Superstitious Death

Also by Peter N. Walker

CRIME FICTION
The 'Carnaby' series (1967–84)
Carnaby and the hijackers
Carnaby and the gaolbreakers
Carnaby and the assassins
Carnaby and the conspirators
Carnaby and the saboteurs
Carnaby and the eliminators
Carnaby and the demonstrators
Carnaby and the infiltrators
Carnaby and the kidnappers
Carnaby and the counterfeiters
Carnaby and the campaigners
Fatal accident (1970)
Panda One on duty (1971)
Special duty (1971)
Identification parade (1972)
Panda One investigates (1973)
Major incident (1974)
The Dovingsby death (1975)
Missing from home (1977)
The MacIntyre plot (1977)
Witchcraft for Panda One (1978)
Target criminal (1978)
The Carlton plot (1980)
Siege for Panda One (1981)
Teenage cop (1982)
Robber in a mole trap (1985)
False alibi (1991)
Grave secrets (1992)

Written as Christopher Coram
A call to danger (1968)
A call to die (1969)
Death in Ptarmigan Forest (1970)
Death on the motorway (1973)
Murder by the lake (1975)
Murder beneath the trees (1979)
Prisoner on the dam (1982)
Prisoner on the run (1985)

Written as Tom Ferris
Espionage for a lady (1969)

Written as Andrew Arncliffe
Murder after the holidays (1985)

Written as Nicholas Rhea
Family ties (1994)
Suspect (1995)
Confession (1997)

THE 'CONSTABLE' SERIES
Constable on the hill (1979)
Constable on the prowl (1980)
Constable around the village (1981)
Constable across the moors (1982)
Constable in the dale (1983)
Constable by the sea (1985)

Constable along the lane (1986)
Constable through the meadow (1988)
Constable at the double (1988)
Constable in disguise (1989)
Constable through the heather (1990)
Constable beside the stream (1991)
Constable around the green (1993)
Constable beneath the trees (1994)
Constable in the shrubbery (1995)
Constable versus Greengrass (1995)
Constable about the parish (1996)
Constable at the gate (1997)
Constable at the dam (1997)
Heartbeat Omnibus I (1992)
Heartbeat Omnibus II (1993)
Heartbeat – Constable among the heather (1992)
Heartbeat – Constable across the moors (1993)
Heartbeat – Constable on call (1993)
Heartbeat – Constable around the green (1994)
Heartbeat – Constable in control (1994)
Heartbeat – Constable along the lane (1995)
Heartbeat – Constable versus Greengrass (1996)
Heartbeat – Constable in the dale (1996)
Heartbeat – Constable about the Parish (1997)

THE 'MONTAGUE PLUKE' SERIES
Omens of death

Written as James Ferguson
EMMERDALE TITLES
A friend in need (1987)
Divided loyalties (1988)
Wives and lovers (1989)
Book of country lore (1988)
Official companion (1988)
Emmerdale's Yorkshire (1990)

NON-FICTION
The Courts of law (1971)
Punishment (1972)
Murders and mysteries from the North York Moors (1988)
Murders and mysteries from the Yorkshire Dales (1991)
Folk tales from the North York Moors (1990)
Folk stories from the Yorkshire Dales (1991)
Folk tales from York and the Wolds (1992)
Folk stories from the Lake District (1993)
The Story of the Police Mutual Assurance Society (1993)
as Nicholas Rhea
Portrait of the North York Moors (1985)
Heartbeat of Yorkshire (1993)
Yorkshire days (1995)

SUPERSTITIOUS DEATH

Nicholas Rhea

Constable · London

First published in Great Britain 1998
by Constable & Company Ltd
3 The Lanchesters, 162 Fulham Palace Road
London W6 9ER
Copyright © 1998 by Peter N. Walker
The right of Peter N. Walker to be
identified as the author of this work
has been asserted by him in accordance
with the Copyright, Designs and Patents Act 1988
ISBN 0 09 478620 8
Set in Palatino 10 pt by
SetSystems Ltd, Saffron Walden, Essex
Printed and bound in Great Britain
by MPG Books Ltd, Bodmin

A CIP catalogue record for this book
is available from the British Library

1

Crickledale's annual ceremony of Shoggling the May could never be contemplated without the eminent presence of the man whose resolute efforts had led to the revival of the custom – Detective Inspector Montague Pluke. That was Mr Pluke's own firmly expressed opinion. There was no denying, however, that it was his meticulous long-term research coupled with his dedication to historical accuracy that had created, deep within his breast, a noble desire to restore the festival as part of Crickledale's municipal calendar.

There had been great rejoicing in the Pluke household with the announcement that the parish council had consented to the revival of Shoggling the May. It seemed only yesterday, but in fact it was fifteen years ago and Montague could well remember his celebratory efforts – he drank at least two large sherries that evening. Now, of course, the annual ceremony was firmly established.

One important factor which had emerged during his research was that, down the centuries, members of the Pluke dynasty had always been to the forefront of the shoggling celebrations. Likewise, they had always held positions of authority and stature in the town throughout Crickledale's long and turbulent history. Ancient records showed that in 1743, when the May Shoggling ceremony had last been held prior to its recent revival, the chief shoggler was none other than Wesley Pluke (1703–1788), one of Montague's renowned ancestors, while Theodolphus Pluke (1697–1756) had donated to the town a full complement of shoggling sticks made from the wood of a yew. Unfortunately, a past incumbent of the parish had used them as pea sticks and they had warped before vanishing during a spring clean of the parochial garden shed. Happily, a new set had been donated by a modern benefactor, a man called Eric Burholme who lived in nearby Barughdale.

Held on the Feast Day of St Eric (18 May) – a Monday this year – this happy occasion always began with a civic reception in the mayor's parlour followed by a service at noon in the Anglican parish church. The service was preceded by fifteen minutes of bell ringing and was attended by the town's civic and other dignitaries. Afterwards, the entire congregation comprising guests and visitors, including the senior class of primary school-children from the town, walked in procession to the historic town centre hawthorn, known locally as the may or may tree.

To this day, the hawthorn stands on Crickledale's central green and, upon the arrival of the congregation, it endures a hectic session of vigorous shoggling, the task being undertaken by the children under the supervision and guidance of the chief shog-gler – currently, Montague Pluke. Food, wine and soft drinks are then distributed on the green if the weather is fine, and in the town hall if it is not; this concludes the celebrations, after which the schoolchildren take the remainder of the day as a holiday.

The present hawthorn, however, is not the original Crickledale May Tree; hawthorns are not renowned for their longevity. The original is said to have died sometime in the fourteenth century due to years of over-vigorous shoggling, but the current speci-men was grown from a fertile haw removed from one of the acknowledged offspring of the very first Crickledale May. Thus the modern descendants of both the Crickledale May Tree and the Pluke dynasty continue to influence the traditions of this pretty limestone-built North Yorkshire market town.

Acutely aware of his position of eminence in the proceedings, Montague Pluke had walked proudly through the town to his office that Monday morning. He hoped a large attendance would enhance the proceedings. As usual, he'd extended his greetings to those he passed *en route*, raising his panama to the ladies and bidding good morning to the gentlemen. He preferred to walk from his home to the hilltop police station, the exercise, fresh air and contact with the public being of immense benefit in his demanding work. He believed the daily perambulation stimu-lated his considerable mental capacity and enabled him to cope with the unrelenting struggle against crime, criminals and petty malefactors. Like Montague Pluke himself, his famous morning walk through the bustling town centre was a vital part of the daily life of Crickledale. Some citizens maintained they could set their clocks by Mr Pluke; others left home to catch their bus or train when he walked past their lounge windows, while the tradespeople regarded his distinctive figure as a living symbol of an ever-vigilant, ever-observant, constantly caring police force.

Extremely prominent in his ancient, tattered and over-large Burberry-style check-patterned coachman's greatcoat with its fitted cape (a family heirloom), his beige spats (heirlooms too), his panama hat with its wide blue hand, his blue bow tie, his heavy black-rimmed spectacles and his profuse, over-long hair, Montague progressed with considerable aplomb. He beamed at Mrs Carstairs, the purple-haired lady who ran Help the Aged; he nodded at the sickly Minskip children at the bus stop and wondered if they would be at the shoggling ceremony; he waved to Whistling Jasper, the town's most active window-cleaner on his ladder in the high street and raised his hat to the new mayor, Councillor Aldrich Thelpe. As he raised his hat, he called to Mr Thelpe, 'See you at the shoggling ceremony, Mr Mayor,' while simultaneously noting that the girl in the off-licence wore a skirt which was far shorter than usual.

He had to deflect his eyes as she dressed a lofty corner of the window and that's when he tripped over a loose paving stone. In his opinion, such things – things like short skirts and low-cut blouses – were bad for the image of Crickledale, a very traditional market town which honoured decency and considerate behaviour. He recovered speedily from his unseemly stumble, just in time to bid a controlled good morning and raise his hat to the portly Mrs Ruth Cholmondeley, one of Millicent's influential friends from Crickledale Ladies' Circle – the president no less. She was most definitely not the sort of lady who would wear a short skirt, although she could justifiably wear a low-cut blouse. Montague blinked at the thought, recalling her visit yesterday evening when she complained that the bay tree in her garden had withered and died. Millicent had said it needed more water but Montague Pluke had placed another more sinister interpretation upon that news, an interpretation he felt he could not divulge to anyone at this stage.

7

Like her busy husband, Millicent – Mrs Pluke – was extremely prominent in Crickledale activities. Her many responsibilities included her work as secretary of several organisations, including the Women's Institute, the Parochial Church Council, the Church Flower Group, the Local History Society and Meals on Wheels, plus being president of the Ladies' Luncheon Club and chairwoman of the Town Hall Entertainments Committee.

As a family unit, therefore, albeit with no children, the Plukes were regarded as personages of considerable stature in this modest and contented market town. In addition to his civic prestige, Montague was a man of professional renown because he was the detective inspector in charge of Crickledale CID; furthermore, he was justifiably famous in another capacity. He was Yorkshire's acknowledged expert on horse troughs and author of the standard work, *The Horse Troughs of Crickledale and District since the 16th Century, fully illustrated by the author.* All his spare time, however limited due to his social and professional commitments, was spent in the never-ending quest to trace and record long-forgotten horse troughs. He had traced and catalogued more than three hundred, maintaining that there were thousands awaiting discovery in North Yorkshire alone, most of which were forgotten, disused and neglected.

In fact, he had been to Scarborough only this last weekend to inspect an exciting new discovery, a wooden horse trough unearthed during excavations at the Spa. It was due to his unrivalled knowledge in this field that he was much sought after as a lecturer on the history and design of horse troughs. His speciality was horse troughs used for ancient and modern civic purposes and he was contemplating a new book on the subject, as well as a further volume about those used for mayoral purposes.

On this Monday, however, Millicent had left home even before washing Montague's breakfast pots, such was the urgency of her mission. In her capacity as a parochial official with several important posts, she'd had to rush off to the church to supervise the preparations for today's ceremony; consequently Montague had left home without kissing her farewell. It was a slightly upsetting start to his day, a break in routine. One of Millicent's responsibilities was to find the parish shoggling sticks in time for the ceremony. Those sticks, the handsome set donated by Eric Burholme, the local philanthropist, were not the Pluke originals of course; those had been seized and destroyed by Thomas Cromwell during Henry VIII's Dissolution of the Monasteries because Cromwell thought they were something to do with the Catholic Mass. Each year the sticks were put away after the shoggling and there was always a last minute search next time they were required. Somehow they invariably got misplaced and top quality shoggling sticks with the required angled tips were not easily obtained in these modern times. In acknowledging the urgency and importance of Millicent's departure, Montague accepted that there were times when one had to put up with disruptions to one's own daily routine, however inconvenient; a day of such civic distinction was one of those occasions.

During his brisk walk to the office, he avoided passing under Whistling Jasper's ladder and bade 'Bless you' to a grey-haired lady who sneezed near the bread shop. Upon arrival at the magnificent stone-built police station, a former manor house, he crossed the threshold with his right foot first, then turned towards the small ground-floor control room.

'Good morning, sir,' greeted Sergeant Cockfield, pronounced Cofield, the officer in charge of the control room. 'It's all very quiet this morning.'

'That is good news,' smiled Pluke. In his late forties, Cockfield was a large man with a bald head whose uniform and spectacles always looked a shade too small. 'Everything's under control, then?'

'Yes, sir, all's very quiet in the town. We've had no reports of overnight crime, vandalism or disturbances.'

'Excellent. That augurs well, a splendid start to the day, although I am somewhat concerned about Mrs Cholmondeley's bay tree. It has died, you know, and yet we have not been too short of water. A very ominous omen indeed.'

'Really, sir? Ominous, eh?'

'For someone, yes. Now, you know about the shoggling ceremony this morning? There are two venues, the first at the church followed by another at the Crickledale May Tree itself.'

9

'Yes, sir. The uniform branch has matters under control. Sergeant Wilson will be in charge. Point duty officers, traffic patrols and traffic wardens will be on duty at both locations – it's all been arranged and a full operation order has been prepared.'

'Traffic cones and crowd barriers in position too?'

'Yes, sir. I think we can cope with the influx of sightseers, sir. About fifty are expected, I believe? The usual number.'

'Yes, sergeant. Personally, I would have hoped for a larger turn-out by the townspeople, but one must remember many will be at work or doing their weekly washing today. Now, what is the official weather forecast?'

'The thundery weather of the weekend has cleared, sir, we do not anticipate any downpours or thunderstorms. Today is expected to be dry and clear, with some high clouds and sunshine, along with a mild westerly wind.'

'That is excellent news. Now, as you know, I shall be playing a leading role in the shoggling ceremony,' and Pluke expanded his chest. 'As founder of the modern ceremonial, I shall be taking a key part in the ancient ceremonial, with my wife, of course. I'm the official shoggler, no less.'

'Of course, sir. I noted your names are on the list of official guests. As you instructed, we made the usual security checks of the invited guests and I don't think there will be any anti-shoggling demonstrations or any unseemly behaviour which is likely to disrupt the proceedings. We are all confident of a smooth, trouble-free event,' smiled Sergeant Cockfield pronounced Cofield. 'But there is one matter of procedure to decide – if a crime is reported during your absence from the office, shall I contact you at the shoggling ceremony, or should I wait until afterwards?'

'Refer any such reported incident to Detective Sergeant Wain. He will contact me if it is a reported crime of some importance and urgency. Murder, rape, robbery, arson, that sort of thing. Detective Sergeant Wain will cope with any lesser problems such as car thefts, burglaries or shoplifters until my civic duties are over. I will instruct him to liaise with you on those matters.'

'Very good, sir.'

10

Happy that well-thought-out and diligently prepared local procedures would keep the Crickledale criminals firmly under control, Montague climbed the stairs to his office. He hung his panama on a hat-stand just inside the door, then removed his baggy overcoat to reveal a jacket of similar colour and style beneath, its breast pocket full of pens, propelling pencils and pocket torches. He hung his coat on a peg fastened to the wall then bowed slightly to the sun which was visible through the east-facing window. Next, he rearranged the items on his desk, making sure the plastic model of a horse trough (his paper clip container) was in precisely the right place.

Then he edged his blotter to a more perfect position, checked that the ancient evil-thwarting hagstone which served as a paperweight was dusted and, once he was satisfied that his desk was absolutely to his liking, he settled upon his chair. As he did so, his substantial secretary, Mrs Plumpton, in her voluminous purple dress, flowed into his office in a cloud of strong perfume and shifting flesh. Some of her bits and pieces seemed to be balanced one on top of the other, like a juggler doing tricks with beach balls, but nothing ever fell off or out. She was bearing a cup of hot coffee.

'Good morning, Mrs Plumpton,' he smiled. 'A very nice day, if I may say so.'

'Very nice indeed, Mr Pluke. And a good day for the shoggling ceremony.'

'Perfect,' he beamed. 'The forecast is good, the flies are flying high which is a sign of good weather and the wind is in the west – you know the saying, "When the wind is in the west, the weather is always best."'

'You have a wonderful knowledge about all sorts, Mr Pluke,' said the adoring Mrs Plumpton as she reached across to place his coffee on the desk. As she did so, the wide neck of her dress fell forwards and he thought again about jugglers and beach balls.

'One tries to learn a little extra every day, Mrs Plumpton. Now, before I give my undivided attention to my civic duties, is there any police matter to which I must address myself?'

Standing upright once again, with everything apparently in

11

place, she assured him that his mail contained a few letters which did require a reply, but that there was nothing of a very urgent nature. Nonetheless, he decided to dictate the necessary responses in order to provide Mrs Plumpton with some work before calling in Detective Sergeant Wain. Ten minutes after Mrs Plumpton had left, there was a knock on the door of his office and Wain entered.

Well over six feet tall, with dark curly hair and a suntan that never faded, Detective Sergeant Wayne Wain was a thirty-three-year-old career detective who served as Montague's very able deputy. Montague, who disliked referring to subordinate officers by their Christian names, felt he could do so in the case of his sergeant because his forename and his surname sounded exactly alike.

'Good morning, Wayne,' smiled Montague.

'Good morning, sir,' said Wayne Wain. 'A very nice day for the shoggling ceremony, if I may say so.'

'Yes indeed, and the forecast is good,' said Pluke. 'It's only rained once in living memory at that ceremony and that was when we misplaced one of the shoggling sticks. So, we should have a splendid day – that's if Mrs Pluke can find the sticks.'

'They're important, are they?' asked Wain, fairly new to the town and its curious customs.

'Important, Wayne? They are indispensable! Yet we always manage to lose them. Somehow, they always get misplaced during the year. Children, I expect. Choirboys will persist in using them as billiard cues or even as dratting poles and nurgling sticks. Now, Wayne, I shall be at the ceremony from ten thirty this morning, for about three hours. You can deal with any emergencies which might arise?'

'Routine emergencies, yes, sir. But what if something serious happens?'

Pluke was thinking of Mrs Cholmondeley's bay tree.

'I will leave that to your discretion, sergeant. Have words with Sergeant Cockfield pronounced Cofield, make some suitable arrangements between you. I do not wish to be disturbed during the shoggling ceremony unless it is a matter of absolute necessity. This is a very important municipal occasion, rich with

12

dignitaries and ceremonial, a vital part of the town's heritage, so we do not want it to be disturbed by rapes and murders, do we?'

'I understand, sir. Not that we've had any rapes or murders, or serious crimes of any kind, in recent months. Not even any routine sudden deaths.'

'That's all due to good policing and crime prevention techniques, Wayne. This town is a noted major crime-free zone. Now, if there are no questions I shall prepare my speech for today. It is my privilege, as chief shoggler, to address the crowds from beneath the tree. A very historic moment in our civic year, Wayne.'

'I understand perfectly, sir. I'll leave you in peace and go down to the control room for discussions with Sergeant Cockfield pronounced Cofield.'

And so Montague's big day began to take shape.

Millicent had managed to locate all the shoggling sticks. After a dusty hunt, she discovered they had been removed to the bell tower along with the parish lawnmower, wheelbarrow and gardening tools, probably by some untutored church helper who thought they were pea sticks or sweet pea canes. It meant that the shoggling ceremony got off to a very good and prompt start.

During the church service, the vicar spoke movingly about the need for such customs to be maintained and expressed delight at the involvement of the local children, saying that without this kind of unselfish commitment, our appreciation of history would diminish and our sense of heritage would vanish for ever. There was also a word of appreciation for the generosity of Eric Burholme in providing a complete set of shoggling sticks of superior quality and design. Burholme, a tall, slender man with a head of thick white hair, was in the congregation and signified his pleasure at the vicar's oration.

The vicar next praised Montague Pluke for his diligence and public-spiritedness in reviving the ancient shoggling custom, then after the final hymn – 'O Holy Tree, O Mighty One' – the congregation moved outside. They walked in solemn procession to the green where they assembled in a wide circle around the famous hawthorn. Beneath it, someone had positioned a small dais upon which Mr Pluke could stand to make his annual speech to the assembly. Standing beneath the blossom-laden branches, Montague spoke movingly about the origins of the custom, reminding the assembled citizens how, around AD 1127, a demented man had ridden post-haste into Crickledale from a distant town with the sole intention of burning down the wooden, thatched church of that time.

Word of his intentions had preceded him, however, and the Crickledonians were waiting with sticks and pick-axe handles, but the man dodged them and fled. He managed to find refuge in the heavily tree-covered common which then occupied the centre of the town. All the stick-wielding citizens entered the woodland and began to poke the undergrowth with the intention of flushing him out. It was during this manhunt that some stick-wielding children began to prod the slender trunk of a young hawthorn with their angled sticks. They pushed and pulled at the slender trunk, soon treating it as a game with the unspoken challenge of making it sway. Eventually, due to their combined efforts, the hawthorn did begin to sway backwards and forwards, the impetus making it sway so powerfully that a man tumbled out. He had secreted himself in the thorny branches high above the ground but had been unable to withstand the wild rocking motions.

Thus the church was saved – and to this day, children surround that tree and, with their shoggling sticks, make it sway backwards and forwards while chanting, 'Shoggle, shoggle, I'll be bound, see the villain hit the ground.' Shoggling is an old Yorkshire word for shaking roughly, hence the name of the custom, although very few shoggle-worthy hawthorns are available in modern times – trees with especially pliable trunks are required.

With Millicent standing proudly before him, Montague Pluke had almost reached the stage where he was about to call, 'Let shoggling commence.' At that crucial moment, he noticed Detective Sergeant Wayne Wain at the rear of the crowd, his height enabling him to tower above their heads. Pluke's first reaction was that Wayne Wain had decided to attend the ceremony in an

14

attempt to learn something of Crickledale's folklore and ancient past, but the sergeant was gesticulating towards him.

Momentarily forgetting the omen of Mrs Cholmondeley's bay tree, Pluke's first reaction was to ignore the fellow – he was probably waving at a pretty woman in the audience – for Pluke believed nothing should be allowed to interrupt the shoggling ceremony, particularly at such a critical stage. He therefore continued with his duties and after declaring, 'Let shoggling commence' to a ripple of polite applause, he descended from his miniature stage and moved aside to allow the children to come closer. Accompanied by some spirited cheering from the crowd, the children moved towards the thickly blossomed may tree with their shoggling sticks held before them like lances. Placing the angled ends around the trunk, they prepared to push and pull, alternately pressing and pulling as the tree began to sway with its own momentum. It would take time and some florets might be loosened but it was all in a very noble and historic cause.

As the crowd pressed closer to watch, Detective Sergeant Wayne Wain pushed through them and managed to gain access to Pluke. Taking him by the elbow, he steered Pluke away from the assembled masses and halted at a point where their conversation would be confidential. In fact, their discussion would not be overheard due to the noise and activity around them for the children were shouting with delight as the audience – mainly their parents – echoed their encouragement.

'Sir.' There was an urgency in Wain's voice. 'I'm sorry to have to drag you away at such an important moment, but I must talk to you.'

'Can't it wait, Wayne? Can't you see that I am about to conclude a most important and historic local ceremony? Shoggling has commenced and I have to supervise it and then declare it complete at the appropriate time, before we raise our hats and drink a toast to the church which was saved—'

'It's a body, sir, of a woman,' Wayne Wain interrupted.

'A body, Wayne? A dead body, you mean? A real human body?' So the omen of Mrs Cholmondeley's bay tree was right after all. If a bay tree dies in a garden, it is an omen of death.

15

'Yes, sir, with injuries. Buried in Harman's Quarry. Very suspicious, sir.'

'Murder, you mean, Wayne?'

'Almost certainly, sir. There is ample evidence to suggest it is murder. We must leave immediately to visit the scene.'

'Oh dear,' sighed Detective Inspector Montague Pluke, reluctantly accepting that police duty took precedence over his shoggling responsibilities. 'That means I cannot formally close this ceremony. It will be the first time I have not been present during the concluding moments!'

'I'm sure His Worship the Mayor will stand in for you, sir,' suggested Wain.

'No, that is not possible. Precedence says it must be a Pluke . . . I suppose I could ask Millicent, although she is a woman.'

'I am sure that tradition and precedent will find that a most acceptable compromise, sir. After all, she is a Pluke, and an eminent one into the bargain,' said Wayne Wain. 'Now we must go. I have a police car waiting.'

2

It was known throughout Crickledale and district, and within police circles, that Montague Pluke possessed very few driving skills. He was able to propel a motor vehicle forwards but was distinctly incapable of guiding it safely in any specific direction. Likewise, he had problems going backwards and his technique was to avoid reversing at any cost; similarly, he had further problems in rapidly halting a moving vehicle when danger threatened. As a consequence, a succession of police driving instructors, charged with the duty of refreshing Pluke's motoring skills, had politely described his problem as a dangerous and life-threatening lack of co-ordination between brain and limbs.

His efforts behind the wheel had caused many driving instructors, both civilian and police, to seek premature retirement. In spite of that, he did hold a driving licence which he had acquired in his more spritely days when the roads were not so busy and when they had fewer direction signs, road markings, traffic lights or a real need to make emergency stops. In a gallant attempt to avoid causing injury and terror to members of the public who might be using the roads, and to maintain the good reputation of police drivers, Pluke always made use of an official driver when engaged on official business, and Wayne Wain was ideal. Pluke found pleasure and pride in having the handsome smart-suited fellow at the wheel, the public perception being that Pluke was a personage of some eminence and that Wain was his chauffeur. On this occasion, therefore, Wain drove through Crickledale and into the countryside with Pluke at his side. They were using an official dark green Vauxhall Astra without any police insignia, a CID car equipped with an official radio.

'So, Wayne,' asked Pluke once he had settled into his seat. 'This is clearly a matter of some importance. Can you give me a situation report?'

'We are heading for Harman's Quarry, sir. It lies on the edge of the moor about four miles out of Crickledale on the minor road to Barughdale. It is disused – years ago, it was a limestone quarry but it has never been active since the end of World War II. It was owned by a quarrying company but when the quarry was exhausted, it was purchased by the owner of the nearby farm, a Mr Eric Burholme.'

'Eric Burholme? Are you sure?' Pluke's eyebrows registered some astonishment at this news.

'Yes, sir, positive. Do you know him?'

'Know him? He is a most generous benefactor to this town, Wayne, a diligent supporter of many local charities. And he supplied the town with its current complement of shoggling sticks. A very fine man, by all accounts.'

'Well, he is the owner of the quarry where the body was found, sir. He runs a business from Harman's Farm; he hires agricultural machinery, as I am sure you know. He uses the quarry to store several heavy vehicles like combine harvesters and other large mechanical contraptions when they are not in use. It also houses a number of those rounded bales that all modern farmers seem to wrap in miles of black pastic. Over the

17

years, the floor of the quarry has become covered with grass and campers sometimes make use of it. The old quarry face is now like a small cliff, and although the surrounding fences have been retained, the quarry has been fully integrated into Mr Burholme's farm. Access by motor vehicle is through the main gate to the farm; once through the gate, the road to the farm forks left and leads into the old quarry.'

'Your local knowledge is impressive, Wayne.'

'I checked some facts before contacting you, sir.'

'And does Mr Burholme know of this untoward development, Wayne?'

'Not yet, sir. He was out when Sergeant Cockfield pronounced Cofield tried to ring him. He wanted to let him know the reason for our impending arrival.'

'He was at the shoggling ceremony, Wayne, but I am sure he will return home in due course. Now, I do have a good knowledge of local footpaths, thanks to my quest for horse troughs, and I can add that there is access to the quarry from the Barughdale road,' Pluke stated with conviction.

'That's true, sir.'

'In fact, the whole area is rich with footpaths, Wayne. It's very good rambling country.'

'That's right, sir. Now it seems that when the quarry was active, there was direct access for vehicles from that road – an unsurfaced track led from the road directly into the quarry. When the quarry ceased to be active, though, Mr Burholme placed a fence across the entrance to effectively close off that means of entry. He incorporated a stile in the fence, however, because the track formed part of a public footpath which leads from the Barughdale to Crickledale road via the quarry to the moors beyond. Today, that path is well signed and in regular use by ramblers. It skirts the southern boundary of the quarry and does not actually enter it. It is one of several public footpaths in that vicinity.'

'And, in your estimation, what is the distance from the Crickledale to Barughdale road to the quarry?'

'Something around a third of a mile, sir. Not far, although you can't see the quarry from that road.'

'From my own local knowledge, I'd say your estimation was about right, Wayne. And the body. Tell me about that.'

'It is female, sir, about thirty years of age and white-skinned. She was discovered by a hiker who was using the public footpath; he was walking past the quarry and heading for the moors. For some reason, he had diverted slightly from the path and found himself in the quarry. He rang from his mobile phone and was asked to await our arrival; a uniformed constable – PC Singleton, the local village policeman – attended immediately and confirmed there was a dead female body with what appears to be a head injury. The body had apparently been buried in a shallow grave but was fully dressed. PC Singleton secured the scene pending our arrival; the man who found the body has remained with him. I have called out our Scenes of Crime team, a doctor and a forensic pathologist. All are *en route* – indeed, some may have arrived already but they will not commence their investigation until you have examined the scene and the body.'

'Well done, Wayne. You have acted with your customary professionalism and your local knowledge is impressive. So what else do we know about the body?'

'Not much more at this stage. I have not viewed it. Preliminary accounts from the scene suggest she has not been buried for very long – it might even be a mere matter of hours, sir. There is virtually no decomposition of the body. The grave is new; it is covered with very fresh earth and sods, and it was that which drew the attention of the hiker to it – he noticed the disturbed earth in the old quarry. In fact, it was his dog which began to dig and partially revealed the woman.'

'And the apparent injury?'

'According to the constable who viewed the corpse it looks like a puncture wound. There is not a great deal to be seen and it has not bled a lot, but he says it is in the right temple. Whatever caused the wound appears to have been removed. There is no weapon near the body.'

'A bullet wound, perhaps?' suggested Pluke. 'With the missile still deep inside?'

'That's a possibility, sir. We do not know whether there are injuries to other parts of her body; her lower body and limbs are still covered with earth.'

'Has Singleton any idea who she is? He is the local constable, you say?'

'He is, sir, but he does not know her. He's never seen her around this area. At this stage, we have no idea who she is.'

'And are any women of her description reported missing?'

'Not in our area, sir. Clearly, we will have to search national records if we can't identify her as a local person.'

'So there are several puzzles to be solved, Wayne.'

'Yes, sir.'

'And those officers who have already gone to the scene – have they been routed via Harman's Farm?'

'Yes, they have. I thought it best if they did not park on the Barughdale road. Thanks to PC Singleton, Control was able to explain about that route through the farm complex – as I said earlier, it's the only way to get into the quarry with a motor vehicle. With Mr Burholme being out, we could not notify him of our intention to enter his land, but will do so the moment he returns.'

'Good. Then, to begin, we shall walk along the footpath, Wayne. I need to view the scene from all angles.'

Under Pluke's guidance, Wayne Wain parked the Astra at the side of the Crickledale to Barughdale minor road, taking care to leave the vehicle some distance from the stile. They had no wish to contaminate the area around the stile, just in case the killer had made use of that route. He might have left some evidence of his activities, a footprint perhaps or some other useful clue.

Once out of the car, Pluke stood on the tarmac road surface for a long time as he studied the route to the quarry, examining the verge around the stile and fence. The fence and stile were fashioned from sturdy wooden rails, the top rail of the fence being adorned with barbed wire.

Beyond was a meadow with the footpath clearly visible as it meandered through the grass. A large herd of red-brown cows grazed in the meadow which rose slightly as it extended from the road until there was a considerable incline ahead, some of it tree-covered. The disused quarry lay out of sight behind that elevated portion, in a hollow which had been created by years of excavations for limestone. The footpath led past the quarry, circling it to the south and passing through a copse of mixed conifers and deciduous trees before heading west on to the moors.

Pluke absorbed all this, then said, 'Very interesting. Now we mustn't keep the others waiting, Wayne, so can you take the car to the scene? I'll walk to the quarry. I will see you there. Ensure that Scenes of Crime examine this footpath, will you, especially the stile and the barbed wire along the top of this fence. There may be relevant fibres clinging to those barbs.'

'Very good, sir,' acknowledged Detective Sergeant Wayne.

Himself wary of the barbed wire, Pluke was unfazed by the cows whose heads turned to gaze upon him as he prepared to walk among them. As Pluke climbed over the railings some yards from the stile, he noted the profusion of mugwort which grew in the lee of the rails. It was not yet in bloom, and he recalled the ancient verse: 'If they'd drink nettles in March and mugwort in May, so many fine maidens would not turn to clay.' But some young maiden – was she a maiden? – had indeed turned to clay. With the cows contentedly watching his progress, Pluke continued through the long grass as he noted the wild flowers of the meadow and listened to the skylarks which sang unseen in the heavens.

The countryside out here on the edge of the moors was so unspoilt and exhilarating. In time, he reached the summit of the elevated patch of ground where he halted to observe the layout of the quarry. From this vantage point, the footpath could no longer be seen as it snaked its way through the copse of hawthorns, birches and conifers to emerge at the far side of the fenced-in quarry. But on the firm floor of the quarry were several large agricultural vehicles, all covered with green tarpaulins as they awaited the time they would be used, while the distant perimeter was adorned with a row of large round bales all wrapped in black plastic. They had been placed end to end until they looked like a huge black pudding or a string of black-skinned, short, fat and gigantic sausages.

The quarry entrance was at one end of the row of bales and

around it there now stood several vehicles, some bearing police insignia. A few policemen and other officials were standing nearby, awaiting Pluke. Wayne Wain had parked his car and joined them. To Pluke's right, in a soft area of the floor of the quarry, lay the disturbed grave of the young woman with the top half of her body now revealed. No one waited close to the grave.

As Pluke approached the waiting group, taking care to avoid any route which might have been used by the killer or his victim, a uniformed constable came forward.

'Good morning, sir.' It was PC Singleton, the village constable from Barughdale. This farm and quarry were upon his patch. 'I have secured the scene pending your arrival.'

'Well done, PC Singleton. So who has been to the graveside?'

'I have, sir, and so has our local GP, sir, Dr Tomlinson from Barughdale. I allowed him to attend the woman, sir, just in case she was still alive. He took great care not to destroy any evidence that might be there. I noted his route to the graveside – he used the same approach as I did which in turn was the one used by the man who found the body. The woman was not alive, sir, and he has certified the death.'

'Good. And who is the person who found the body?'

'Mr Michael Wardle and his dog, Sam. They are waiting to talk to you, over there near our cars. He is a hiker, he was passing through here on a long trek. Scenes of Crime are also awaiting your arrival before they begin their work, but the pathologist hasn't arrived yet. He told us he should be here within the hour. And the shell has been ordered; the Task Force is standing by too.'

'Good. Now show me the body. Come with me, Wayne,' Pluke called to his deputy who detached himself from some earnest discussion with an attractive policewoman. PC Singleton escorted Pluke and Wain to the remains, taking the circuitous route he'd previously used.

They approached the grave, Pluke making mental notes as he progressed, and then they halted.

'That is exactly how she was found, sir,' said PC Singleton.

Pluke saw the upper torso of a young white woman with blonde hair. In life, she would have been beautiful and for some reason he realised it was Monday, thinking of the verse 'Monday's child is fair of face', but she was no child and she might not have been born on a Monday. Whatever her past, she was now lying in a shallow grave with only her shoulders, neck and head exposed, the lower half of her body being covered with soft earth. There was no apparent decomposition of the flesh and the grave was only some two feet deep. It had been dug in soft grass-covered earth, then filled in and re-covered with turves, some of the surplus soil being scattered across the grass.

From his vantage point, Pluke could see what appeared to be a puncture wound in her right temple. It was roughly circular in shape, about the size of a little fingernail and marked by a tiny patch of dried blood, its edges softened with dampness. Very little blood had apparently escaped to mark her skin although one or two particles of earth were adhering to the wound. A lack of blood was sometimes a feature of deep and dangerous puncture wounds and he did not lose sight of the fact that this could have been caused by a large-calibre bullet. If so, it did not appear to have made an exit wound.

'From external appearances, it does seem she died from that wound, Wayne,' Pluke said softly. 'And very recently too.'

'It is too early to speculate about the precise cause of death.' Wayne exercised all the necessary cautions. 'We must await the post-mortem.'

'You're absolutely right of course, Wayne,' Pluke smiled. 'Now, is there any sign of a digging implement or the murder weapon? Or other people hanging about the scene?'

'The surrounding area has not been thoroughly searched yet, sir,' PC Singleton told him. 'I did a brief visual examination, eyes only, sir, but did not see any weapons or tools, and there was no one here when I arrived. Apart from Mr Wardle, that is.'

'Right,' said Pluke. 'I think we had better not disturb anything until the forensic pathologist has made his examination, then we'd better call in the Task Force to undertake a fingertip search of the scene. The Task Force is standing by, I am told. Call

Control and have them sent here, will you, Wayne? While I'm waiting, I can speak to Mr Wardle. Introduce me to him, would you, PC Singleton?'

Michael Wardle was a slender man in his mid-fifties with a balding head of dark brown hair, a small dark moustache and gold-rimmed spectacles. With a healthy tanned face and standing about five feet nine inches tall, he was dressed in hiking gear – light brown boots, corduroy trousers, a multi-coloured sweater – and he carried a small haversack containing his provisions for the day. His dog, Sam, was a black and white border collie, and it lay at his feet, patient and well-behaved.

'Good morning, Mr Wardle,' Pluke greeted him after the introduction. 'Thank you for being so patient on our behalf.'

'I am just passing through. I am not restricted to a particularly tight schedule so time is not too important.' Wardle's smile revealed his nervousness. 'It was such a shock, dreadful ... but if I can help at all ...'

'The person who finds a dead body is always of help in our enquiries,' returned Pluke. 'So what time did you make this awful discovery?'

'About three-quarters of an hour ago, perhaps. I reported it immediately.'

'Good, I am delighted no time was wasted. Now, if you would be so kind, can you tell me how you came to find this unfortunate young lady?'

'Well, it was pure chance, really. Sam, that's my dog, found her, not me. I went into the trees, the call of nature you understand, and while I was there Sam wandered off. He found his way into the old quarry, it's only a few yards behind the copse of trees and there is a gentle descent into the floor of the quarry, not a vertical cliff face as there is at the other side. Anyway, Sam began to dig and bark ... I went to see what he was doing and, well, that's it. I saw the young woman he'd partially uncovered ... A terrible shock, Inspector Pluke, and I touched her. She was cold ... buried like that ... I made Sam sit as I brushed a bit of earth away from her, just to be sure it was a real woman and not a dummy or a wax head. I carry a mobile telephone, as it happens, in case I fall and break a leg or get

24

delayed for any reason ... So I rang the police, 999. That's all I can tell you ... What an awful shock, inspector ... dreadful ...'

Each time the dog's name was mentioned, it pricked its ears and thumped its tail on the ground, but never moved from its master's side. A well-trained animal, Pluke thought, but it was showing no undue distress in the presence of violent death. Indeed, it was behaving perfectly normally. Pluke was acutely aware of stories of dogs seeing ghosts or being afraid to enter haunted places, or howling and whining in the presence of sudden or violent death. But this dog was showing none of those signs.

'I am obliged to you for your courtesy in ringing us.' Pluke's appreciation was genuine. 'Now, can you show me the precise route you used to reach the grave? PC Singleton has shown me but I would like you to show me too. I need to know exactly where you placed your feet, and if you can bear it, I would like you to show me how you brushed away the dirt from her face ...'

'Must I do that again?'

'It would be of immense help to us,' said Pluke.

It was with some reluctance that the hiker retraced his steps and repeated his actions, but his acquiesence did please Pluke who noted his route, signified his approval and thanked Mr Wardle for his courage.

'Now,' continued Pluke, 'I will need your full name and home address, and something to prove your identity. Then we shall need a formal written statement from you. My sergeant will attend to that, and once that is over, I need not detain you any longer. We might want to talk to you at length in due course, just to clarify any further points that might arise. You're just passing through, you said?'

Wardle provided Pluke with his full name and address – Michael John Wardle, 77 Wolverdale Avenue, Parkland Estate, Portrack-on-Tees, adding, 'I was made redundant – I was a process worker in the chemical industry, Imperial Chemicals. Now I occupy my time walking. I got the bus to the road end this morning, and will catch one home this evening. In the meantime, I hope to do about twenty miles. I'm doing all the footpaths in North Yorkshire, one by one. I need to achieve something in my dotage!'

'Far more satisfying than sitting at home watching television!' nodded Pluke.

'I never expected to find a dead body, though. What a shock! I'm not used to such dramas. I prefer to look for interesting examples of wildlife. I do try to identify the birds I see . . .'

'Clearly a man of the countryside! Now, I must ask you this – is the young lady known to you?'

'Good heavens no! I've never seen her before, ever.'

'You've done this walk before?'

'A long time ago, fifteen years perhaps. With a party from our ramblers' club. The Tees Valley Ramblers.'

'And you were alone on this occasion?'

'Yes, most of my friends are still holding on to their jobs. I join them at weekends for organised rambles.'

'You are not married then?'

'No, I never found anyone who could make me happy. Except my dog.'

'Well, Mr Wardle, before I hand you over to Detective Sergeant Wain, I need to complete one unpleasant task,' Pluke told him.

'Unpleasant?'

'I need to search your haversack, Mr Wardle.'

'Am I under suspicion?' A look of horror crossed his face.

'In the case of a suspected murder, Mr Wardle, everyone is under suspicion until formally eliminated. I have to see if there is anything in your belongings which might have been used to either kill the woman or bury her.'

'Good heavens . . . I mean to say . . . I'm not sure I like this . . .'

'If there is nothing in your bag, Mr Wardle, it would indicate you are not under suspicion.'

'Well, of course I am not guilty . . . by all means search my haversack!' and he swung it from his back and held it out for the detectives to take. Wayne Wain carried out a swift but thorough search before saying to Pluke, 'Nothing incriminating, sir. Food, drink, extra socks, a bird book and a map.'

He returned it to its relieved owner.

'That pleases me immensely, Mr Wardle. So, Detective

Sergeant Wain, can you take Mr Wardle to our car and obtain a statement?'

'Yes, sir,' nodded Wayne, indicating the car to Wardle. Mr Wardle, with his obedient dog at his heels, walked towards the knot of police vehicles at the quarry entrance as Pluke turned to PC Singleton.

'So, PC Singleton, you were the first to meet that man. What do you make of him?' asked Pluke.

'He seems very genuine to me,' returned the constable.

'You are new to this kind of major enquiry?' asked Pluke.

'I've never been on a murder enquiry before, sir.'

'Then I hope you can learn from this experience. The first thing to appreciate is that I have not yet confirmed this is a murder enquiry but in spite of that, we shall mount a murder-type investigation. The next thing to learn is that the person who finds the body is automatically a prime suspect, an important fact which the investigating officer must bear in mind. We shall examine Mr Wardle's life, movements, personal friends and contacts in very great detail. I must admit he could have killed her – a middle-aged man not married ... his sex life must inevitably be of interest to us – but before we tear his life apart, we need to have the scene photographed as it is now in advance of the arrival of our forensic pathologist. Can you call Sergeant Tabler and ask him to come here? He's waiting at the entrance.'

'Yes, sir.'

'Before you go, PC Singleton, note the condition of the grave. At the moment, it is virtually as it was discovered. Once the forensic pathologist arrives, he will eventually brush away the remaining earth. He will change the appearance of the grave and of its sad occupant. So I need to have everything recorded on film as we see it at this very moment. Now, as you were the first police officer to arrive at the scene, will you inform the coroner on my behalf? Do it through the control room, give him my compliments and ask if he will approve a post-mortem examination.'

And so began Detective Inspector Pluke's formal murder-type investigation.

3

As Pluke awaited the pathologist, Wayne Wain returned, having interviewed Michael Wardle and released him.

'Well, Wayne, what do you think of Mr Wardle?' asked Pluke.

'An honest man, I believe, sir. An ordinary fellow who happened to find a person dead in suspicious circumstances. It happens all the time – lots of murder victims and suicides are found by ordinary people.'

'He's not a suspect, you feel?'

'I don't think so, sir. But I do appreciate his background will have to be researched.'

'That's a good job for one of our incident room teams when we assemble them. Now, PC Singleton,' and Pluke addressed the constable. 'I understand this quarry is owned by Eric Burholme, who also owns the adjoining farm. He was in Crickledale when I left to drive here, so he is not aware of our presence or the reason for all this unseemly activity on his land. Can I ask you to inform him when he does return?'

'He is back, sir, just. He drove in minutes ago. I explained matters to him and assured him we'd keep him informed of developments. He raised no objections to our presence and said he would be around the premises all day if we wanted to talk to him. This farm is on my beat, sir, as you know; I am known to him.'

'Yes, indeed. So what do you know of Mr Burholme?'

'Not a great deal, sir, he keeps himself very much to himself, although he is widely known as a philanthropist, a regular supporter of charities and good causes.'

'I believe so,' nodded Pluke.

The constable continued, 'Although he runs a thriving farm machinery hire business, he's not one for unnecessary socialising. Because he doesn't keep livestock, I rarely have to visit his farm.

He's lived here a long time, sir, he came to the area long before I was posted here. Before I was born, in fact.'

'And he lost his wife, I understand,' commented Pluke. 'He lives alone?'

'Yes, sir. She died some years ago, before I was posted here, and there is no new wife or partner. He is well regarded locally, sir, everyone agrees he is a very nice man and I know nothing against him. He's never given me cause for concern.'

'And local gossip?'

'I've never heard the local farmers criticise him or gossip about him. He's always fair in his dealings with them, never gives them reason to complain and always pays his bills on time. If there is gossip, it's only because he lives alone and never has people in for a meal or a party. Although he is very generous, he is a natural loner, sir, but none the worse for that. I reckon his business keeps him busy round the clock. His life is his work, in other words.'

'That's a fair assessment to start our investigation.' Pluke thanked the constable, then turned to Wayne Wain. 'I do remember his wife dying, Wayne, although I cannot recall the precise details. There was something strange about her funeral ... it'll come to me before long. Now, in spite of the universal high regard for Mr Burholme, we shall have to interview him in depth but I prefer not to do so just yet. Ah, I see our forensic expert is now arriving.'

A smart red Rover 820 Si had turned off the road and was cruising slowly towards the farm; it turned along the track which led into the quarry and eventually halted near the assembled police vehicles. From it emerged Dr Simon Meredith, a slightly built individual with half-moon spectacles, thinning fair hair and a matching moustache. Clutching a large black case, he walked towards Pluke, instantly recognisable in his heavy overcoat, spats, blue bow tie and blue-banded panama.

'Good morning, Mr Pluke,' the pathologist greeted him. 'So what have we this time?'

Standing with the grave and its occupant in view, Pluke explained and provided an outline of what had transpired since the discovery. Meredith nodded, noting that some photographs had been taken, and that the scene had been subjected to some disturbance and contamination, however minor it might be.

'Right,' said Meredith. 'I will begin immediately. Perhaps your photographers will accompany me to record my examination?'

Under Pluke's guidance, Meredith approached the grave by using precisely the same route as Michael Wardle and the others. After placing his case carefully on the ground, he stood for a few moments to silently absorb the macabre scene, then produced a small plastic sheet from his case, spread it on the ground beside the grave and knelt upon it. Gently, he touched the dead woman's face, fingered a pinch of soil and then began to remove the remaining earth. For this he used a small brush and shovel; after lifting aside the turves which remained, he slowly removed the layers of soil, placing some samples in plastic bags and casting the unwanted earth some distance away. The soil was fairly dry, the outcome of a few weeks without rain – the thundery rain of the weekend had not penetrated the ground to any depth, having run from the surface to disappear down natural drains.

In time, the girl was completely uncovered; she lay on her back with her legs straight before her and her arms down the sides of her body, squeezed between her torso and the sides of her shallow makeshift grave. Meredith ordered photographs at this stage, showing her clothing and the position in which she lay. Then he examined her injures, initially without touching them.

'Mr Pluke,' he called to Montague. 'First, note the distinct lack of decomposition and then the puncture wound in her right temple. It is rather like the wound one would expect from a captive bolt humane killer on a pig, is it not? There is very little blood, however, and that suggests the wound is a very deep one. So what on earth caused it, Mr Pluke? Your guess is as good as mine at this moment but even without the benefit of a post-mortem, I would guess it caused her death.'

'So you feel this is murder followed by a crude and unsuccess-ful attempt to dispose of the body?' invited Pluke.

'That is a very distinct possibility, Mr Pluke.'

'It is a starter theory,' Pluke smiled. 'I think it is good enough for me to launch a murder-type enquiry and set up an incident room.'

'I would think so, but I need to examine that wound in laboratory conditions. It is a most peculiar wound, Mr Pluke, and we must not lose sight of the fact that it could be accidental. It doesn't look like a bullet wound to me.'

'And it cannot be self-inflicted,' suggested Pluke. 'The instrument is not here, not with the body.'

'I agree with that. Now, let's consider her clothing. Blue denim jeans, white trainer shoes, white socks, a pale blue blouse with short sleeves. Inexpensive, I'd say, mass market stuff, not designer clothing. Once she's undressed, I can give you the manufacturers' names so you can check the retail outlets. No jewellery around her neck, no ear-rings, no spectacles, but there is a watch on her left wrist . . .' and he lifted that arm from its resting place. As he did so, the earth around it fell away and revealed a small pink plastic-framed hand mirror, the sort a young girl might use in her bedroom. It had been lying close to the fingers of her left hand.

'A watch,' continued Meredith, 'still functioning, a Timex – inexpensive, I would say, in keeping with her clothing – plastic strap. And this mirror. Pink plastic frame and handle, round glass about three inches in diameter, cheaply manufactured . . . Would you think the mirror is relevant, Mr Pluke, or has it been lost by a child on a picnic here and got mixed up in the earth which was eventually used to fill the grave?'

'It could be very relevant,' said Pluke with due solemnity. 'It must be retained.'

'Really? What do you think is its relevance? People do have picnics here, don't they? Someone could have lost it. This quarry is beside a popular public footpath.'

'People rambling and hiking do pass by this way on a regular basis,' admitted Pluke. 'I believe the route is one of the most popular in this area and I am sure some will enjoy picnics among those trees, or even down here in the quarry, or at least around the edge of the quarry.'

'Quite, so we should not attach too much importance to that

31

mirror. I do not want it to deflect us or mislead us in our enquiries. We could waste hours examining the mirror and trying to discover its source when it may have no relevance whatsoever. It might have been lost by a camper.'

'It was found beside the body, Mr Meredith, and as the investigating officer I consider that to be of some importance. Perhaps you know that in some cultures, even today, it is customary to place objects in the grave, objects which might be useful in one's long and uncertain journey to the Hereafter.'

'I don't think that is done in any civilised society, Mr Pluke. But a mirror? Why would a mirror be relevant? This is England, remember, not a primitive country where logical things like food, tools and travel requirements are buried with the dead for their journeys into eternity! And I would venture to suggest that this girl is English – her clothing, her watch and her general appearance would suggest that.'

'Nothing is impossible, Mr Meredith – but even if she is English, her killer might not be. Furthermore, the person who buried her might not be English either – the killer might have had an accomplice, and either of them could be foreign. That is why the mirror is relevant, even in England.'

'I will note what you say, Mr Pluke. The presence of the mirror will be recorded. Now, have we anything else down here?'

Before asking for assistance in lifting the body from the grave, he removed the loose earth which had fallen down around it, commenting, 'This is a very shallow grave, Mr Pluke, because the ground below the body is solid rock. Chummy would not have known that when he started to dig. There is every possibility he wanted a deeper grave but circumstances appear to have defeated him. You'll also note that it is a well-dug grave; it has been cleanly cut with a spade, not scraped out of the earth with stones or even bare hands. Note the clean cuts – and it was cut to the correct size as well. I'd say this grave was well planned and executed, Mr Pluke.'

'I would agree with that, Mr Meredith,' acknowledged Pluke.

'I will examine her clothing in more detail when I get her to the lab but I do note it is damp,' continued Meredith. 'And I will make a closer examination of her injury, internal as well as external. It might have occurred after death, although the presence of blood would indicate otherwise. She might have been exposed to rain around the time of death too, the damp clothing and spread of blood around the wound suggest that. The good state of preservation of the body means she has not been dead very long and has not been buried very long. A very interesting case.'

Pluke said, 'I heed what you say, but in addition, I would like you to note the orientation of the grave, Mr Meredith. East to west. The head is towards the west, the feet towards the east.'

'Is that significant as well?' asked Meredith, who had not regarded the position of the grave as having any particular relevance.

'That, the presence of the mirror and the careful digging of the grave combine to make me believe the grave was intended to be permanent,' said Pluke. 'The person who buried her did not believe she would be discovered. It has long been the practice in many cultures to orientate graves on an east to west axis. I believe the person who dug this grave exercised some thought in its preparation with a degree of permanence in mind, although I was initially puzzled by the fact it is so shallow. That question has now been answered – it has a base of solid rock – but its position so close to a busy footpath means it could be very easily discovered. I fear there are some contradictions here, Mr Meredith.'

'Well, you are the investigating officer. But could the orientation of the grave have happened by pure chance, Mr Pluke?'

'In the investigation of a murder, Mr Meredith, nothing can be assumed to be the outcome of pure chance. Not even cheap plastic-framed mirrors.'

'*Touché*!' grinned the pathologist. 'Now I must remove her from the grave – I need to turn her over to see if there are any other wounds, a bullet in her back perhaps, or a knife wound. Your men can help me, can they?'

'Of course,' said Pluke. 'You'll carry her feet first from the grave? All corpses should be carried feet first.'

'I do know your little quirks, Detective Inspector Pluke,' beamed Meredith. 'And I can see no reason to contradict your wishes. So, yes, feet first as always.'

Pluke then called PC Singleton and Wayne Wain to render the necessary assistance. The victim was lifted carefully from her grave and placed face down on a large plastic sheet produced from the pathologist's case. After a careful examination, albeit without removing any of her clothes, he concluded there were no further wounds on her body and there was no other helpful evidence in the earth which had contained her. Meredith then made a cursory search of the pockets of her jeans but found only a small white handkerchief. There was nothing which would identify her, no wallet, diary, or other written matter.

'She has very few personal belongings, Mr Pluke, which does not surprise me. The killer has done his best to remove identifiable items, I suggest. I think we can remove her to my laboratory now,' said Meredith. 'The coroner has been informed, I presume? And have we the necessary transport?'

'Yes,' said PC Singleton. 'I have notified the coroner and he ordered a post-mortem. The shell has arrived too, Mr Meredith. PC Browning is the driver, he'll act as coroner's officer.'

The brown plastic coffin-shaped receptacle known as the shell was brought from an unmarked blue van and the remains of the once beautiful girl were placed inside, along with the plastic mirror and the samples of soil secured by Meredith.

'One thing, Mr Meredith,' Pluke hailed him. 'Would you care to state whether or not she was killed here? In your opinion, is this the scene of her death or did she die elsewhere before being brought here for burial? And am I right in thinking her death was comparatively recent?'

'I cannot be adamant about any of that, Mr Pluke, but my first impression is that there is nothing to indicate she died here. And I think she died within the past forty-eight hours, perhaps less. Sometime on Saturday, early evening at a guess.'

'I tend to agree. Now, you will note that this quarry is used for a variety of purposes and by a variety of people,' Pluke pointed out. 'Many people know of it, campers, local lovers, litter louts and the like – and you can see that a number of agricultural machines are stored here.'

'Are they also relevant, Mr Pluke?'

'There could be a link, Mr Meredith. For example, I must consider that a component part of one of the machines might have caused that injury – a bolt, spindle, something of that kind.'

'You're thinking of some kind of accident followed by an attempted cover-up, are you?'

'It is one of the options I shall be bearing in mind, Mr Meredith.'

'I have no doubt you will closely examine all such machinery to see if a part is missing. If you discover anything of relevance, give me a call. I can check to see whether the wound is the same shape and size as whatever part you find, and of course there might be identifiable deposits in the wound. Meanwhile, I shall be carrying out the post-mortem. The sooner the better.'

Minutes later, the blue van, driven by PC Browning of Crickledale, left the scene *en route* to the pathologist's laboratory. Meredith followed in his Rover as Pluke turned to PC Singleton and said, 'PC Singleton, Scenes of Crime and the Task Force will now carry out their detailed examination of the scene and fingertip search of the surrounding area. As you know, they will be seeking the murder weapon and the tool used to dig the grave. I shall ask them to examine those machines too. Can you remain here to secure the site against anyone who might try to enter – press, photographers, hikers?'

'Yes, sir.'

'Good. Now, Detective Sergeant Wain, we shall talk to Mr Eric Burholme, a preliminary interview at this stage. And our officers will have to examine his heavy machinery, every piece of it, to see if a component part could have caused that odd wound.'

'Yes, sir.' Wayne Wain was looking forward to this investigation. A successful outcome, crowned by the arrest of the killer, would enhance his chances of promotion for surely old Pluke was heading for his pension? Soon, there must be a vacancy for a young, energetic, modernised and successful detective inspector.

35

As they walked towards the farm buildings, Wain warmed to his task while Detective Inspector Pluke glanced around. The complex was an amazing place, extremely tidy and well maintained but full of colourful decorations and large bold advertisements. Huge lengths of pale blue plastic sheeting with yellow lettering advertising 'Harman's Agricultural' adorned the outer walls of some buildings. Fluttering in the moorland breeze, a large blue flag with a similar message flew from a flagpost at one end of the big house. It was complemented at the other end by a huge weather-vane comprising a golden-headed cockerel perched above a slender arrow which in turn was above the letters which indicated the four points of the compass. The body of the cockerel was painted light blue; the beautiful vane was in excellent condition considering its exposed position. In fact, the entire farm was immaculately maintained with fresh paint on the doors and windows, and not a speck of rubbish in sight.

The weather-vane, Pluke noted, indicated that the wind, more powerful up here than in the valley, was still blowing from the west. The displays of plastic sheeting and the flag were fluttering noisily, making a sound rather like that of a yacht at sea. Before them was the massive farmhouse; this also had a sign outside, a wooden one above the door saying 'Harman's Farm' in yellow letters on a clean blue background. An array of stone buildings surrounded the house, like a clutch of chicks around a mother hen, and they provided a degree of shelter from the fierce moorland weather.

'A likely place for interesting horse troughs, Wayne!' said Pluke with enthusiasm as he strode towards the front door.

'Some of these places have been modernised, sir, and all unwanted artefacts removed.'

'Some, but not all, Wayne. Many old farms of this kind, with the original buildings still intact, are the perfect sites for unadulterated horse troughs. There's none of your modern metal or plastic monstrosities in these places – good old stone troughs serviced by spring water which never ceases to flow.'

'Sir, this is a murder-type investigation. We have rather more serious things to concern us just now.'

'But even murder enquiries are ephemeral, Wayne. Stone horse troughs are not. Now, when we interview Mr Burholme, we will not suggest, at this early stage, that we suspect a piece from any of his machines could be responsible for the girl's injuries. If it's flown off a machine at high velocity, we don't want him looking for it, finding it and getting rid of it when we've gone!'

'But he will know eventually because we shall have to examine every one of them,' Wayne stressed.

'Indeed we shall and we shall also have to search his farm for the tools used to dig the grave. I think you will agree that a person could walk from the quarry and help himself, or herself, to a spade or pick-axe from these buildings without anyone knowing. The doors appear to be left permanently open – they're open now. Few farmers lock away all their tools or even keep them under cover, but this is an exceptionally tidy place.'

As they crossed the neat forecourt towards the house, Mr Burholme emerged from the front door. Framed in the opening, he appeared to be exceptionally tall and upright with a splendid head of pure white hair and a very fresh, pink complexion. His slender body was casually dressed in a patterned green shirt and light slacks. He appeared to be in prime condition for he walked without the aid of a stick and without any sign of a stoop. He could be in his late sixties, Pluke guessed, a fine specimen of manhood and living confirmation of the ancient belief that a luxuriant head of hair was an indication of life and vigour.

'Ah, Mr Pluke. They have sent you!' His crisp well-spoken voice held just a trace of a North Yorkshire accent.

'Good morning, Mr Burholme. Yes indeed, I am the investigating officer and this is my deputy and my assistant, Detective Sergeant Wain.'

'So the call of duty dragged you away from the shoggling ceremony, Mr Pluke. A shock for us all, but how can I help?' and Burholme extended his hand in a gesture of warmth and hospitality. Pluke and Wain shook his hand, each noticing a very strong, dry grip.

'May we come inside?' suggested Pluke.

'By all means, how discourteous of me,' and Burholme turned and led the way towards his kitchen. Inside, it was spacious and light with a tiled floor and oak-panelled walls; a large table on which lay a plate, cup and eating utensils dominated the centre of the room while a wood-burning Aga worked ceaselessly in the background, casting its heat about the entire house. A kettle was singing on one of the hot plates, its lid bubbling up and down as steam puffed into the room. The place was immaculately clean, with every kitchen utensil in place and no dirty pots in the sink, although Pluke did notice the absence of fresh flowers. The woman's touch was missing.

'I trust we are not interrupting your lunch or your family meal?' Pluke indicated the used plate.

'Not at all, I have just had lunch. I live alone in this great barn of a place. I have seven bedrooms, one for every day of the week,' he smiled. 'But can I offer you a drink of something? Tea, coffee? Wine? Fruit juice?'

'No, thank you,' said Pluke even before Wain could express his delight at the prospect of a cup of coffee. It seemed they would not get any lunch today: when interviewing suspects, Pluke regarded offers of food and drink as potential bribes and rejected every one.

'As you wish, Mr Pluke,' and Pluke then noticed the intensity of the cool blue eyes of this handsome farmer.

'We shall not detain you long, Mr Burholme,' continued Pluke. 'Now, I know you are aware of our activity in the quarry – your quarry, I believe?'

'Yes, PC Singleton explained. He said a body had been found by a hiker, buried in my quarry.'

'It is the remains of a young woman.' Pluke exercised considerable care in presenting the information, conscious of the fact that this man was his second suspect until he had been eliminated. 'She had suffered a head injury and was buried in your quarry, not far from the public footpath. The body has now been removed for a post-mortem to be conducted, and my officers are undertaking a careful search of the quarry and surrounding area. We have to search for a potential murder weapon and any other material evidence.'

'You are saying she was murdered?' A frown appeared on Burholme's face.

'That is a distinct possibility, but it has not yet been determined,' Pluke said. 'But I must be frank and say that this has all the hallmarks of a suspicious death. We are treating it as murder until the contrary is proved. That means we must question you, Mr Burholme, about your movements, about people you might have seen on the farm or in the quarry, whether or not the girl is known to you . . .'

'Of course, I understand perfectly, inspector. Please feel free – I wish to help all I can. Do sit down.'

Pluke and Wain each eased a dining-chair from beneath the table and settled upon them, with Pluke beginning the questioning.

'Your full name, sir, to begin with?' he asked politely.

'Eric Burholme, just Eric, and this is Harman's Farm, as I am sure you realise from the displays outside. The postal address is Barughdale, as I am sure you know. I am a widower – my dear wife died fifteen years ago this very week, and I have no children. An old war injury, you understand. As I said, I am alone in this huge place, Mr Pluke.'

'You still work, though?'

'I need to keep myself fully occupied. But you think I am too old to work?' He smiled at the detectives, those bright blue eyes laughing with pleasure. 'I am eighty years of age . . .'

'Eighty?' Pluke expressed genuine surprise. Burholme could have passed easily for someone ten or even twenty years younger.

'I know I do not look it. I reached eighty in February. I have aged well, Mr Pluke, and I owe that to a careful lifestyle of hard work in the open air. But you will note there are no animals or livestock on the farm, not any more. I sold them all after the death of my wife, to raise capital which I have invested to provide me with an income. I like to be kept busy, so I occupy myself by hiring my wide range of agricultural machinery to those who need it, when they want it – farmers just beginning their careers cannot afford to pay thousands of pounds for something like a combine harvester which they use only for a few days each harvest time. So I hire my machinery to them – everything from ploughs to combines by way of seed drills and mowers, tractors and forage harvesters, hence the rather gaudy

39

advertising. And I lease my land to those who wish to make use of it, either for crops, silage or livestock grazing. I do work, Mr Pluke, just sufficient to keep me agile, but no longer do I tire myself out with hard manual labour. That's a young man's game.'

'And I do know that, in addition to what you have told me, you are a generous benefactor to many local causes.'

'I like to share my good fortune, Mr Pluke. I have no family to inherit my wealth, and I like others to benefit from it. It is my way of giving something back to society.'

'A very nice thought, Mr Burholme. Now, you store some of your machinery and bales in the old quarry?'

'I do indeed, but not all my machinery is kept in the open air. Most of it is under cover, in the buildings which you can see around this complex. You are welcome to have a look at anything you wish. The bales in the quarry are not mine, by the way – I allow a neighbouring farmer to leave them there. I have ample room and besides, they do create a useful shelter for small animals and also provide a solid wind barrier.'

'My officers will have to search your premises, Mr Burholme, in case the person responsible has concealed any evidence around the farm. I cannot divulge the precise cause of death, except to say there are indications of violence upon the victim. That means we need to find the weapon which caused her death, and the implement which was used to dig the grave.'

'Of course, Mr Pluke. I shall help in any way I can. This is a dreadful thing to happen, and it is made worse for me because it is on my land.'

'I do understand, and thank you,' said Pluke. 'Now, the victim is a young woman, blonde hair and very attractive in life, aged about thirty. We should have a photograph before the day is out, but can you recall any such visitor here? A customer perhaps? The wife or girlfriend of a customer maybe? Or someone merely passing through?'

Burholme creased his brow in thought a while, and then he shrugged his shoulders. 'Lots of people come here on business. Many of them are either ladies or accompanied by ladies, but I

40

cannot identify any of them from such a brief description. I'd like to see a photo, if that can be arranged?'

'We will do that,' promised Pluke. 'Now, have you had any visitors out of normal hours? I am thinking of the quarry in particular. I believe the only way into the quarry by motor vehicle is through this farm?'

'When I bought the quarry, many years ago, I closed its entrance from Barughdale lane, for security reasons. Then I made a new entrance across my own land. One reason was to deter uninvited visitors from trespassing in the quarry – courting couples, campers, caravanners, people lighting fires and using the place as a toilet or to dump their household litter. I have no objection to bona fide campers using my quarry but so many selfish people would come to dump old chairs, settees, mattresses, oil drums and worse. Anyway, the point is that lots of people made illegal or nuisance use of the quarry but once I bought it, I was determined to stop that kind of low person. I was bound by law to keep the public footpath open, however, although my action did reduce the numbers using the quarry illicitly. Now, it is only possible to enter it with a motor vehicle by coming through my main gate and then crossing my land. It's much more private now, although passing hikers still head for it, for picnics and overnight camping in tents, that sort of thing. I don't mind that provided they leave the place clean and tidy and do not cause damage. I don't always hear them, sometimes I do not know they are there – it's only when they've gone that I find evidence of their presence, bonfires and, sadly, litter, used condoms, and picnic waste like beer cans and plastic wrappers. The route into the quarry does not come near my house, however. I made sure the road avoided my buildings!' He grinned.

'So anyone taking a vehicle into the quarry must cross your land and must enter by the main gate. Did you hear or see anyone visiting the quarry over the weekend, or at any time recently, without your permission?'

'I don't hear everything, but yes, there was a motor vehicle on Saturday night,' said Burholme. 'Late, it would be. Eleven o'clock

41

or thereabouts. I heard its engine once or twice, moving about, but it was impossible to say whether it was on the road outside my premises, or in the quarry. I peeped out of my bedroom window but saw nothing, no lights or movement. I have no idea whether it stayed a while or left immediately. I was not particularly concerned, such noises are not unusual here. In spite of my efforts to isolate the quarry, I do get courting couples using it. Saturday nights especially. I do know that some married men have brought their mistresses here . . . I disturbed one only last Easter.'

'Who was it?' asked Pluke. 'The dead woman might be someone's mistress.'

'I have no idea. When I disturbed him, he drove off saying his wife must never find out . . . It was a dark blue car, a large one, but I did not note any other particulars. And I believe his woman was dark-haired.'

'We shall make enquiries of our night patrolling constables,' smiled Pluke. 'It is amazing how much information they gather about traffic movements during their duties. Now, did you visit the quarry this morning?'

'No, I did not. I do not visit it every day – I must admit I had forgotten about the vehicle I heard on Saturday.'

'And the rest of Saturday and Sunday, Mr Burholme? Were you here?'

'I left home fairly early on Saturday morning, half-past ten or thereabouts. I went to a demonstration of a new combine, in Harrogate. At the Great Yorkshire Showground, an invitation event. I am thinking about buying one or two of the newer models and it is important that I examine them first. I remained there all day, then had a meal with some colleagues in the early evening and returned here around nine o'clock. Sunday, I was here all day, doing maintenance most of the time, and this morning, I attended your shoggling ceremony. Like you, Mr Pluke, I do like to keep old customs alive – Christianity hijacked a lot of them, you know, from the pagans . . .'

'But not this one, Mr Burholme, not Shoggling the May. Now, I must inform you that we shall want to check your movements over the relevant period.'

'I understand. I know I am under suspicion, Mr Pluke. But I have no fears. Check all you want, search my entire premises. I have a clear conscience and you must do your duty.'

'Thank you for being so co-operative, Mr Burholme. Now, do you know the names of anyone who might come to the quarry at night?'

Burholme smiled. 'By night, it's usually courting couples, Mr Pluke, lads and lasses who know their way around the countryside. Campers sometimes use it, hikers carrying their own tents. Picnickers popping in during the daylight hours. But I can't give you names, I'm afraid.'

'You are not afraid of thieves, either here or in the quarry?'

'No. No one could remove any of my machines without me being aware of it. Nor have I suffered from vandals – we're too far from what some regard as civilisation for vandals to operate.'

'And the bales lining the edge of the quarry? Who do they belong to?'

'Brian Preston, my neighbour at Hollins Farm.'

'Might he pay a late night supervisory visit to the quarry, do you think?'

Burholme shrugged. 'It's highly unlikely, Mr Pluke. He has no cause to visit the place unless he wants to check his property. No one's going to steal any of those huge rolls, not without the necessary lifting gear. It's hardly likely he would visit the quarry late at night to check anything. But it's not impossible, of course.'

'I shall have to interview him,' noted Pluke, pleased to receive the name of another suspect. 'And I expect you have regular customers for your hire business?'

'Yes, of course. You'll want a list of them? Preston's one of them, he's got one of my forage harvesters, he took it only a couple of days ago. Early on Saturday morning, actually, before I went off to Harrogate.'

'I would like a full list, Mr Burholme. They and their contacts are precisely the sort of people who might make use of your old quarry, for lawful or unlawful purposes.'

'I'll get the list now,' offered Burholme.

4

After thanking Eric Burholme for his list of customers, Pluke asked for a guided tour of his outbuildings. These proved to house a bewildering variety of heavy and extremely intricate equipment whose functions were beyond the imagination of Pluke. During the tour, Burholme told the officers that many of the machines were currently not in use. The combines, for example, were used only in the autumn for harvesting grain; when idle, they were serviced and then stored in readiness for the following season. Burholme hired the necessary expertise for this, although some of the work was done on these premises for there was adequate room and facilities to permit that. Nevertheless Burholme said he could, and frequently did, personally undertake some of the minor repairs and basic servicing tasks. He added that he enjoyed working with metal and undertaking light engineering tasks.

'At this time of year,' Burholme went on, 'the farmers are producing silage and so they need our forage harvesters. We have six, and they are all out with customers at the moment. Soon, they will not be required – haymaking is the next seasonal activity, only a week or two away, when our hydraulic mowers will be in demand.'

'I note none of your outbuildings is locked?' said Wayne Wain.

'There is no need; who can steal these monsters without me knowing?'

'But if you are away, people could wander in and out of the buildings . . .' began Pluke.

'To hide a murder weapon or steal a spade to dig a grave?' countered Burholme.

'Precisely,' nodded Pluke.

'Quite clearly, I cannot deny that,' admitted Burholme. 'I never consider my machinery at risk from either thieves or vandals, not at this remote place, but if I am honest, I cannot say no one

44

has been here to steal tools or hide things. It is possible someone could enter my buildings without my knowledge.'

'I have to consider that likelihood,' said Pluke. 'My officers will have to make a detailed search of all your buildings, Mr Burholme, but meanwhile perhaps you could check your tools to see whether anything is missing? Particularly something like a spade, shovel or pick-axe. And if you find something has been added to your complement of tools without your knowledge, perhaps you'd alert us? Don't touch it, though, leave it for my men to deal with.'

'I will check all my gardening tools and other implements at the earliest opportunity, Mr Pluke.'

'Then I think we can leave now. Thank you for your co-operation,' said Pluke. 'My officers will come later for a formal written statement. We shall also want to confirm your movements on Saturday, Sunday and on Monday prior to the shoggling ceremony.'

'I'll be here,' promised Burholme.

As they left, the tall slender figure of the snow-haired Eric Burholme disappeared indoors.

Pluke and Wain returned to the quarry where the Task Force had arrived; the Scenes of Crime officers also awaited Pluke's orders. He addressed them all by clambering on top of a convenient bale and speaking from the elevation it provided. After outlining the circumstances of the discovery, he ordered the Scenes of Crime officers to undertake a meticulous search of the quarry and its array of machinery, highlighting the need to find the murder weapon and the grave-digging tool or tools. He reminded them that the girl's injuries might have been caused by a bolt-shaped, pointed component of an agricultural machine which, if found, might bear incriminating evidence – blood or minute particles of skin, for example. The likelihood of some other weapon being used had also to be considered. Working in conjunction with the Scenes of Crime team, the Task Force had to undertake the necessary fingertip search of the quarry and its surrounds. When that was complete, both teams should meticulously examine the machinery within the farm buildings, and the buildings themselves, either for the instrument which had caused her death, or for a spade, shovel, pick-axe or other grave-digging tool. Those implements did exist, consequently they must be somewhere – and that being so, they could be traced. The footpath must be searched too, along with the surrounding vegetation, for any items of thrown-away evidence, while the barbed wire on top of the roadside fence near the stile must be examined for fibres and other possible evidence.

Pluke told his officers that the press would be informed of the death, but in the event of any journalists speaking to officers other than Pluke or Wayne Wain, then they must be told the girl had died from a head injury. The precise nature of that injury must not be given to anyone not involved with the investigation.

'And now,' said Pluke, 'I shall radio the control room at Crickledale to give a brief situation report for onward trans-mission to interested parties such as the Chief Constable and Headquarters CID, and to formally request the establishment of an incident room. Then Detective Sergeant Wayne Wain and myself will interview our first witness – a local farmer called Brian Preston – and this evening at 6 p.m. I shall arrange the first formal briefing. That will be in the incident room. Our priority is to get the deceased identified as soon as possible and for that, Sergeant Tabler, I shall require you to take the fingerprints of the deceased and a photograph which is decent enough to be viewed by members of the public.'

'No problem, sir, I'll do that when the post-mortem's finished. So can I treat this as murder?' asked Detective Sergeant Tabler, the officer in charge of the Scenes of Crime officers, known as SOCO.

'I am treating the case as possible murder at this stage,' countered Pluke. 'I am awaiting the pathologist's report. Mean-while, we are conducting a murder-type investigation.'

'But with all due respect, sir, if the woman is suffering from a head injury which might have been caused by something from an agricultural implement, then she might have sustained it accidentally. She might have got caught in some moving machin-ery or something might have flown off at high velocity and struck her.'

'I am aware of that . . .' began Pluke.

'Balers have very powerful flywheels, remember, and such occurrences are not uncommon in this part of the world. Agricultural accidents are a sad feature of country life during the summer months.'

'Indeed they are,' agreed Pluke.

'I have dealt with many such accidents,' continued Sergeant Tabler. 'Some were caused in the most unbelievable manner . . . bizarre really . . . but deadly.'

'Precisely, Detective Sergeant Tabler, I have that very point under active consideration,' agreed Pluke. 'But if the death was the result of an accident, why arrange a secret burial? And why dispose of the object which caused the death? And why not summon medical help? In the absence of any substantial answers to those questions, I must consider murder to be a possibility until the contrary is proved. A possibility, but no more. You and your colleagues must consider this a murder-type investigation for the time being – no more and no less.'

'Point taken, sir,' acknowledged Tabler. 'I just need some authority for my involvement and my teams' expenses.'

'Once we get a name for her, sergeant, I feel sure her mode of life and her personality will produce some sensible answers, but in the meantime I want a full investigation. So as your teams undertake their work at the scene, Detective Sergeant Wain and myself will visit a Mr Brian Preston at Hollins Farm. He owns those rounded bales which line the edge of the quarry. From there, I shall return straight to my office, sergeant; if your officers find something of interest, report to me as soon as practicable.'

'Yes, sir,' said Detective Sergeant Tabler.

As Pluke and Wain drew to a halt in the muddy yard of Hollins Farm, Pluke spotted the massive horse trough which appeared to be built into the base of the heather-clad hillside towering behind the buildings. The trough was full of fresh water and the inlet was flowing generously, the trough spilling its overflow into a drain beneath.

'Look at that, Wayne!' he enthused. 'What a monster . . . a true giant among troughs!'

As they parked the car, Pluke rushed out with his coat flaps open and his hat on the back of his head, having had it knocked there during his exit from the vehicle. He stood beside the trough, looking up the hillside where another trough had been placed . . . it was also large in comparison with most and it was also brimming with water which overflowed into a drain. And there was another above that . . . a triple-decker!

Then they heard a voice behind them.

'Now then, gentlemen, what can I do for you? Interested in our water system, are you?' The new arrival peered quizzically at Pluke's overcoat, hat and bow tie.

'I am indeed,' stated Pluke with some conviction. 'Might I ask if that upper trough services the one beneath, and if that in turn services this lower one?'

'Aye, they do. We get a lot of folks coming to inspect our water supply, university types usually. They reckon it's quite unusual. Now, the spring which serves 'em all also supplies the house, it gives us all the water we need, for baths, kitchen, washing clothes, the lot. Supplies the humans and all the animals and poultry. It always has done, down the years. What's left over from the house comes into yon top trough up on the bank side, and it overflows into t'next one which overflows to fill this 'un in the yard and they reckon the overflow from this, near where your foot is, runs underground to service the farm in the dale below us . . . and the spring which supplies 'em all never dries up. Never. That's what baffles folks. Nobody can fathom where all that water comes from. There must be some sort of reservoir underground, a mighty big 'un if you ask me.'

'This is limestone country, underground caverns are quite likely, but this trough is fantastic – it reminds me of the Five Rise Lock at Bingley,' enthused Pluke, and within seconds he had produced a small camera from the pocket of his baggy overcoat. He began to take photographs of the series of troughs, and then, as Wayne watched helplessly, he pulled a notebook from his pocket and made a note of the location and description of these magnificent working examples of horse trough history.

'Sir.' Wayne Wain was anxious to proceed with the matter in hand. 'With all due respect, we are not here to examine horse troughs. Mr Preston, this gentleman is Detective Inspector Pluke from Crickledale and I am his deputy, Detective Sergeant Wain.'

'Oh, police business, is it? You don't look like policemen to me, leastways your mate doesn't. What am I supposed to have done? Not filled in my stock register or summat? Or been parking my tractor on double yellow lines somewhere?' and he grinned wickedly.

'Are you Brian Preston?' asked Wayne Wain.

'Aye, that's me.' He was a sturdy weathered fifty-year-old with a brown flat cap, grey flannel shirt with long sleeves, black boots and corduroy trousers held up with red and white braces. 'So what's up? What brings the plain-clothes constabulary to see me?'

'We've come from your neighbour, Eric Burholme.' Pluke spoke slowly. 'The body of a woman has been found in his quarry – she was discovered earlier today. We have reason to believe her death is suspicious. We are making routine house-to-house enquiries, and also visiting all Mr Burholme's customers.'

'You mean that quarry where I store my bales?'

'That's the one,' Wayne Wain told him. 'She was found buried on the edge of the quarry, near the trees which span the footpath.'

'But that's terrible! Poor bloody woman! Who is she then? Somebody local?'

'We don't know,' Pluke admitted. 'That is our most important task – to get her identified. Maybe you have some idea? She is about thirty, with blonde hair, average height and build . . .'

'Could be anybody, there's plenty of good-looking blondes in these parts,' muttered Preston. 'So why do you want to talk to me?'

'Two reasons, Mr Preston,' said Pluke. 'First, those wheel-shaped bales in the quarry. Do you check them regularly for any reason?'

'No, no need. They're not going to go anywhere.'

'So when was the last time you paid a visit to the quarry?'

'Weeks ago. I can't be too accurate but it would be five or six weeks back – I went to see if the plastic covers had been damaged. Folks do use that quarry, campers and courting couples. And Eric doesn't seem to mind so long as they behave.

I'd be more worried about strangers if I was him – I'm not saying they'd all vandalise things, but you can't be too careful. Even a small cut in them plastic covers would cause problems – I don't want rainwater seeping in.'

'And you've not been since that time?' Pluke wanted to be sure about this.

Preston shook his head. 'Nay, Mr Pluke. So how long's she been there, this lass?'

'We are not sure, it's probably a very short time, but she was buried there. It would take some time and effort to do that.'

'Buried? In that quarry? I thought the base was solid rock, that's why Eric keeps some of his machines there, they won't sink into the ground.'

'Whoever buried her found a soft patch of earth, a shallow piece,' said Pluke. 'So you've never noticed anyone in the quarry, say in the last couple of days or late at night? Or a disturbed piece of ground?'

'Sorry, no, Mr Pluke. By gum, this is dreadful . . . poor lass . . . what a way to end your life.'

'And the other reason for my visit, Mr Preston, is that I understand you are one of Mr Burholme's customers. You've hired a forage harvester from him recently?'

'Aye, a couple of days back. It's down my fields now, cutting silage. There's no problem with it, is there?'

'We want to trace all the machines currently on hire from Mr Burholme,' said Pluke. 'And we'd like our officers to examine them. Was yours damaged in any way when you took delivery of it? That was on Saturday morning, I believe? A part missing perhaps? Something like a bolt or a spindle?'

'Took delivery? I collected it myself on Saturday morning, early on. Half-seven or thereabouts. But no, I checked it over before I towed it away. There was nowt wrong with it, no damage, nowt missing.'

'Did you notice anyone else around the premises? Apart from Eric Burholme?'

'No, never saw a soul, Mr Pluke.'

'Thank you. Now, can we have a look at your machine?' asked Pluke.

'Aye, if you like. Follow me. It's a fairish walk.'

In spite of wearing such a heavy and cumbersome coat, Montague Pluke enjoyed the rapid walk down the fields of Hollins Farm, although it caused Wayne Wain to pant rather more than he would have wished. The open fields provided an extensive view of the moors behind Crickledale, and in time, having discovered that a fairish walk in Yorkshire was a long walk by most other standards, the three men entered a field where a tractor was moving slowly through the long grass. Preston hailed the tractor driver who halted and awaited the arrival of the three oncomers.

'Hang fire a bit, Harry,' said Preston. 'These chaps want a look at your harvester.'

Under the farmer's guidance, Pluke examined the machine and decided nothing was missing – it wouldn't have functioned with a part missing – but because the working parts were smothered with chopped grass and other vegetation, it was impossible to see whether any of them bore signs of blood or skin or minor damage.

'It was clean when you collected it, you said?' Pluke confirmed.

'Not immaculate, not like a new machine,' said Preston. 'You can't expect that when you've a machine which is doing this kind of mucky work. There's nowt worse than fresh grass for clarting up forage harvesters. Just think of a lawnmower. But it was as clean as I'd expect, and in good working order.'

'Right, well, thank you very much for your help,' said Pluke, wondering whether a forensic scientist would be able to locate blood or skin on any part of such a used machine. 'I'm sorry to have caused a break in your work.'

'Think nowt of it, Mr Pluke. Mind you, you'd have a job to get trapped in one of these, but nowt's impossible. I just hope you catch the bloke responsible. Right, Harry, back to it. We can't stand around all day when there's work to be done.'

And so the forage harvester resumed its silage making while Pluke, Wain and Farmer Preston walked back to the farm buildings.

'If you can think of anyone who might have used the quarry,

or who the blonde girl might be, give us a call, would you?' asked Wayne Wain.

'Sure,' said the farmer, waving them off.

After a long, lingering look at the magnificent series of horse troughs, Pluke fastened his seat belt and said, 'To the office now, Wayne, if you please. I wonder if our pathologist has produced any surprises?'

When Pluke returned to the police station, his first task, after crossing the threshold with his right foot first, was to visit the control room where he asked Sergeant Cockfield pronounced Cofield if there had been any messages.

Wayne Wain waited at his side.

'Yes, sir, Mr Meredith rang, from the path lab. Could you call him back?'

'I will indeed. Now, is the incident room being established? If so, where?'

'Yes, sir, in the parade room. Detective Inspector Horsley of Headquarters CID is in charge as usual, and he's already got the furnishings, telephones and computers organised. He's put out calls to draft in thirty detectives from across the force area.'

'Then I must pay him a visit. I shall proceed immediately to the incident room, sergeant, and I shall be there for a while. If anyone from the press rings, tell them I shall issue a statement very shortly. Have there been any press calls, sergeant?'

'Not yet, sir.'

'Good, I need to present them with accurate information – I may need their help to get this victim identified.'

As they moved through the corridors to the room normally used by the town's constables for parading on duty, Pluke turned to Wayne and said, 'Wayne, call the force press officer at Headquarters. I'd like him to join the team in the incident room, as soon as he can arrive.'

'You think this is going to be a runner, sir?'

'It has all the hallmarks of a long-lasting investigation, Wayne. Consider the facts – there is a most curious injury which is likely to have caused death, a distinct and thought-provoking lack of clues at the scene except for a pink hand mirror, no ready identification of the victim, no obvious motive, a well-dug grave

52

at an isolated location with no witnesses ... The ingredients are all there, Wayne. A mystery for us to solve.'

'A mystery, sir? Not a murder?'

'Not necessarily, Wayne. But thinking of our crime figures and detection statistics, we do not want an undetected murder on our books although that worry does not colour my judgement in this case. I continue to have a very open mind.'

'I understand. Right, sir, I'll call the press officer immediately. It's a new man, by the way – an Inspector Russell, Paul Russell,' and Wayne Wain headed upstairs to make the calls from his own office.

As Pluke entered the parade room, littered with unplaced desks, filing cabinets, telephone engineers and administrative personnel, all of which or whom were required for the creation of an incident room, someone picked up a phone which was already ringing and said, 'Detective Inspector Pluke, it's for you.'

He accepted the instrument and identified himself.

'Hart, Headquarters,' came the brusque reply. 'What the hell's going on in Crickledale, Pluke?'

'Barughdale, sir, to be precise.'

'Stop being pedantic, Pluke. It's within Crickledale sub-division. I have a garbled message here at Headquarters to say you've requested Horsley to set up an incident room in Crickledale.'

'Yes, sir—'

'Now the force is involved in a cost-cutting exercise and we want no unnecessary expenditure ... so is this murder or not?'

'I am treating it as murder, sir.'

'I don't care how you are treating it, Pluke, I want facts, not your bizarre theories. Is it murder or isn't it? That's all I want to know. It's a simple question which requires a very simple answer – yes or no. And while I am talking to you, I must say that you're not exactly in the top league of operational detectives, Pluke – your record of dealing with murders is pretty thin to say the least and your record of solving them is even thinner. I'm not sure you are the man to deal with an extended investigation, murder or otherwise, and it wouldn't surprise me if you didn't know a murder from a bit of malarky—'

'This is a highly suspicious death, sir,' Pluke interrupted this flow of venom as he tried to reason with Detective Superintendent Jack Hart. 'The woman was found in a shallow grave with head injuries—'

'All sorts can cause head injuries, Pluke. Falling off a bike can cause head injuries, banging your head against a brick wall can cause head injuries . . . I do it all the time!'

'This one looks like a puncture wound, sir. The pathologist is examining the victim at this moment. I don't think it was a self-inflicted wound, it was far too deep, consequently I am awaiting his judgement.'

'But is it murder, Pluke? That's all I want to know.'

'I must be honest and say I am not sure at this stage, sir. The injury is in her right temple, a deep hole in the head to be rather crude, a puncture wound by an object yet to be identified.'

'She fell on something, maybe?'

'I had not ignored that possibility, sir. Furthermore, she was buried in a disused quarry and found by a hiker. And her identity is not known. It all suggests something highly suspicious.'

'Go on, Pluke.'

'Well, sir, those circumstances compel me to treat the death as a possible murder. I should know the pathologist's opinion very soon, and this will assist me to determine the matter. Meanwhile I am conducting a murder-type investigation. I do need that kind of commitment from my officers if I am to bring this case to a satisfactory conclusion.'

'Well, if it's not murder we can't go to the expense of running an incident room and all the costly trappings that go with it, Pluke. Dozens of detectives on overtime, high telephone bills and all that. We have a budget for serious crime, remember. We can't go spending money as if we've won the lottery.'

'I am very aware of the financial restraints, sir, but I am also anxious that justice is done. The administration of justice should not depend upon the limitations of provincial police budgets, sir, with all due respect.'

'Well, it does depend upon precisely that,' snapped Hart. 'And I have to work within that budget, like it or not. So keep me informed, call me the minute you have the pathologist's report. If this is not murder, then I can't approve an expensive long-running investigation of murder-type proportions, can I?'

'No, sir.'

'And I should not have to remind you that unauthorised or unconventional burial isn't necessarily an indication of murder, Pluke, especially if it's preceded by accidental death ... People who hide secrets are not always murderers,' and he slammed down his handset.

Smarting from Hart's vitriol, Montague Pluke sought Detective Inspector Horsley, his colleague from headquarters CID and the man whose job it would be to administer the incident room. He would also allocate actions to the detectives when they assembled. Running an incident room was the equivalent of being in charge of the operational enquiries in a case of murder, hence the equal ranks.

'Ah, Detective Inspector Horsley,' beamed Montague. 'Glad you could make it.'

'Has Hart been on to you?' was Horsley's first question.

'Just now,' said Pluke. 'A very rude man, if I may say so, very lacking in courtesy, a sad thing for a man at the height of his professional career.'

'He's under pressure from the Chief Constable. Budgets, the low detection rate, the increase in recorded crime ... you name it, poor old Jack Hart's got worries about it. So we are treating this as murder, Montague?'

Montague Pluke never referred to other officers by their Christian names, especially in the presence of subordinates and particularly those with whom he was not on close friendly terms. He said, 'There are sufficient very good reasons for this death to be investigated with all the vigour of a murder enquiry.'

'Fair enough, it's your decision, you are the operational detective in charge of this sub-division. So what are your plans?'

'I understand you have called out thirty detectives? I shall address everyone in the incident room at six o'clock this evening. The most immediate and important task is to get the victim identified. Very soon, I should have the result of the pathologist's examination, and we shall then know the cause of death. Our teams need to be thoroughly updated, so you will have the incident room fully operational by six o'clock?'

'I will,' said Horsley. 'You seem to have made a good start – that's if it is murder! If not, you'll have to send them all home again.'

'Monday is not a bad day to begin a new enterprise,' Pluke told him in all seriousness, and then the telephone rang again. Pluke answered it.

'It's Meredith here from the pathology department.'

5

'I was going to ring you,' beamed Pluke. 'So what is your news?'

'A fascinating case, Mr Pluke,' began Meredith. 'First, the girl's physical appearance, you'll need this if you're to get her identified. White skin, five feet six inches tall, that's 165 centimetres; taller than average. Well built, thirty-six inch bust and hips, twenty-eight inch waist. Not slim by any means. Very good physical condition, no operation scars and every indication of being well cared for – nails in good condition, nicely manicured without any varnish, good natural teeth and hair all in first-class condition. The hair is thick and blonde, bobbed to just below the ears, not a fashionable or very expensive cut, Mr Pluke, not according to my secretary anyway. She has blue eyes, no spectacles or contact lenses. No ear-rings and her ears are not pierced. No lipstick or discernible perfume, no rings on her fingers – in fact no jewellery of any kind. Somewhat unexpectedly, she is a virgin, unusual for a woman of her age, if I may be so bold. There is no sign of any sexual attack, nor was she raped. That fact alone raises a question about the motive. Now to the injury, Mr Pluke. It is most peculiar. Some rigid object has penetrated her right temple and skull; it penetrated to a depth of at least three inches, even three and a quarter, that's eight centimetres or so. Beyond doubt, that – and the associated shock – killed her.

56

The object was removed before burial and I did not find it in the grave. Death would have been swift but not necessarily instantaneous – I would not place an estimate on how long it would have taken her to die, however. An hour might be too extreme – it could have taken mere minutes – but I think she would have been unconscious from the moment of injury until the time of death. There is bruising around the entrance to the wound as one might expect and other bruises about her head and shoulders, some with broken skin. If we find the object which caused the puncture wound, we might find it is attached to something else which made those cuts and bruises. Obviously, if the object is traced, I can make a match – but an agricultural machine might be what we are seeking. There are also minor lacerations to both her hands, rather as if she had fallen to the ground and tried to protect herself.'

'Fallen?' queried Pluke.

'It's one possibility, Mr Pluke, and it could fit your accidental falling-into-an-agricultural machine theory. Got herself impaled on a spike which was among some other metal sections perhaps? Fell on to iron railings even? Those with spikes? But that's not a positive theory, Mr Pluke – to be honest, I have no idea what the object could be.'

'There are no iron railings with spikes at Harman's Farm, they're all wooden ones.'

'Whatever caused the wound, I think it was made of metal, it was heavy in weight and solidly constructed, and I think that the pointed section which produced the wound was painted black. There are minute traces of black metal paint in the wound. The spiked object has a diameter of four-tenths of an inch, that is nine millimetres, and it has a sharp point.'

'It does sound like something from an agricultural machine, Mr Meredith.'

'We must not let ourselves be persuaded by what we saw near the grave, Mr Pluke. That missile, whatever it was, could have come from anywhere or anything. It wasn't a bolt from a humane killer, though – they have hollow tips and this weapon was pointed. I would add that considerable force would be required to drive it into her head. In trying to guess what the object might

57

be, beyond a fall on to something spiked, I must confess to being baffled.'

'So either she fell into it, was knocked into it, or it knocked her over, or someone used it to knock her over ... My men will conduct a very meticulous search of the locality, including the machinery and the places in which it is stored, Mr Meredith. Rest assured you will be the first to know if we find anything likely to have caused that injury.'

'Good. Now, Mr Pluke, I sought deposits on her body and clothes and found some items of relevant interest. For example, there were tiny pieces of gravel in the lacerations on her hands, consistent with her putting out her hands to save herself as she fell on to a hard surface. Similar gravel was found in the fabric of her jeans, on the left side, again consistent with falling on to that side. Her clothing was damp too but that might have been due to her lying in the moist earth of the grave – or, of course, she might have been caught in one of Saturday's thunderstorms. The soil samples I took from the grave were remarkably dry, Mr Pluke – the rain had not penetrated that far down – and the soil was not the same consistency as the pieces of gravel in her hands and clothing. I think that she might have got wet in the rain and that she was alive at the time of the shower.'

'So the question which faces me, Mr Meredith, is whether this is an accidental death or murder. That is what I must establish if I am to be allowed to continue this investigation.'

'There is every indication it is murder, Mr Pluke. The absence of the instrument of death, the force required to kill her with it, and the circumstances of her burial all add up to a murder. It is difficult to envisage how such an injury could have been caused accidentally.'

'I must state that I believe she could have fallen and impaled herself on something,' said Pluke. 'There is some evidence to suggest that. The gravel in her hands and clothes, and the accompanying minor wounds.'

'Then where is the object which caused that fatal wound, Mr Pluke? Indeed, what is it? And why did no one call in the emergency services to give her medical aid? Why hide the body, why bury it in an isolated quarry without notifying the authorities?' asked Meredith. 'All those factors indicate murder, Mr Pluke.'

'Then if my supervisory officers try to prevent me carrying out my investigation, you will support me by agreeing that this is a murder hunt?'

'I will indeed, Mr Pluke. I am as intrigued as yourself.'

'Fine, although privately, I must say that I have doubts. But if we can treat it as murder, it means I can avail myself of professional expertise in order to determine how she died. Now, the time of death, Mr Meredith? Can you give me any indication of that?'

'Taking everything into account – weather, temperature of the body, burial, the rain, the lack of advanced decomposition – I'd say she has not been dead more than two days. If you ask me to be more precise, I'd say probably she died sometime on Saturday, later in the day rather than earlier. I'd support my earlier estimate of around tea-time. Her damp clothing might be a factor, too, and I think the blood of her wound was exposed to rain. Maybe she lived and died in the rain.'

'There was a new moon early on Saturday morning.' Pluke spoke softly, almost to himself. 'A Saturday new moon is never a good omen, Mr Meredith, it heralds bad weather, heavy rain, storms at sea and bad fortune in general.'

'In her case, she did have some appalling bad luck, didn't she?' There was a tone of dismissiveness in Meredith's voice.

'We should not mock or ignore such omens, Mr Meredith. So often do they prove to be accurate.' Pluke now paused to reflect upon the information which had been passed to him, then asked, 'So, Mr Meredith, in your expert opinion, shall I launch a widespread search for a component part of an agricultural machine?'

'You can't ignore that likelihood, Mr Pluke. I cannot be more positive than that, but remember a highly polished or oily part was not responsible. The part you seek is covered with black paint, and it has a sharp point. I've already said I believe it was not a humane killer. To do the damage it did, I think it would be fairly heavy and applied with extraordinary force. That doesn't sound like a bolt or a spindle from a piece of machinery – and I think it was part of something heavier and rather complex in its construction. Remember her other cuts and bruises.'

'We can have photographs of those, can we?' asked Pluke. 'To help match the object when we find it?'

'By all means,' agreed Meredith.

'What we do need here, Mr Meredith, is some very imaginative thinking. I'll work on that. In the meantime, what about her clothing? Is there anything else you can tell me?'

'I feel sure she was wearing it when she was injured – there were some tiny tears in her blouse which match the bruises I mentioned earlier. Don't overlook the gravel particles either: I can match those with control samples if you find the place she fell. Because she was wearing those clothes when she died, you can publicise details – someone might recognise the clothing or may have noticed her wearing it. That is something you may wish to stress when you issue a description to your officers. And your officers might wish to trace the source of her clothing, Mr Pluke, although there is nothing which adds greatly to our knowledge. All her clothing, and her underwear, are of mass market manufacture, easily obtainable in department stores and high street shops. Modest in price, not fashionable items. The only thing in the pockets of her jeans was a single small white handkerchief – no money, make-up, combs. Nothing.'

'Nothing that would lead to her identification?' asked Pluke.

'No, I'm sorry, nothing. You'll want to take her fingerprints, I suppose?'

'Yes, I have already asked Detective Sergeant Tabler to arrange that,' Pluke said. 'He will contact you to arrange a time.'

'You have informed the coroner?'

'Yes, but the inquest cannot be opened until we have an identification, and that might take time. And we'd like a photograph for showing to the public during our enquiries, that's if we can get one which doesn't make her look as if she's dead.'

'I am sure all that can be arranged. She will remain in our refrigerated unit until the body is required again,' said Meredith. 'So, Mr Pluke, I don't envy you as you search for the device that killed her even though it might be fairly close at hand. Do remember that people get impaled on railings and spikes of all kinds, while bolts and other pieces of machinery can fly out under pressure, rather like the bolt from a crossbow. Lethal things, bolts from crossbows. You might consider that, Mr Pluke – a crossbow bolt, I mean.'

Pluke pondered on this, then said, 'If it was a mere accident, it might have been in abnormal circumstances which caused her to be buried secretly.'

'Like being a man's mistress, you mean? She sustained her accident on his premises while his wife was away . . . Someone who's trying to urgently and desperately cover up his tracks and his deception?'

'Something along those lines, Mr Meredith. Someone with a big secret to maintain.'

'But accidental death followed by unauthorised burial of a corpse is hardly the crime of the century, Mr Pluke!'

'Whatever happened, Mr Meredith, someone knows all about it. Someone took the trouble to bury her secretly and to remove or conceal the instrument of death . . . and I shall find that person or persons.'

'Then consider yourself with a major enquiry on your hands, Mr Pluke. I wish you good luck.'

'To help me, I shall establish a four-leaved clover in my office just as soon as I can find one,' Pluke told him, and replaced the telephone.

While Pluke left the office to obtain a four-leaved clover from a nearby field in which he knew they could be found, Detective Inspector Horsley completed the preliminaries for the incident room. By five thirty, it was ready to receive the thirty detectives and the civilian staff who would add their clerical expertise to the enquiry and as six o'clock approached, they began to filter into the premises. Inevitably, it became known as the Plukedom.

When everyone was present and recorded on the duty sheets, Pluke, with Wayne Wain at his side, strode into the room, called for silence and stood upon a chair to address his teams. After introducing himself and his senior officers, he provided a detailed outline of the discovery and of the work currently under way at the scene, then continued:

'To all intents and purposes, this is a murder investigation and

61

as usual in such an enquiry, I require two detectives per team. Detective Inspector Horsley will allocate your actions, but there are certain priorities. First and foremost, we need to identify the victim. Make yourselves familiar with her appearance and dress. Who is she? Where is she from? How did she travel to the quarry? Was she dead upon arrival at the quarry or did she die there? We need to trace her movements during the latter days of last week, Saturday in particular. Who was she with? Where is her family, who are her friends ... you know the sort of things we must establish. Check all missing persons lists, local and national. Her fingerprints and a photograph of her will be available shortly, they might help, she might have a conviction of some kind. She is a virgin but that does not rule her out from being a prostitute. Prostitutes provide services other than normal sexual intercourse. Find out who has been using the quarry and question them closely to establish reasons and times – campers, picnickers, hikers, people dumping household litter, courting couples. They might have seen the blonde on a previous visit, or they might even have seen her over the recent weekend, alone or with someone. A camper might have arrived with her and left without her after some skylarking in the machinery sheds or elsewhere. She might have been sheltering, her clothes were wet. And there were particles of gravel in lacerations on her hands and in the leg of her jeans, these suggesting a fall. If she fell, where did it happen? What did she fall on to? There are no metal railings with spikes at Harman's Farm.

'Next, we need to find the weapon which caused her injuries. Mr Horsley will allocate teams to that task, to examine all the agricultural machines on Burholme's premises, and indeed any others that might be in the district. In particular, we need to trace any component part which could have caused her injury. But the object could come from anywhere else. Think about that as you go about your enquiries – think of large bodkins, tent pegs or some other camping or hiking device, a bolt from a crossbow, an awl of some kind, a stone or metal punch – this is a rural area full of craftsmen and craftswomen, so consider a craft tool of some kind, one for making deep holes. Try to envisage such a device which could be part of some larger

62

fabrication, then try and work out what it might be. It might bear traces of blood although that will not be easy to find, and it will be covered with black paint. It is likely to be made of metal with a sharp point, nine millimetres wide, and capable of penetrating to a depth of at least three and a quarter inches, which equals eight centimetres. How did such a large object manage to penetrate her skull? It would require great force. Mr Meredith, the forensic pathologist, will examine anything you discover and once we identify the object responsible, we might be able to trace its recent movements and those of the people who have had access to it. Mr Burholme, the owner of the quarry where she was discovered, hires a wide range of machinery to local farmers. We have a list of his customers – each must be visited in an attempt to identify the deceased. Is she a girlfriend of one of them? She's a virgin, so she's hardly likely to be a wife ... but she could be a girlfriend who likes to say no. Is that a motive for murder, perhaps? So, ladies and gentlemen, we have a lot to be going on with. We can make a start this evening. We shall work from 9 a.m. to 9 p.m. daily until further notice, and overtime will be paid. It means we have fewer than three hours' work left this evening but even that could produce a wealth of information. Now, any questions so far?'

'Sir ...' A detective in the crowd raised his hand. 'You said a mirror had been found in the grave. Are we to try and trace its source?'

'Yes. It is being examined by Scenes of Crime at the moment, but once they have finished, I shall have photographs distributed. It is a small pink-framed mirror, plastic-framed that is, with a round glass. It has a handle too; rather like a child's toy mirror in fact. We need to find out where it was made or purchased, and who bought it. Did the girl buy it, did she bring it with her, or was it bought by the person who buried her? Detective Inspector Horsley will allocate a specific action for a team to trace the mirror's history, but I would ask you all to bear it in mind during your enquiries. Now, is Inspector Russell here?'

'Sir,' and a youthful, dark-haired man in civilian clothes raised his hand.

'See me when I dismiss the others, will you, inspector? We need to draft a news release this evening.'

'Yes, sir.'

Considering that this initial briefing contained sufficient information to launch the investigation, Pluke dismissed the detectives.

He reminded them to update the incident room records before going off duty, and then to parade for duty tomorrow morning at nine. With a bustle of activity, the detectives, male and female, began their work as Paul Russell, carrying a briefcase, followed Pluke into his small dark office which adjoined the incident room. A small glass vase stood on Pluke's desk; it contained a freshly picked four-leaved clover which stood in water.

'Sit down,' invited Pluke, and the inspector obeyed, placing his briefcase on the floor.

'You are new to this job?' Pluke asked.

'I've been press officer for six months now, Mr Pluke. I was drafted in from the Crime Prevention Department. But this is my first murder enquiry.'

'I am sure you will be a great asset to my investigation, Mr Russell, and I feel sure we will not encounter too many problems. First, I must inform you that I am not convinced this is a murder, but I shall deal with the case as if it is. I say that because I need the co-operation of your friends in the media as well as the dedication of my own officers. Now, it is too late for us to catch the regional evening programmes on television, and of course, the evening papers will have been printed too. So we are thinking of tomorrow's dailies, radio programmes and television news.'

'Yes, sir.'

'You heard my briefing?'

'I did, sir, yes. You want me to concentrate on the victim? Is there any chance of photographs which are suitable for use by the media?'

'Talk to Sergeant Tabler, he's making the necessary arrangements. Happily, our victim is not disfigured about the face. Otherwise, an artist's impression might be useful. Initially, a verbal description should be sufficient to commence our publicity campaign. That will provide the necessary element of

64

intrigue. Now, I do not want any mention in the press of our theory about components of agricultural machines. That is one very localised line of enquiry we are actively pursuing and I don't want to frighten people into disposing of good evidence. Should you receive any queries, just say she was suffering from a head injury and that we are seeking the object which caused it. Leave it as vague as that.'

'I have drafted a news release, sir, for your approval. I got the facts from Sergeant Cockfield pronounced Cofield,' and Russell opened his briefcase to produce a typewritten sheet. It said, 'The body of a woman was today found in a shallow grave in a disused quarry on land at Harman's Farm, close to the Crickledale–Barughdale road. She was suffering from a head injury and police have launched an investigation. The identity of the victim is unknown but Detective Inspector Montague Pluke, head of Crickledale CID, said, "She is about thirty, well built with blonde hair and blue eyes. She is wearing a light blue blouse, blue jeans and trainer shoes. I should be pleased to receive any information which might lead to her identification." Thirty detectives have been drafted on to the enquiry and an incident room has been established at Crickledale police station. The telephone number is 456654.'

'That's fine,' agreed Pluke, noting that the word 'murder' did not feature in the release. 'You can circulate it now on the usual media distribution list. You can work in the incident room if you wish, rather than your own office at Headquarters. That will enable you to answer the press calls which will inevitably follow as the enquiry progresses. I shall hold news conferences at 10 a.m. and 4 p.m. daily, which should enable you to plan your press campaign, and between us we shall deal with any matter which might arise in the meantime.'

'Can news photographers visit the scene, sir?'

'Once Scenes of Crime and the Task Force have concluded their work, yes, of course they can. In fact, I have no objection to them taking pictures of my men working at the scene, provided they do so from a distance and do not interfere with the scene or the progress of the investigation. You'll supervise those who do approach you?'

'Yes, sir.'

'Good. Well, the sooner that news release gets into print or on to the radio networks, the better. Let's hope it leads to her identification.'

When Russell left to go about his part in the enquiry, Pluke opened the door and called for Wayne Wain. Wain, who had been explaining to a pretty secretary the system for abstracting computer data from the incoming statements, hurried to Pluke's office.

'Close the door and sit down, Wayne,' invited Pluke as he entered. 'There is something I wish to do, but I do not want the entire incident room staff to know, not at this stage. But I feel you, as my deputy, should be informed.'

'Sir?'

'First, the victim. There is evidence to suggest she is not British, or alternatively, that the person who buried her is not British. Or that neither is British.'

'How on earth did you reach that conclusion, sir?'

'The mirror which was buried with her. When that came to light, I had some such suspicion in my mind but when the pathologist confirmed she was a virgin, it lent more weight to my supposition.'

'Go on, sir.'

'It used to be the custom in Sweden, when a maiden died, to include a mirror in her coffin. It was believed that young girls and maidens should be able to tidy their hair on Judgement Day. Married women did not require mirrors because their hair was braided, and they were buried with it in that condition. I know of no other European country who clung to that belief – indeed, I believe the Swedes have largely abandoned the superstition although it could linger in some areas, especially among the older generation.'

'She has the look of a Swedish girl, sir, white skin, blonde hair, blue eyes, well built. But her clothes were typically British. High street stuff.'

'And she is a virgin, Wayne.'

'I find that astonishing, sir, really I do!'

'Quite. I would expect that from you. So perhaps she had been

66

in our country for some time? Or perhaps a Swedish burial-person wanted us to believe she was British?'

'Are you saying this death could have some careful planning behind it, sir? In other words, it is not a spontaneous burial, not one of urgent necessity?'

'I am sure her death was not planned, Wayne, because the cause of death is very odd to say the least, hardly the sort of thing a murderer would plan. I cannot ignore the possibility of a tragic accident. But the means of burial does suggest some careful and reasoned planning.'

'Surely that strengthens our belief that we are dealing with a murder?'

'Perhaps yes, perhaps no. I retain an open mind at this stage. So, Wayne, for your ears only at this stage, that is my prognosis. Now, I shall ring the office of the National Central Bureau of the International Criminal Police Organisation – Interpol to you, Wayne – with a request that they contact the Swedish police in the hope we can learn whether any Swedish ladies are missing or not accounted for, or whether any are known to have come to Britain in recent times. Or Swedish men – might she have come to this country with a male friend? Did a man travel from Sweden especially to kill her? There are many permutations, Wayne, and you may remain here while I make the call.'

Pluke was quickly connected and in careful terms explained his case to Inspector Binn, the duty officer at Interpol's Scotland Yard office. Pluke was told that enquiries would be made, but that when the woman's fingerprints were available they would be of great value; a photograph of the victim, even in her present condition, would be welcomed too.

Pluke was told that checks would be made with the immigration authorities in this country and with the emigration authorities in Sweden, but it was explained that it would be most difficult to trace the victim's movements and family without knowing her name or home address, and without any idea of the dates she might have travelled, her mode of travel, whether or not she had one or more companions, or her port of emigration, whether by sea or aircraft, or through other countries. But if such a blonde was known to be missing by the Swedish authorities,

Pluke would be informed and Binn asked that Interpol be updated on any relevant developments during Pluke's enquiry. Confirmation in writing was requested and Pluke said his secretary would prepare the necessary paperwork.

'It will be like searching for the proverbial needle in a haystack, sir,' said Wayne Wain. 'They can't trace her unless we give them a name, and we can't get a name until she's traced. Catch-22 and all that.'

'Did you know that the original phrase was "looking for a needle in a bottle of hay", Wayne? Haywain ... I like that. I might even have added "constable" had you not been a sergeant. But joking aside, that was the original phrase, the word bottle coming from the French *botte* meaning bundle ...'

'I had no idea, sir,' and Wayne's eyebrows rose to the heavens.

'But finding a needle in a bundle of hay is not too difficult, Wayne, far easier than finding one in a complete haystack or, shall we say, a spindle or bolt in a haymaking machine ... So let us not be prematurely defeated by the magnitude of our task.'

'I am sure we can cope, sir.'

'Indeed we can. If it is possible to put a name to that girl, then we shall do so, with or without the help of Interpol. And remember, without a name for her, we will have immense difficulty in tracing her movements. I want you to liaise with the teams who are trying to establish her movements.'

'No problem, sir. But if she is Swedish, it is quite likely she has been touring this country. Back-packing perhaps? With or without a companion? Youth-hostelling? Hitch-hiking? English girls know that it is dangerous to hitch-hike unaccompanied. Maybe girls from overseas do not realise this? I know hitch-hiking is still a popular means of travel in southern Ireland, and safe there. Or she might have been camping, alone or with someone else. She could have used that quarry as a resting place overnight, like so many other people appear to do. I can imagine her with a violent man, things went wrong because she refuses him, and so she's murdered and left in a grave ...'

'Absolutely, Wayne. In light of that possibility, I wonder if a tent peg might have caused her injuries ... there are some with points at the end of long metal stems, although that would not explain the accompanying bruises . . .'

'And if she was back-packing or camping, she would have her belongings with her all the time. Camping gear, sleeping bag, passport, money, spare clothes . . .'

'Absolutely right again, Wayne, and she might have possessed a small pink mirror. So she could tidy her hair when she was travelling on this earth rather than in the next.'

'Of course, sir. If that mirror has survived, then where is the rest of her luggage? And especially her passport. She could not travel all the way from Sweden without having a bag or haversack or suitcase of some kind, or a sleeping bag. A large handbag, even. We've not found a handbag, sir, nor any personal belongings.'

'Precisely, Wayne. Perhaps you would bear all those factors in mind as you make your own enquiries, and as you liaise, carefully, with the teams?'

'Yes, sir, I will.'

'Right. Well, off you go and keep me informed of developments. I am now going to see if our esteemed Mr Eric Burholme is known to the police, although from what I have seen of him both recently and in the past, he does not seem the sort of gentleman who would have a criminal record.'

When Wayne had gone, Pluke picked up the telephone once again, and this time rang the Criminal Record Office at his own Force Headquarters.

'Detective Inspector Pluke, Crickledale,' he announced himself. 'I want you to carry out a search of criminal records for me, please – local first, then national. It is in connection with a murder enquiry within my sub-division.'

'No problem, sir. Who is the subject?'

'A man called Eric Burholme of Harman's Farm, Barughdale in this county. I do not have a confirmed date of birth but he claims to be eighty years of age, with a birthday last February. He is well over six feet tall, slim build with a good head of white hair. He might describe himself as a farmer or agricultural engineer.'

'Is he under arrest, sir?' returned the voice.

'Not yet,' said Detective Inspector Pluke.

6

'Hold the line, sir, the local search won't take many moments.'

Pluke waited and then, after a lull of some two minutes, the voice returned. 'Your Eric Burholme, Mr Pluke. He's not in our records. We've checked on the computer among the names of suspected criminals too – but nothing's known. He's as clean as a whistle. There are no Burholmes of any age, old or young, male or female, in our local criminal or traffic offence records and I have checked the alternative spellings. Sorry I can't be more helpful.'

'Can you do likewise in the national records? I appreciate it will take longer.'

'No problem, Mr Pluke. I'll call you the moment I have news.'

Meanwhile, in spite of the fellow's philanthropic behaviour and his particular gift of the shoggling sticks to the community of Crickledale, Pluke knew he must carefully research the background of Eric Burholme. His lonely life did lend an air of mystery to him, but Pluke and his teams should be able to unearth a good deal about his background. Pluke then returned to the incident room and saw that both Detective Sergeant Tabler, the officer in charge of the Scenes of Crime department, and Inspector Newton in charge of the Task Force had arrived with the results of their searches at the burial scene.

'Well done,' Pluke greeted both. 'Let's start with you, Inspector Newton. You'd better each hear what the other has to say, and I would like Sergeant Wain to be present.'

He called to a secretary and asked her to send Wain into his office; when he arrived, Pluke asked Inspector Newton to proceed.

'It's a case of many negatives, Mr Pluke.' Newton checked from a pad in his hands. 'We examined all the combine harvesters and other machines in the quarry. They've not been used for months, not since last autumn in fact. The dust and cobwebs confirm no one has moved them or interfered with them recently. One of our officers is experienced in agricultural machinery and he found no reason to think any component part had been removed or in any way involved in the woman's death. That applies only to the machines in the quarry, however. We have not yet examined those within the farm buildings, but spiked components of the kind we are seeking are rarely, if ever, used.'

'Spiders' webs are very good for stemming bleeding in an emergency, gentlemen,' Pluke reminded them, having heard the reference to spiders' webs. 'Not that I think one was used in the case of our victim. But go on, Inspector Newton.'

'We examined the plastic covering of the bales along the edge of the quarry. These plastic wrappers are fitted precisely by machine, Mr Pluke, rather like those plastic-covered joints of meat you get from supermarkets, and none had been opened or cut in any way. They were fitted prior to the woman's death. I wondered if either the murder weapon or the grave-digging tools might have been concealed there. But the answer is no in both cases.'

'Good, so we can eliminate that possibility.'

'Yes. Next, my team of eight officers, men and women, searched the ground area of the quarry, a fingertip search. We did find various objects which may or may not be relevant – I have handed these to Sergeant Tabler for scientific examination but my gut feeling is none can be linked to the death. There are used condoms, a man's black plastic comb, a pair of sun-glasses, a pair of women's knickers and a bra, both black, one or two coins, several empty beer and lager cans, and three bottles of cheap German plonk – empty.'

'Nothing can be ruled out at this stage so have the items examined,' cautioned Pluke. 'Although our victim's underwear was not missing.'

'Quite. I am aware of that.'

'You did not find anything that might have caused her injury or which could have been used to dig the grave?'

71

'No, Mr Pluke. Nothing, in spite of the meticulous fingertip search.'

'All right. Proceed, Mr Newton.'

'We found the remains of several camp fires, some with evidence of cooking, but we believe none was lit after Saturday. The fires were from different dates, some very old, but the ashes in all cases were wet, they've not dried out since Saturday's rain. We found no dry ashes – there was no rain on Sunday.'

'And what time was the last rainfall on Saturday?' asked Pluke.

'Six fifteen in the evening, sir,' Sergeant Tabler chipped in.

'Before the grave was dug?'

'I think so. The soil in the grave was very dry, the rain hadn't penetrated the grass covering. A short, sharp shower, sir,' said Tabler. 'The bottom of the grave had not been exposed to rain either.'

'Thank you, sergeant. Now, Mr Newton. Campers? Apart from the fires, is there any other evidence of campers?'

'Yes, Mr Pluke. Our fingertip search found several sites. The holes from tent pegs and tent poles made them easily identifiable, but in most cases, the sides of the peg holes and the base were damp, suggesting they were made before Saturday's showers. We did find evidence of one small tent which was on the site on Saturday. The rectangular outline was dry, the tent peg holes were dry too, so we think it was in position during Saturday's thunderstorm, being removed sometime after the rain had stopped. Unfortunately, there is nothing to indicate the identity of the camper or campers – it was a two-person size tent, Mr Pluke.'

'And was there any evidence of tent peg holes near the grave?'

'There was. The grave was in the centre of where a tent had earlier been pitched, although evidence of its presence had been largely obliterated by activity around the grave, much of it our activity.'

'I wonder if the tent had been erected as the grave was being dug, Mr Newton? In other words, did a tent conceal the body as it lay there, and then conceal the work of grave-digging?'

'It's a possibility, Mr Pluke. Most certainly.'

72

'Good. So, if the campers, i.e. the persons who erected those tents, arrived on foot, there would be no tyre marks from a car, motor cycle or pedal cycle nearby. Yet Mr Burholme did say he heard a car in this vicinity late on Saturday night,' Pluke reminded Newton.

'It did not enter the quarry, Mr Pluke. There would have been tyre marks in the covering of earth, the rain would have softened the ground which forms the thin covering of the quarry floor. There was sufficient rain to cause softness which would retain those marks. There were none.'

'Burholme did say the car might have been on the road outside the quarry, sir, along Barughdale lane,' Wayne Wain reminded Pluke.

'Yes, that's true,' nodded Pluke. 'So, Inspector Newton, anything else?'

'No, nothing. My conclusion is that there is a very noticeable lack of material evidence with absolutely no sign of a likely murder weapon or any grave-digging tools.'

'OK, thanks for that. Now it's your turn, Sergeant Tabler.'

The sergeant began. 'We commenced our examination of the scene at the graveside, once the body had been removed, sir. Bearing in mind the careful activity by our own officers in and around the grave, there were indications of other footprints in the soft earth but it was clear that an attempt had been made to eradicate them. They'd been raked over, sir. Some of the surplus earth had been raked over too, then spread around quite widely so that it merged with the grass. Marks had been made in the vicinity of the grave during the digging, during the lifting of the victim into the grave, during the re-covering of the grave with earth and grass – but all those marks had been quite deliberately removed or obliterated to such an extent that we could not photograph any of the prints or marks, nor could we take plaster casts. If there had been any tyre marks close to the grave, they'd have been obliterated too.'

'Tyre marks?'

'Well, sir, if she'd been killed away from the quarry, a vehicle of some kind would have been needed to convey the body there for burial.'

'Thanks for that, sergeant. Go on.'

'We did note small holes in the ground made by tent pegs and tent poles, these providing indications that a tent had been on the same site as the grave, although we could not state that it had been there at the very time the grave was being dug. It's a possibility, sir, that's all. But any other evidence of its presence had been obliterated by the actions I mentioned earlier.'

'In all, a deliberate attempt to conceal the evidence, you think?'

'Undoubtedly, sir, this burial was not done in a great hurry, sir, great care was taken, along with considerable thought, and I agree the work of burial might have been concealed within a tent which covered the site.'

'Most interesting. Now, you have photographs of the attempts to cover the grave-digger's tracks or wheel marks or the presence of the tent?'

'Yes, we have, sir.'

'So, in spite of these attempts to conceal evidence, the holes made by the tent pegs or tent poles had not been filled in?'

'No, sir. Perhaps they got overlooked?'

'By someone as meticulous as our grave-digger? Yet, if he was as careful as we believe, why would he leave the holes in the ground? Now, the grave itself? Did you examine the soil in the bottom? It did occur to me that the murder weapon could have been concealed there, hidden beneath the body.'

'Yes, sir, we thought so too, but only an inch or so below the level where the woman rested, there is solid rock. Nothing else was in the grave. We sieved the soil which remained in the grave as well as that which had been removed by the pathologist. We did so with great care but we found nothing.'

'And the items referred to by Inspector Newton? They will be given a very careful examination?'

'They will, sir, but none was close to the grave site and there is no discernible link with the burial or the body. Now, as you instructed, my officers examined the barbed wire along the fence which borders Harman's Farm and the Barughdale road.'

'Yes, that is important. If the body had been lifted over that fence, or if someone had climbed over instead of using the stile

– I doubt if anyone carrying a corpse would use a stile – then there would be evidence on the barbs. Fibres in particular.'

'In fact, there was nothing, sir, except a few cattle hairs. They came from the cows in that meadow, the red ones. We compared some from the barbs with samples from one of the animals. Then we checked with Mr Burholme. A cattle dealer called Cooper from Carston rents that field for his herd of Red Polls. We are satisfied the hairs came from those cows and not from a human being or an article of clothing.'

'Good. Sergeant Wain, make a note to interview that cattle dealer called Cooper from Carston. Establish whether he was anywhere near the quarry during the weekend, and ask if he has ever seen the blonde girl, with or without a partner, during any of his visits.'

'Very good, sir,' said Wayne Wain.

Pluke was musing now, as he said, 'Red cows are very important in some pagan cultures, gentlemen. They are the personification of the dawn, some are said to herald clouds and others to herald lightning . . .'

'It did thunder on Saturday, sir,' smiled Wayne Wain. 'With rain.'

'It rained around tea-time, sir, I remember one shower around six fifteen, I got caught in it,' Sergeant Tabler said.

'Yes, but was there lightning?' asked Pluke.

No one knew whether there had been lightning during Saturday's storm but such thoughts were relegated to the back of the detectives' minds as Tabler continued.

'We found nothing else, sir. The burial scene was amazingly clean, surprisingly devoid of evidence.'

'So we all agree the burial was carried out by someone who took immense pains to cover his tracks?'

'We do,' said Tabler. 'Although it was such a shallow grave, it was done with immense care.'

'But it was close to that public footpath, don't forget. Placing it there could hardly be regarded as the work of a very careful planner.'

'If it was done at night, sir, under cover of darkness by a

person unfamiliar with the surrounding area, he might not have been aware of that public footpath,' Wayne Wain said.

'A very good point, Wayne,' Pluke had to concede. 'Yes, a very good point indeed. Well, gentlemen, incorporate your findings in statements and have the details included in our records. Now, Sergeant Tabler, you are going to arrange finger-prints and photographs of the deceased?'

'Yes, I've fixed a time with Mr Meredith. Tomorrow morning at eleven.'

'Make sure there are plenty of copies available, I shall require some copies for my own use,' said Pluke. 'We need sufficient for circulation within our own channels, but in addition, we need some photographs for press purposes, provided she does not look too dead.'

'I will do my best, sir.'

'Well, gentlemen,' smiled Pluke. 'Thanks for your efforts. This is an interesting case.'

And with that, they left his office; Wayne Wain remained behind.

'So, Wayne, what do you make of what you have heard?'

'I am beginning to wonder if the girl camped in the quarry on Saturday night, accompanied by the man who killed her. I think the killer was a man due to the strength required to make the wound and to manhandle the dead body into the grave. The killer could have used a tent peg, hammering it in with a mallet . . .'

'I doubt if she would lie still long enough for that to happen, Wayne!' commented Pluke. 'And besides, tent pegs are not usually covered with black paint.'

'There's always a first time, sir, like someone using one to stir a pot of paint and then taking it on a camping expedition . . .'

'True, true. But I think you will agree that she was not carried over that barbed-wire-topped fence, dead or alive?'

'Yes, I would go along with that.'

'So either she was camping in the quarry on Saturday night, died there and was buried on the spot as you suggest, or she was killed elsewhere and brought to the quarry after death, probably in a motor vehicle. Burholme says he heard a vehicle moving about somewhere nearby late on Saturday night but there is no evidence it actually entered the quarry. If she was not carried across the field and through that herd of red cows, she must have come by motor vehicle, which in turn means she arrived through Burholme's farm, along his roads. If we can trace the vehicle responsible, it will have to be forensically examined.'

'There is no way of proving a particular vehicle used the farm tracks, is there, sir? We can't identify tyre marks on those farm roads, they've got tarmac surfaces. And there are no tyre marks in the quarry.'

'Precisely, Wayne. Another example of the surprising lack of evidence in this case. So, you are going to arrange an interview of that cattle dealer called Cooper from Carston, while I examine the information already on file. I need to think carefully about this case, Wayne. It is more complex than at first appears.'

'Because of the mirror in the grave, you mean?'

There was just a hint of sarcasm in Wayne's voice, but Pluke silenced him by remarking, 'That is exactly what I mean, Wayne.'

Afterwards, a trickle of detectives began returning to the Pluke-dom to file their reports in readiness for booking off duty at nine o'clock. They came also for the final conference of the day which would be around eighty forty-five followed by another in the morning before they embarked on tomorrow's investigations. Much of this paperwork was a necessary chore. It involved filing statements once they had been typed so that teams of statement readers could plough through them and abstract factual details for entry into the computer system. Facts like names, descriptions of motor vehicles, descriptions of suspects, days of the week and a host of other non-contentious data would be entered so that they could be retrieved quickly and processed by computer instead of relying on fallible human memory.

At eight forty-five, therefore, Pluke gathered everyone for his final address of the day. Quite deliberately, he added little to his earlier statements, although he did confirm that photographs of the deceased would be ready for distribution tomorrow, along with her fingerprints. Satisfied that he had done a good day's work, he bade them goodnight. A small contingent invited him to join them for a drink before going home but he declined, as always excusing himself on the grounds that he was not a lover of alcohol – neither did he believe that senior officers should socialise with their subordinates.

Apart from any other consideration, Millicent would have his supper ready; upon leaving her so abruptly at the shoggling ceremony that morning, he'd anticipated a late session, and said she could expect him home at half-past nine.

Promptly at nine-thirty, therefore, Montague Pluke walked through the back door of his modest home right foot first, wiped his feet on the mat and shouted, 'I'm home, dearest.' As he went to hang his commodious coat upon its hook, deposit his hat on the window ledge of the hall and take his jacket upstairs to the wardrobe, Millicent called, 'Well done, Montague, reliable as always . . .' and went to take his meal from the oven. Upstairs, he hung his jacket in the wardrobe, went to the bathroom, washed his hands and face, combed his hair and returned to the dining-room where his meal was on the table, a hot and steaming casserole of flavoured beef and vegetables. It was one of Millicent's specialities and one of Montague's favourites after a hard day of detecting crime. He settled on his chair, tucked his serviette into his collar above the blue bow tie, lifted his knife and fork and said, 'Thank you, Millicent, for being so patient with me in the trials of a detective's life. I was so sorry I had to rush off this morning and burden you so unexpectedly with the shoggling finale.'

'I enjoyed it, Montague, truly I did.' She smiled at him from behind her heavy spectacles, a grey-haired lady of modest appearance. 'It made me realise how well you cope with some of the pressures of your life, the responsibilities you carry and the high demands that are placed upon you.'

'Being in charge of the shoggling arrangements is a heavy responsibility,' he agreed. 'There are times I wonder how the town will cope when I am no more, and you are no longer at my side. I dread the time when there are no more Plukes in Crickledale.'

'Maybe a distant cousin will appear, Montague. There must be some other Plukes in the world apart from us.'

'I am sure there are,' he mused. 'Perhaps there are distinguished branches of our illustrious family that I do not know about? Some African cousins, maybe? Or Canadian settlers with genuine Pluke ancestry? But we must not be gloomy, there are years of service left in you and me. Between us, we will cope with everything that life throws at us.'

'So how was the rest of your day?' She was clearly pleased he was enjoying his meal; it seemed he was extremely hungry.

'There are certain advantages to my job, particularly when I am away from the confines of my office,' he assured her. 'I found a wonderful horse trough,' and he told her about the splendid and unusual triple example he'd found at Brian Preston's farm, saying it warranted further examination and exploration with due emphasis upon the source of the never-ending water supply. 'But,' he added with caution, 'I must not make any such approach until I have eliminated him from my current enquiry. One cannot appear to be showing friendship to a criminal suspect.'

'A criminal suspect, Montague? Oh, of course, you were called to a suspicious death, weren't you? Is it serious, Montague?'

Normally, Montague Pluke never discussed with anyone outside the office the finer or more confidential aspects of his work. Not even Millicent, his utterly faithful spouse, was privy to his workaday secrets. But ever since the omens of death which had surrounded the bathtime saga at the Druids' Circle, he felt that Millicent, through her contacts within every stratum of Crickledale society, might from time to time have something to offer in the way of assistance with his enquiries. Not that he would interview her in any kind of formal manner, rather would he listen to what she had to say after her day mixing with the town's most prominent ladies. For this reason, he felt he could tell her just a little about the events in Harman's Quarry.

'I was called to Harman's Quarry,' he told her. 'That's along the Barughdale road. A body was found upon land within a farm owned by a businessman called Burholme. Eric Burholme.'

'Eric Burholme? How odd,' she exclaimed. 'Especially with today being the feast day of St Eric!'

'By Jove, so it is!' He expressed surprise that he had not appreciated the significance of that small fact. 'He is an Eric and our shoggling ceremony is always on the feast of St Eric! What an odd coincidence.'

'He is such a kind man, that Mr Burholme,' enthused Millicent. 'Generous to a fault. He provided wonderful support to the Town Hall Entertainment Fund and to lots of other local causes. People say he is rather old-fashioned, Montague, a bit strait-laced in some ways, according to one or two of my friends.'

'Old-fashioned, Millicent?'

'Well, honourable is perhaps the better word, Montague. He is very proper in his conduct; he always maintains a discreet distance from the ladies, you know, he never gets familiar, never takes advantage of anyone . . .'

'He did love his wife dearly, you know. He thought a lot of her . . .' A fleeting memory of her burial came to him, but he could not recall the precise circumstances of her funeral, except that it was somehow different. If it was at this time of year, of course, he'd have been extremely busy with arrangements for the shoggling ceremony – and fifteen years ago, it was the very first of the current series. With such demands on his intellect and time, it was not surprising he could not recall the details of Mrs Burholme's funeral.

But Millicent was talking. 'So what was the body, Montague? Are you engaged in a major murder investigation? If so, my friends will be so impressed.'

'I am engaged upon a very difficult enquiry featuring a very suspicious death,' he explained. 'But you must not inform your friends of any of the confidential details that I might impart during our conversations . . .'

'Of course not, Montague, you know I would never dream of betraying a confidence.'

He decided he could relate to her the facts as given in the news release and accordingly provided Millicent with a fairly brief but factual account of the day's activities, including a description of the dead girl. She listened intently and when he had concluded with a statement of his intention to have the girl identified, she said, 'Montague, that is very odd, very odd indeed. You know Mrs Cholmondeley's bay tree died for no accountable reason?'

'I am very aware of that fact, Millicent,' he said. 'A sad occurrence by any standards – as you know, it is said to herald a death, either of a royal person or someone within the household in whose grounds it grows, or of course some other person unknown who might have associations with the tree or its owner. Bay trees were planted to protect the household against lightning, you know, that is why they were regarded as very important assets.' And then he remembered the Red Poll cows along Barughdale lane. They heralded lightning. So had Mrs Cholmondeley's bay tree been struck by lightning? Surely, that was impossible . . .

'That's just what Mrs Cholmondeley said when I had a cup of tea with her following the shoggling ceremony, and she wondered who it might be. She has no family, you see, her husband died five years ago and there were no children.'

'Perhaps it was the omen associated with the quarry girl's death,' commented Pluke as he chewed a piece of gristle.

'Well, that is why I think it is most odd,' said Millicent. 'When Mrs Cholmondeley was telling me about the tree, she said she'd had a young woman in the garden, a stranger wanting to know local bus times. She had seen Mrs Cholmondeley watering her borders and had come into the garden to ask about buses. The girl commented on that bay tree, in fact she stroked its trunk and said it didn't look very healthy . . .'

'When was this?' asked Pluke.

'Friday,' said Millicent. 'Friday afternoon. The girl had come to Crickledale by hitch-hiking and was wanting to know the bus routes and times in case she did not get a further lift. She asked Mrs Cholmondeley the way to the bus station, or if she knew local bus times.'

'Where was she going, that girl?' Montague Pluke was so excited that his fork wobbled and he dribbled some gravy down his serviette.

'Oh, I have no idea, Montague, you'd have to ask Mrs

81

Cholmondeley. She said the girl spoke very nicely and was most pleasant; she was blonde and quite a big girl, in her late twenties or early thirties, according to Mrs Cholmondeley.'

'This could be our victim!' cried Pluke, coughing on a piece of potato. 'Even though I am off duty, I must speak to Mrs Cholmondeley without delay.'

'At this time of night, Montague? Do wait until you have finished your meal, dear,' advised Millicent, and Pluke decided his enquiries could wait just a few minutes longer. 'And whatever you do, don't invite Mrs Cholmondeley to the house. Once she gets into a house, she'll never leave until she's drunk all the sherry.'

'Then perhaps a telephone call to open our discussions?' suggested Pluke, and Millicent thought it was a fairly good idea. At least she would not have to find sufficient sherry to accommodate Mrs Cholmondeley's drinking habits.

'On second thoughts,' said Montague, 'I might visit her at her home.'

'Make sure she doesn't get you tiddly, Montague,' said Millicent. 'I know it is getting late, but she will be in, she always watches *News at Ten* with a nightcap.'

'I think I can justifiably interrupt her news viewing on a matter of such importance,' beamed Montague, cleaning his plate and wondering what there was for afters.

When he knocked on Mrs Cholmondeley's door with her highly polished brass knocker in the shape of an eagle's head, she called through the letter box, 'Who's there?' and when he identified himself, she admitted him. She was a substantial lady of sixty-five years at least, with a head of iron grey hair tied back in a bun, and thick, horn-rimmed spectacles perched on a rather large red nose. She always wore dark clothes, spacious dresses and cardigans which tended to disguise her height, width and depth. She was probably six feet tall, he reckoned. He wondered if she'd been a shot putter at some stage of her life.

'Oh, Mr Pluke, what a surprise, and at this time of night too ... I was all locked up and almost ready for bed, just watching *News at Ten* with my nightcap. Will you join me in a nightap? It

82

is very seldom I get gentleman callers so late in the evening, so very seldom indeed . . .'

Because it was possible that a large sherry might persuade her to provide him with the information he sought, he decided a nightcap would be in order for him too, particularly as he was not on duty. He did not think it would impede his line of enquiry; rather, it might enhance it.

'A sherry would be very acceptable . . .' he began. 'A dry one.'

'Large of course, Mr Pluke. One must not be too abstemious on such occasions . . . Now, what can I do for you at this time of night?'

There is little doubt that his unexpected arrival had generated some excitement deep within Mrs Cholmondeley and that she was very curious about his motives. The papers had warned attractive women about opening their doors to strangers but Mr Pluke was no stranger. After all, he was Montague Pluke, a middle-aged man of distinction in the community, and hardly the sort to take advantage of a lonely woman, whatever her attractions. But, being a woman, she knew that still waters ran deep. Very deep in some cases. Was there just a hint of passion in the deep and meaningful Montague Pluke?

'Millicent said you had a caller at the house on Friday,' he began as she led him into her lounge. 'A young woman, a blonde.'

'Indeed I did, Mr Pluke. A very handsome young woman too, if I may say so.'

She poured him a huge glass of sherry, more of a tumblerful than a small schooner.

'Who was she?' he asked, noting that his line of questioning had stemmed the flow from her tongue while she helped herself from the same bottle.

'That I cannot say, Mr Pluke. A total stranger. She had hitch-hiked into Crickledale, and I do not know from whence she came. She asked if I knew the times and destinations of local buses and when I expressed my ignorance – I do run a new Volvo, you know, I never use buses – she asked for directions to the bus station.'

'What time did she call?'

'Mid-afternoon, Mr Pluke. Three o'clock or thereabouts, I'd say.'

'Where was she going? Did she give any indication?' He sipped from the glass.

'She spoke very well, Mr Pluke, with hardly a trace of an accent. An educated young woman, I would say. She wanted to know if any buses went to Barrowdale.'

'Barrowdale?'

'That's what I am sure she said, Mr Pluke, and that's why I thought the bus station was a good idea. They have printed timetables – the written word is more easily understood by visitors.'

'Can you remember what she was wearing?' was his next question.

'Yes, I can. Blue jeans, and a white anorak over a pale blue blouse. And she was carrying a small haversack, a black one, over one shoulder.'

'If I showed you a photograph, tomorrow all being well, do you think you could recognise her?' He drank again, recognising the quality of Mrs Cholmondeley's superior sherry.

'I will do my best, of course, Mr Pluke. Might I ask, is this an important enquiry?' She sipped from her glass, her big eyes admiring him as he dominated her lounge.

Taking his customary care with words, he outlined the discovery at Harman's Quarry, at which Mrs Cholmondeley sat down open-mouthed but still-tongued as he unfolded the saga of the shallow grave. This would give her something to talk about tomorrow, and he felt she might get out of bed much earlier, in order to do the rounds of her many friends in town, imparting news of a staggering nature. And, he hoped, her efforts might, in return, produce some information of value to him. When he'd finished his account, he took several large mouthfuls of sherry, not quite a series of gulps, but precariously close to them.

'Mr Pluke, what a drama! And you are in charge. My word, Millicent will be proud of you!'

'Until tomorrow, then, Mrs Cholmondeley,' he smiled. 'I will call once we have developed our photographs, but I cannot give a specific time. But don't wait in for me, I will catch you at some stage during the day, probably in the afternoon.'

'Don't be afraid to call late, Mr Pluke. I can always have another nightcap ready for us. I find your company so exhilarating. You are such an interesting man. You don't have to go just yet, do you? I mean, your life is so full, so packed with matters of great and dramatic moment, and I am dying to know more about your work. I am sure you could make me a very educated and well-informed woman.'

'Sadly, duty calls and I must go, Mrs Cholmondeley,' and he gulped another huge mouthful of sherry as he rose to his feet. With that gallant effort, he managed to completely empty his capacious glass which he placed on the mantelshelf. 'You have given me hope!'

'Have I really,' she oozed, following him to the door.

'Until tomorrow,' he said, struggling to emit the words while simultaneously tripping over the step as he attempted to leave.

As he hurried home with his feet persistently interfering with one another, he tried to steer a straight course and did avoid a couple of troublesome lamp standards and a grinning pillar box. But his mind remained alert and it seemed the only discrepancies between Mrs Cholmondeley's visitor and the girl in the grave were the white anorak and the black haversack. In spite of those minor differences, his keen detective instinct told him this was surely the same young woman.

He walked home with a bounce in his stride, but fell over his front doorstep and hit his head on the doorbell.

7

Responding to the late-night shrilling of the bell, Millicent rushed to the door with just slight apprehension due to the hour; in the glow of the porch light through the frosted glass, she saw the figure of a man. He was leaning against the outside wall beside the door, but the distinctive colouring of his clothing immediately told her it was Montague. Relieved, she unlocked the door to admit him.

'Montague! Are you all right?'

'Yesh, dearesht, I am. I tripped over shomething and shtumbled againsht the bell . . . I don't think it ish anything to do with Mishish Cholmondeley's sherry, merely a momentary lack of conshentrashion on my part. But thank you for your loving conshern.'

He did appear to be somewhat unsteady on his feet and she helped him over the threshold where his feet performed some strange gyrations before he stomped along the entrance hall. Although his speech was rather different from usual, he was able to stand upright without hanging on to anything. She did not think he was drunk, although he was perhaps just a little tiddly? Unless he was dreadfully tired? He had been working so hard lately. To be frank, Montague was not the sort of man to get himself drunk nor even to indulge in the over-consumption of alcohol – and apart from anything else, he'd not had sufficient time to drink a lot. Unless Mrs Cholmondeley had spiked his drink with something? Something potent and secretive with his seduction in mind? Millicent was aware of the man-eating reputation of Mrs Cholmondeley.

Oblivious to her concerns, Montague disrobed, smiled charmingly and said, 'I think a nightcap would be an exshellent idea, dearesht.'

'As you wish, Montague. I think it had better be cocoa.'

'Under the shircumshtancesh, yesh, that will be fine.'

As she went to prepare the drink, he settled on the settee in his lounge. The room did appear to be revolving ever so slightly but not enough to prevent him considering the information imparted by Mrs Cholmondeley. If her visitor had been the deceased girl, then it seemed she had arrived in the district with some objective or destination in mind. She knew where she wanted to go. The fact that she had asked about buses to Barrowdale might support his belief that she had a particular reason for her journey. On the other hand, it could suggest she was completely lost because there was no Barrowdale in this part of the world; of similar name, there was a Borrowdale near Lake Derwentwater in the Lake District but that was more than a hundred miles away, and no regular buses serviced that route from Crickledale. Surely the girl was not looking for the Lakeland Borrowdale?'

On the other hand, mused Pluke, the girl's lack of knowledge of local pronunciations could have disguised the fact she was *en route* to Barughdale because that was pronounced Barfdale. Barrowdale might be her erroneous way of pronouncing Barughdale. People did make such mistakes. He recalled a Japanese visitor at Heathrow Airport who asked for directions to Turkey and found herself in Torquay, while many English place-names did present difficulties, even to the English. For some odd reason, Londoners pronounced Holborn as Hoeburn and plenty of Yorkshire tourists had problems with Wass, Sleights and Ruswarp. On one occasion, Pluke had tried asking a Yorkshireman the way to Yockenthwaite ...

So far as Barughdale was concerned, however, buses did run twice every weekday from Crickledale, and three times on Saturdays, although he was not sure of the exact times. In contemplating those buses, he could not ignore the fact that Harman's Farm and the adjacent quarry were situated between Crickledale and Barughdale along Barughdale lane. Precisely upon the bus route in fact. As the girl's visit had been during the middle of the afternoon, there might not have been any buses; they tended to run at times convenient to office workers and shoppers rather than tourists.

So had she been hitch-hiking along that road when she'd met her attacker? Or was she walking due to the absence of a convenient bus? Or had she decided to camp overnight in the quarry? But Mrs Cholmondeley did not say the girl had carried anything as large as a tent or sleeping bag. According to Mrs Cholmondeley, she'd carried nothing more than a small haversack. An added factor, of course, was that when seeking help from Mrs Cholmondeley, she had been alone. Mrs Cholmondeley, whose house stood beside the main road out of town, had not referred to the girl having a companion of any kind and this compelled Pluke to think the girl was raither naïve, for hitch-hiking was not suitable for an attractive young woman on her own.

'Was your visit to Mrs Cholmondeley of any value, Montague?' Millicent returned to the lounge bearing two mugs of steaming cocoa and a plate of biscuits. The room had ceased to revolve now and he accepted a mug and some biscuits from Millicent, after which she settled on her own chair and smiled at him. 'She must have been very generous towards you, Montague, you are quite flushed.'

'It wash a mosht fruitful ekshperience,' he agreed. 'I am encouraged by the poshibility that Mishish Cholmondeley both shaw and shpoke to the victim. Tomorrow, I shall show her a photograph which might help determine the matter.'

'Do be careful if you drink any more of her sherry, Montague, especially if you have to walk home afterwards. You are not very experienced in the skills of drinking strong liquor ...'

'I do not think Mishish Cholmondeley's sherry ish a danger-oush shubstance or a nokshious fluid, Millishent,' he said. 'It ish merely a meansh of oiling the wheelsh of social intercourshe. But if I do call tomorrow, I shall be on duty and in that cashe will not be able to acshept any drink from her. Now,' he continued, 'one fearful point hash preshented itself to me.'

'It doesn't mean you have to go out to work at this time of night, does it? I have already put the hot water bottle in your bed.'

'No, it doesh not mean going out at thish late shtage, but if Mishish Cholmondeley did shee our victim, then she ish prob-ably the lasht pershon to shee her alive. That meansh, Millishent, that I musht treat Mishish Cholmondeley ash a shushpect for murder.'

'Montague, no! Surely not!'

'It'sh a fact and really, I should not have acshepted that sherry, not from a criminal shushpect ...'

'Oh, Montague, don't be silly! You know she is of aristocratic ancestry; she would never kill a young woman or anyone else for that matter. And she does attend the Church of England.'

'On the other hand,' he mused as the room executed another

minor wobble, 'shomeone at the bush shtashion might have sheen her afterwardsh, that'sh if she called there. Yesh, that ish a poshibility too. Tomorrow, I musht have enquiriesh made at the bush shtashion. If she wash sheen there, it will remove a lot of shushpishion from Mishish Cholmondeley.'

'You do have a lot to think about, Montague.' Millicent sipped her cocoa as she admired her husband. 'It is no easy job, being a senior detective.'

'One ish highly trained over many yearsh in order to qualify for high office,' he assured her as he munched a biscuit. 'Well, I think it ish time for bed, Millishent. I shall shleep shoundly tonight in the knowledge that my enquiriesh are prosheeding very well indeed.'

'Yes, you must get some sleep, you have a busy day tomorrow.'

'For the poleesh, Millishent, every day ish bishy. There ish no relief from the relentlessh fight againsht crime. Now, ish the housh locked?'

'Yes, dear, you go to bed and I will put out the lights,' she smiled, wondering what had really transpired between Montague and Mrs Cholmondeley. His face was definitely more ruddy than it had been for a long, long time and he did seem inordinately cheerful. It reminded Millicent of that time Mrs Cholmondeley had cornered that tea salesman – Millicent had arrived just in time to save his reputation.

Next morning, Tuesday, Montague climbed out of his single bed at the same side he had entered; he had no wish to get out of bed at the wrong side and remain bad-tempered for the whole of the coming day. In so doing, he took care not to slip his right foot into his left slipper or his left foot into his right slipper because that would bring bad fortune. He did not have a headache, so Mrs Cholmondeley's sherry must have been of the finest quality, and the room was no longer swimming around him. After his blood-free shave, ablutions and vigorous session of teeth cleaning, he went down to breakfast. Millicent had prepared a healthy meal of cereals, toast and honey and, on this occasion, black coffee in case his head was aching after banging it on the doorbell last night.

But Montague was in fine fettle. He ate his breakfast with enthusiasm, kissed her farewell and cheerfully embarked on his morning walk to the police station. As it was a Tuesday, he had no fears about meeting a left-handed man although he was careful not to sneeze, because to sneeze on a Tuesday meant he might have to kiss a stranger. Today was also the feast day of St Yves, a French saint well known for his interest in forensic expertise and legal knowledge, another good omen in Pluke's continuing quest for justice.

As usual, his passage through the town was met with lots of goodwill and greetings to which he responded with his own voluble good mornings, accompanied by added hat raising if the person before him was a lady. One ill-mannered man did lower the tone of things, however, by calling, 'Saw you sneaking away from Mrs Cholmondeley's late last night, Mr Pluke, with a happy smile on your face. On form, was she? Did she ask for a look at your truncheon?' But Montague, being a man of sound principles, responded with, 'She was helping me with my enquiries,' at which the man raised his eyebrows and laughed. 'A likely story, Mr Pluke. A likely story! A good one, though, yes, a very good one.'

By contrast, one or two people with a more responsible attitude did pass comment about the discovery in the quarry, saying, 'I see you've got a big job on your hands, Mr Pluke,' or 'I hope you catch the killer, Mr Pluke,' or 'We're all relying on you, Mr Pluke. This is a safe town, I hope you're not going to let this develop into a crime wave.' Through comments of this kind, Detective Inspector Pluke knew that the suspicious death had been featured in the morning papers and on local radio.

These exchanges also proved that the Crickledonians had great faith in his detecting ability. Full of fresh air and *bonhomie*, therefore, he arrived at the police station in a good mood with no sign of a headache, crossed the threshold by leading with his right foot and, as usual, paid a visit to the control room where he found Sergeant Cockfield pronounced Cofield in charge.

'Good morning, sergeant,' greeted Montague Pluke.

'Good morning, sir, not a bad morning by May standards.'

'A very pleasant morning, sergeant. As they say, "A May wet is never kind yet" although another belief goes, "The haddocks are good if they're dipped in a May flood." But, weather apart, what has transpired overnight?'

'Overnight? Not a great deal, sir. One incident of car breaking, a radio stolen by smashing the driver's window. A travelling thief, I think, hardly the sort of thing a Crickledonian would stoop to. That's all. Already this morning, however, we have been busy, thanks to reports in the newspapers. Several people have rung in with suggested names for the girl in the quarry.'

'Excellent. Are any of them positive leads?'

'I didn't examine them, I passed the list immediately to the incident room, sir.'

'Good, then I shall proceed to the incident room. You can contact me there if there are any truly dramatic developments.'

'As you wish, sir,' and Sergeant Cockfield pronounced Cofield returned to his work.

A quick visit to his own regular office showed there was nothing which demanded Montague's urgent attention; Mrs Plumpton was quite capable of handling the routine enquiries and dealing with the mail, and so he adjourned to the incident room. Already the Plukedom was humming with activity, many of his detectives having arrived early in order not to miss any developments.

He found Wayne Wain leaning over a red-haired secretary, deep in conversation about the means by which a virile man can help a shy woman to develop a good singing voice. Montague decided not to interrupt him because the young lady seemed genuinely interested in what Wayne was suggesting, a curious means of clearing the air passages, and in any case, it was not yet nine o'clock, the official starting time for today's duties. Apart from those considerations, Pluke would inform Wayne of Mrs Cholmondeley's development at the same time as he told the others.

He busied himself for a few minutes with minor administrative matters and then with a perusal of possible identities for the blonde. A final check of the duty rota showed that everyone was

91

now present. Thirty detectives with their supervisory officers plus the necessary civilian staff had assembled in the incident room and he called for the conference to begin.

'Good morning, all,' he began, to which they all replied, 'Good morning, sir,' in the manner of a class of schoolchildren at morning assembly.

'There has been an important development overnight,' he told them and outlined what had transpired between Mrs Cholmondeley and the visiting blonde, although he did so without making any reference to the informalities which had transpired between himself and Mrs Cholmondeley.

An enlarged map of the town and surrounding district was displayed on one of the walls; upon it, he indicated the location of Mrs Cholmondeley's house in relation to the town, the bus station and the road out to Barughdale. Now it was time to allocate specific duties.

'Detective Inspector Horsley,' he addressed the officer in charge of the incident room. 'You need to allocate actions which will enable further in-depth enquiries to be made throughout the town. In particular, I want enquiries at the bus station to see if anyone recalls seeing the blonde woman there on Friday after, say, lunchtime, or even on Saturday morning, asking about bus times, destinations, routes, or even boarding a bus. And I need to know whether anyone saw her hitching a lift or walking along the road to Barughdale around those material times. There must be some regular users of that road. And we shall need enquiries making in Barughdale itself, to see whether anyone in the village was, or is, expecting a visit from a blonde woman. Furthermore, we need to know whether that lady ever arrived in Barughdale. Barughdale is a small village, Mr Horsley, it has a mere two hundred inhabitants, therefore someone should know the answer.'

'Right, sir.'

'And while we are discussing the allocation of actions, I require a couple of teams to revisit Harman's Farm because we are still seeking grave-digging tools which may have been concealed afterwards. Those farm buildings are an ideal hiding place and some discreet further examination of Burholme's machines might not be amiss, bearing in mind the marks on the girl's body and clothing. It might be wise to recruit the further services of the Task Force – Inspector Newton, who is sitting at the back of the room to the right, will give every assistance, I am sure. Now, I shall personally interview Mr Burholme in depth at a later stage, so you need not worry about that action just yet. I have operational reasons for delaying that interview, reasons I shall not divulge at this stage of the enquiry. Next, Detective Sergeant Wain?'

'Sir?' responded Wayne Wain.

'You are keen to consult that cattle dealer called Cooper from Carston, I believe?'

'Yes, sir.'

'Then that is your next task. When doing so, consider that the deceased might have been walking past, or even through, the field which contains his cows. Was he around at the time? If so, did he notice her? Where was she heading? Was she alone? Cycling? Carrying anything? Where are her haversack and her anorak?'

'She might have come to Crickledale particularly to visit Harman's Farm, sir,' suggested Wayne Wain.

'I cannot see her wishing to hire any of his machines, Wayne, and Eric Burholme says he has never seen the woman and does not know her,' countered Pluke. 'Of course, he has based that assertion upon our description of her rather than a photograph or any personal inspection of the body. I do intend to show him a photograph when one is available.'

'He would deny knowing her if he had something to hide, sir, so can we believe him? He might still deny knowing the girl even if shown a photograph. I accept he might not know her personally, but she might have sought shelter in his barns and, well, to be blunt, he might have tried his hand with her.'

'He is eighty, Wayne!' Montague sounded appalled and slightly embarrassed by Wayne's suggestion.

'So what does that prove, sir? He's a fit old devil, by the look of things. I bet he hasn't lost the urge. I hope I'm as fit when I'm his age – but I do keep in practice, sir, one has to. Use it or lose it, that's my motto.'

'There is a considerable age gap between you and Mr Burholme, Wayne, but quite clearly, in view of what you say, Mr Burholme is in the frame, as we tend to phrase it. Nonetheless, I need a little more evidence, or lack of it from other places, before I present him with any indication that he is a prime suspect. You could be right. She might have been heading for Harman's Farm for one of several reasons or she might have come across the farm by chance and made use of its available facilities to shelter in a storm. But if she was deliberately making for the farm, why would she be going there? She does not seem the sort of woman to want to hire a forage harvester or anything else, especially not all the way from wherever she has come. And why would Mr Burholme deny knowing her? Only he can answer that – but let's keep him dangling on our hook for a little while longer. I would like Mr Burholme to think we are interested in his buildings as possible hiding places, rather than being interested in him. I will elaborate on that statement later,' Pluke said with an air of mystery. 'Now, to return to Detective Inspector Horsley. Mr Horsley, we need to interview the finder of the body, Mr Wardle, and we need to do so in considerable depth for the usual elimination purposes. Check his background, will you?'

'Yes, no problem.'

'And don't ignore his sexual proclivities, his movements immediately prior to finding the grave – you know what to look for.'

'Of course, Montague.'

'Then we need full house-to-house enquiries in and around Crickledale, especially along the various routes the girl might have used. I shall be visiting Mrs Cholmondeley later in the day when photographs of the deceased are available, and if she confirms her identity, then we need to find the girl's missing white anorak and black haversack. Sergeant Tabler?'

'Sir?'

'Photographs and fingerprints. What time can we expect them?'

'Lunchtime at the latest, sir.'

'Officers on house-to-house enquiries will benefit from a photo and perhaps an artist's impression which includes a white anorak and black haversack. But that might come later. There is another task for someone, Mr Horsley – tent pegs and tent poles. Can we obtain a sample of every type of tent peg and tent pole in an effort to establish that one of them could have caused the wound in the girl's temple?'

'Yes, sir,' said Horsley, making rapid notes of all the specific enquiries being demanded by Pluke.

'And,' continued Detective Inspector Pluke, 'we need to establish whether anyone in this part of the world possesses a crossbow. To my knowledge, there have been five murders with crossbows in this country in recent years. I know there are restrictions on their purchase but do ask at the sports suppliers. If there are crossbows in use in this district, then someone somewhere will supply their owners with bolts and spare parts. We need to trace any crossbow users and establish their movements on Friday and Saturday, and we might have to confiscate a bolt or two for forensic comparison. And finally, the press has published some details of this case, so the public is aware of what we are doing.'

Pluke paused to allow Horsley to complete his scribbling and for his officers to digest his comments, then he flourished the list of possible victims he had received from the public.

'This is a list of girls fitting the description of the deceased,' he told them. 'Local girls mainly. In all these cases, the girls have either gone missing from home or have not been seen in their usual haunts during the past few weeks. There are seven names here. One is of particular interest – a Dutch girl called Marijka de Jong, 5'6", blonde and about twenty-five years old. She came to Crickledale as an au pair and left without warning a week ago. The name of her employer is here – he has not heard from her since, although he has contacted the agency which supplied her, to acquaint them with her absence. Mr Horsley, can we put a team on to checking all these girls? Get photos of them if possible, for comparison with the deceased.'

'Yes, sir.'

'Now, first, are there any comments, observations or inputs

from the floor?' asked Pluke. 'It is early days of course, and I do not expect much to have been gleaned from the few enquiries that were possible last night.'

'Just one, sir,' said a detective constable. 'I was making enquiries about Mr Burholme's list of customers, sir, and I discovered one with a secret girlfriend, a big blonde. His name is Hebden, from Pasture House Farm on the outskirts of the town.'

'Do we know anything about this man Hebden?' asked Pluke.

'Not a lot at this stage, sir, except that he is known as a Romeo, he's wealthy, travels a lot to agricultural shows, gymkhanas and the like, leaving his wife at home to look after the farm. Whenever he's away from home, he usually has a blonde in tow.'

'Right, a good suspect to work on. Check him out, will you? And you are?'

'Detective Constable Brett, sir.'

'I'll leave that in your hands, DC Brett,' said Pluke. 'Now, any more comments or queries?'

There were none, so Pluke dismissed his officers to go about their duties, and turned his attention to Inspector Russell and this morning's news conference. Pluke had little to add to last night's news release, other than the possibility that the deceased had been seen in Crickledale on Friday. That would be his theme for this morning's news conference and he hoped it would be supported by Mrs Cholmondeley when he called to see her later.

As promised, Detective Sergeant Tabler did have the photographs and fingerprints ready for distribution before noon. Pluke was supplied with sufficient for what he described as his personal requirements; this included Inspector Binn at Interpol as well as repeat visits to Mrs Cholmondeley and to Eric Burholme. He decided he would undertake the Cholmondeley duty on his way home to lunch. That would enable him to stipulate a reason for not remaining long with Mrs Cholmondeley and her sherry bottle.

When she greeted him just after twelve thirty, she was as gushing as always and invited him inside.

'Oh, Mr Pluke,' she said. 'I do admire you and your work. I

saw it in the *Yorkshire Post* this morning, such a tragedy for a young woman. And what a lovely photograph of you with that spade. I cut it out. I shall keep it, Mr Pluke, as a memento. Now, if I can be of any assistance, any at all, in helping you to catch the man responsible, then I shall be most honoured to assist, most honoured.'

'I have a photograph of the girl,' he told her. 'In colour. Now, it is not a particularly pleasant photograph . . .'

'I do think I shall have to have a sherry, Mr Pluke. A large one. How about you? I do recall from last night that you enjoy a really good sherry . . .'

'Not on this occasion, thank you, Mrs Cholmondeley.' He adopted his most firm voice. 'I am on duty, you see, and cannot drink alochol until I come off duty. Apart from that, Mrs Cholmondeley, Millicent will have my lunch on the table. I am on my way home, you see, so I dare not linger . . .'

While talking to her, he had placed the enlarged colour print of the deceased woman on Mrs Cholmondeley's table top and she could not take her eyes from it.

'She is dead, is she?' Mrs Cholmondeley's voice was hushed and somewhat throaty. 'She looks as if she is asleep . . .'

'She is dead, I am sad to say,' confirmed Pluke. 'Now, look at her carefully. Consider her face, the colour of her hair, her clothes . . . She has no anorak, you will note, nor have we found any haversack, but, Mrs Cholmondeley, is this the young lady who called at your house on Friday last to ask about bus routes and destinations?'

'Yes, Mr Pluke, yes it is, that's her. Oh, the poor dear . . . what a dreadful thing to happen . . .'

'One of my officers will have to come to take a formal statement from you, Mrs Cholmondeley,' he told her. 'In the meantime, can you try and recall if you have seen this woman anywhere else? In town perhaps? Walking in the street? Shopping? In Crickledale on another occasion perhaps, recent or otherwise? Alone or with someone? If this picture does trigger a memory, Mrs Cholmondeley, perhaps you would acquaint my officer with the circumstances when he arrives. We do need to trace her movements and all possible contacts in town.'

'Oh, Mr Pluke, I never thought I should be of valuable assistance in a murder enquiry – and to think I was one of the last people to see that charming young woman alive ... It is a terrible world, Mr Pluke, a truly terrible world. Who could do such a thing to another human being? I think I shall have to have another sherry.'

Buoyed by this modest success, Pluke took his leave of Mrs Cholmondeley as she poured herself another very large comforting sherry, and made his way home for a light lunch with Millicent.

As he walked home, Montague realised that if Mrs Cholmondeley had noticed the girl in town, then surely someone else must have seen her. She must have been seen somewhere, she was quite striking in appearance. It was the duty of his teams to find any such witness. He felt sure they would not let him down.

And then, after lunch, Montague would visit Septimus Warbeck, the man who kept Crickledale's weather records. Montague knew that Septimus had maintained Crickledale's detailed weather records for more than fifty years and he could discover when almost every drop of rain had fallen. From him, Montague wanted to know the time of Saturday's thunderstorms, particularly the time they had passed over Harman's Farm. He also wanted to know if any flashes of lightning had accompanied those storms, and if so, what time they had occurred.

Montague felt the enquiry was now growing more intriguing by the hour.

8

Over a light lunch with Millicent, Montague continued to confide in her as he related his morning's work. Bearing in mind that she was a genuine Pluke, albeit through marriage, and that she had proved her worth by successfully replacing him at yesterday's shoggling ceremony, he felt she could be trusted with a limited selection of operational police data. This would apply especially to that which relied upon assistance from members of the public. This was one such example.

Accordingly, he told Millicent that the girl seen by Mrs Cholmondeley was undoubtedly the Harman's Quarry victim and that attempts would now be made to trace her movements for the duration of her stay in Crickledale. At Millicent's request, he showed her the photograph but she shook her head, saying she had not encountered the young lady and did not recognise her. However, she would mention it to her many friends and acquaintances. There was scarcely anyone of significance in Crickledale who was unknown to Millicent. Montague therefore left a photograph for her to use if she felt inclined – the more people who examined it, the better, he felt, and he had sufficient for that purpose.

Before returning to the incident room, he rang Septimus Warbeck to ensure he was at home and arranged an immediate visit. Septimus was in a potting shed that was so full of weather-recording equipment that it looked like a meteorological station. But it was heaven to Septimus, a retired gas inspector. A lanky individual in his early seventies with long unkempt grey hair, a thin face and half-rimmed spectacles, he opened his door and bade Montague enter.

'I'm just tracking a deep trough of low pressure over Birmingham,' he said. 'And there are some delightful cirro-cumulus clouds over Newcastle. May is a fascinating month from the weather perspective, Mr Pluke, truly fascinating.'

'There is always a lot of weather around in May, Mr Warbeck,' smiled Pluke. 'But I am here on police business.'

'How exciting, Mr Pluke. So how can I, a humble weather recorder, be of assistance to the might of the local constabulary?'

'I am interested in the weather on Friday and Saturday, Mr Warbeck. Last Friday and Saturday, that is, in and around this part of Britain. Crickledale in particular, with some emphasis on the road between here and Barughdale.'

'I do keep a very detailed diary, Mr Pluke, but I also keep a more general notebook, more for amateurs than professionals like myself. In my detailed log, I record atmospheric pressures, wind strength, air and ground temperature and much more besides, in rather technical terms ... but I don't think you need all that.' And Septimus reached to one of his shelves and withdrew a leather-bound book of considerable size and weight. Quickly, he opened the volume.

'This is my general record. Now, Friday, 15 May, you said,' and he muttered to himself as he found the right page. 'Fine morning, fresh westerly breeze ... hum, hum, hum ... some clouds appearing around noon. More clouds later in the day and a dull evening, but mild for the time of year ... no rain, though.'

'And no thunderstorms or lightning?'

'No, Mr Pluke. Not on Friday. So to sum up Friday in brief. It was a fine day with no rain, but a fresh westerly breeze and some clouds later in the day, resulting in a dullness by early evening. Mild for the time of year. If you need more detail than that, I can search my other diary.'

'No,' exhorted Pluke. 'This is just what I require. And Saturday?'

'Yes, Saturday, 16 May. The day started dull and very mild with a strengthening wind coming from the west. Dark clouds and a threat of rain were apparent around noon. There were isolated showers during the afternoon, but no thunder, then a thunderstorm broke out at 5.30 p.m. It began as isolated rumbles to the west, but the strong westerly wind drove the storm clouds nearer, and by five thirty, there was a heavy shower accompanied by rumbles of thunder and some lightning. The thunder rolled round and round for about forty minutes on and off, Mr Pluke, with the heaviest of the rain lasting about ten minutes. Light sprinkles of rain followed over a period of half an hour or so. Rather a damp evening, Mr Pluke.'

'I was in Scarborough for the day, Mr Warbeck, examining a sixteenth-century wooden triple-header horse trough which was recently discovered near the Spa. I missed that storm.'

'Well, it continued for a while, the rain eased off and then returned for a second bout around quarter-past six, with further thunder, lightning and another heavy shower. That lasted for half an hour, and then slowly moved east, towards the coast. It was followed by a fine and very clear evening, Mr Pluke, with cooler conditions.'

'And while I am here, what about Sunday?'

'Sunday was fine and clear all day with clouds and bright patches of sunshine. It was slightly cooler than the previous days with a gentle breeze from the south-west, but no thunder, rain or lightning.'

'And the two heavy showers which descended on Crickledale, Mr Warbeck – do you think they would have extended as far as, say, Barughdale, or at the least, Harman's Quarry?'

'Undoubtedly, Mr Pluke. The storms were widespread, not isolated. There may have been fractional time differences between the constituent elements of those storms – that would be due to the distance between each location – but we are talking about a matter of minutes. So in short, whatever we received in Crickledale on Saturday, then so did Barughdale and the Harman's Quarry area at about the same time.'

'And are you aware of any storm damage, Mr Warbeck? Lightning strikes, flood damage, that kind of thing?'

'I do know there was some minor flooding on the roads, Mr Pluke, but only short-lived. There was no flood damage, no houses or walls washed away, nothing like that. As we'd had a dry spell prior to those storms, the rainwater ran off the surface of the ground and the drains accepted it with a few localised exceptions. We did not have a cloud-burst, Mr Pluke, merely a heavy spring shower accompanied by thunder and lightning.'

'Thank you, Mr Warbeck. This is precisely what I wish to know. Might I inconvenience you later by having a detective call round to take a written statement detailing what you have just told me? We need it for our records.'

'Might I ask what records those are, Mr Pluke? This is the first time I have been questioned by the police about local weather conditions.'

'You have not heard about the events in Harman's Quarry, Mr Warbeck?' Montague was amazed that someone in the town did not know of the mystery blonde.

'No, what's happened, Mr Pluke? I never listen to the news, you know, nor do I read a newspaper or watch television, except of course for the weather forecasts.'

Thinking that such a lamentable lack of interest in local affairs was hardly conducive to the solution of major crime, Montague Pluke told Septimus Warbeck all about the dead girl, and then showed him the photograph.

'So, Mr Warbeck, we are trying to identify this woman and to trace her movements in Crickledale since Friday afternoon. There is a suggestion that she was caught in a thunder shower on Saturday evening, or perhaps that she sheltered from the storm, hence my visit to you. I need to determine the times of any significant rainfall.'

'Ah, well, I hope I've been useful. But I cannot say I've seen her around nor do I know who she is, Mr Pluke. Sorry about that. In my gas board days, I got into most houses in the town, but can't say I ever saw a girl like that – mind, it's five or six years since I retired, but even so, she would have been grown up at that time, eh?'

'Yes, she would, in which case I am sure you would have recognised her, Mr Warbeck.'

'So, Mr Pluke, if she was seen in the town on Friday afternoon, where was she between that time and being caught in a thunderstorm early on Saturday evening?'

'That is precisely what we are trying to establish, Mr Warbeck. With some difficulty, I might add.'

'Well, if I hear anything, I'll let you know. Glad to have been of some help.'

'Yes, indeed, Mr Warbeck. You have been most helpful, and thank you for all your assistance.'

Pluke left the meteorological potting shed to walk to the police station and *en route* found himself passing the bus station. Although he knew his officers would have made the necessary enquiries here, he decided to pop in for a chat with Mrs Harvey, the lady in the information office, who was one of Millicent's friends. It was good to show one's presence at a time like this; his arrival at the office would be a powerful reminder of the importance of this investigation.

'Well, hello, Mr Pluke,' said Mrs Harvey, a small middle-aged woman with shiny jet black hair of the kind not found naturally upon many British female heads of half a century old or thereabouts. 'What brings you here? We've just had two of your officers in, not long ago.'

'I'm pleased to hear it,' and he raised his panama in greeting. 'I was just passing – I had another important enquiry not very far from here – and thought I would pop in to see the outcome of my officers' visit.'

'And very rightly too, Mr Pluke. Now, would a cup of tea be in order?'

'No, thank you,' he declined with his customary politeness. 'I cannot stay long. So did the young lady call here? The blonde woman who is the subject of my officers' investigation?'

'She did, Mr Pluke, and I remember her well. As I told your officers when they showed me her photo, she came on Friday afternoon, three thirty it would be or thereabouts, and asked about buses to Barughdale. It was Barughdale, Mr Pluke, she showed me the name on a map she was carrying, but she did not pronounce it properly. She called it Barrowdale, so I knew she wasn't local. Fancy anyone not knowing how to pronounce Barughdale! It takes all sorts ... but she'd missed the two fifty. It meant she'd have to wait until five fifty for the next one, we only run two a day to Barughdale and two in from Barughdale, getting here at ten to nine and ten to eleven, for office and shopworkers, you understand, then shoppers.'

'And did she wait?'

'Oh, no, she said she would hitch-hike. She went into our cafeteria and I saw her at a table, having a cup of coffee and a sandwich. That would be getting on for four o'clock. Then next time I looked, she'd gone.'

'And was she alone all the time she was on your premises?'

'Oh, yes, Mr Pluke. Entirely. I did not get the impression she was waiting to meet anyone either. Not looking repeatedly at the door or at the clock like people do when they are waiting.'

'And was she carrying anything?'

'Just a small black shoulder-bag type of thing. Not a lot.'

'A handbag?'

'No, Mr Pluke, just the shoulder bag.'

'And not a portable tent for example? Or a ground sheet?'

'No, nothing like that. We do sometimes get people in like that, carrying their house and home on their backs, but not this young lady.'

'And her clothes, were they the same as those in the photograph?'

'Except for her white anorak, Mr Pluke. Yes, just the same. She was travelling light, there's no doubt about that.'

'You said she had a map, Mrs Harvey. Could you say whether it was a tourist map, or one in more detail, like an Ordnance Survey?'

'Oh, it was very detailed, Mr Pluke. Yes, an Ordnance Survey map, the sort most experienced hikers and ramblers use. It had all the minor roads and things on it, I noticed those when she pointed Barughdale out to me. She knew which road she wanted to take out of Crickledale, she showed me while asking about buses.'

'There is only one road she could use from here to Barughdale, of course.'

'That's right, Mr Pluke.'

'And did you have much of a chat with her, Mrs Harvey? When she was asking about bus times and destinations?'

'Not a lot, Mr Pluke. I think she was quite shy, not used to chatting to strangers. Besides, another customer came in.'

'I wonder if she gave any clue which would indicate her point of departure, Mrs Harvey?'

'Newcastle, Mr Pluke. She said she'd come down from Newcastle-upon-Tyne that day, Friday, hitched all the way down the A19. Did it in two lifts, she said, an articulated lorry carrying furniture all the way to Thirsk, then a gentleman's private car into Crickledale.'

'Newcastle-upon-Tyne? And she did not give any other clues?'

'No, Mr Pluke, just Newcastle. I've no idea where she came from before that.'

'And would you know whether she tried to hitch-hike from here to Barughdale? Did she thumb a lift from here?'

'Once she left the cafeteria, I never saw her again. I never saw her thumbing, Mr Pluke, all I know is that she said she couldn't wait for the five fifty so she'd set off and would hope to obtain a lift. She said she'd been lucky so far that day, getting lifts without much trouble, and with such decent men.'

'Well, that does give us a further important lead, Mrs Harvey. I am sure someone must have seen her on the road at some point. You told all this to my officers?'

'Oh, yes, Mr Pluke, they were very thorough in what they asked. They said they would start asking Newcastle police to see if they could help.'

'Good. Well, I must thank you for being so observant and for talking to me and my officers. You have been extremely helpful, Mrs Harvey.'

As he walked back to the police station, Montague Pluke decided that a time chart would be a useful asset to the investigation. Upon it, he could record all the positive sightings of the victim – already, the gaps were narrowing. After Mrs Cholmondeley's meeting with her, she'd been seen at the bus station around four o'clock on Friday, but there remained a massive gap between that time and the discovery of her body on Monday morning.

To date, the only fact they could be fairly sure of during that interval was that she was alive on Saturday, even until fairly late on Saturday according to the pathologist. And that tied in with the likelihood that she had been caught in a thunderstorm on Saturday evening, her damp clothing further suggesting that likelihood, combined with the possibility that she had taken shelter at Harman's Farm, or in the quarry, probably around five thirty. In a tent, perhaps? But where had she been and what had she been doing between four o'clock on Friday afternoon and, say, five o'clock or six o'clock on Saturday afternoon? Twenty-four hours and more, with a night in between? Had she been in Barughdale during that time? Overnight perhaps? Or camping in the quarry? Or elsewhere? And had she been alone, or with a companion, known or unknown to her? Had an unwanted travelling companion imposed himself upon her? Or had she come down from Newcastle to meet someone or to visit a particular place? Hitch-hiking could be very dangerous, especially for a young and attractive woman, and so he might issue a news release seeking help from motorists who might have seen her on the road, or getting into a vehicle between Crickledale and Barughdale.

In between leaving the police station before lunch and returning now, Montague Pluke felt his enquiry had moved forward at a fairly brisk pace but, at the same time, it had left unanswered a lot of vital questions. Nonetheless, he entered the police station with a jaunty bounce in his step, checked with Sergeant Cockfield pronounced Cofield for his messages, and then returned to the incident room. Wayne Wain had just returned too.

'Ah, Wayne,' Pluke greeted him. 'Did you make contact with that cattle dealer called Cooper from Carston?'

'I did, sir, but he could not help us. He does visit his herd near the quarry twice every day, morning and evening, and he did go out especially during the thunderstorms on Saturday. He got there around five thirty. His herd were taking shelter under some trees, but he did not see the girl.'

'So he did not enter either the quarry or the grounds of Harman's Farm? There was no likelihood of him seeing the girl there, either dead or alive?'

Wayne shook his head. 'No, sir. We can eliminate him from our enquiries, I feel sure.'

'Good. Now, I have news for you,' and he acquainted Wayne Wain with the detailed results of his recent investigations. 'So we know the girl was intending to travel along that road, Wayne, past the quarry and the farm, and onwards to Barughdale.'

'Or to the farm only, sir,' said Wayne. 'You said she had an Ordnance Survey map – it would show the farm and even the quarry. We do not know that she intended to travel all the way to Barughdale. Suppose she fully intended visiting Eric Burholme at Harman's Farm? It is within easy walking distance of Crickledale, especially to someone accustomed to walking.'

'I do have that possibility in mind, Wayne. Now, we do have a team in Barughdale, checking to see whether she ever got to that village, or whether she was even expected there. Have they reported in yet?'

'Not yet, sir, no.'

'Is that something you would like to do now? Go to Barughdale and help them in their enquiries? The sooner we establish that she was never intending to travel that far, or that she never reached the village, the better. And some Barughdale people might have seen her on the road.'

'Right, I'd like that, sir. I want to get this one solved. I'll get a car and go now.'

As Montague Pluke went to his own office in the incident room to write up the result of his investigations for the files, the telephone rang.

'It's for you, Mr Pluke,' said the secretary who answered it. 'I'll put it through to your office, shall I?'

'Who is it?' he asked.

'Previous Convictions,' she replied.

'Right,' he said, hurrying towards his desk to lift the receiver, then answering, 'Detective Inspector Pluke.'

'DC Lester, sir, Previous Convictions. Reference your enquiry about Eric Burholme. I've got the result of the national search.'

'Well done, DC Lester. So what does it reveal?'

'No convictions, sir, nothing. A clean slate both locally and at national level, no minor or major crimes recorded, and no traffic offences. But there is one thing of note, sir.'

'Relevant to my enquiry, you think?'

'His record is flagged, sir.'

'Flagged?' puzzled Pluke.

'A security device, sir, on his national record. It means that Mr Burholme is of interest to the security services. I have no further information on that nor do I have the necessary security clearance to investigate further. But your enquiry will have automatically triggered off a computer reaction; you may get a call from someone in Security.'

'Then who does have the clearance to investigate further?'

'You will have to make contact with the eighth floor at New Scotland Yard in London, sir, through the necessary channels, and take it from there. I am authorised to pass this information to you so that if you feel his past is of relevance to your present investigation, you may request access to the relevant information. That doesn't necessarily mean you will gain access to the relevant information, but you are entitled to ask. It all depends how sensitive the information is, or, of course, it would depend upon the precise involvement of your Mr Burholme.'

'I must admit,' said Pluke, 'that your information is not a great surprise. During the course of my enquiries I have encountered several indications which have led me to suspect there may be a complication of that kind . . . but thank you for confirming that. I have not mentioned my reservations to any of my officers but, in the light of further enquiries and information which I gather, I shall consider whether or not I should contact the eighth floor.'

'Very good, sir. Pleased to be of assistance,' and DC Lester rang off.

Pluke sat for a few moments to absorb the full implications of this news and then the telephone rang again. He picked up the receiver and identified himself.

'Detective Superintendent Bromley, C.1, New Scotland Yard,' said the strong southern voice at the other end. 'You've been making enquiries about Eric Burholme?'

'I have, sir, yes. A routine enquiry from the Criminal Records Office.'

'What's he supposed to have done, Pluke?'

'He's not supposed to have done anything, sir,' responded Pluke with just a hint of indignation. 'The body of a young woman, who has not been identified, was found in a disused quarry which he owns. She had head wounds, sir, consequently we are treating the death as suspicious. As the body is on Burholme's land, he is clearly a prime suspect although at the moment he is on the periphery of my investigations. Nonetheless, I intend to commence enquiries into his movements and background, for routine elimination purposes, and my recent enquiry from CRO at Scotland Yard is just the beginning of that process.'

'It's also the end, Pluke,' said Bromley.

'The end, sir?'

'Yes. Whatever your enquiries turn up, Pluke, keep Burholme out of your frame. I shall be contacting your Chief Constable to acquaint him with this. By all means continue your enquiries if you believe someone else is responsible for her death, but keep

Burholme out of the frame. And that applies even if the evidence points to him. Never forget that. Now, Detective Inspector Pluke, this conversation never took place. Is all that understood?'

'But, sir, with all due respect, if my enquiries produce evidence that this man is guilty of murder, then he should be brought to justice—'

'No arguments, Pluke. Just obey orders,' and the phone was replaced.

9

While Montague Pluke sat alone in his office to digest the implications of the aura of secrecy which now appeared to surround Eric Burholme, there was a knock on his door. He called upon the visitor to enter. It was Detective Sergeant F. L. Tower, known as Eiffel to his colleagues.

'I saw you were in your office, sir,' began the sergeant, a tall thin man with dark skin, fair hair on a very small head and feet of considerable size; he was a person who lived up to his nickname. 'I thought I'd update you on the bus station enquiries at this early stage because they were so positive.'

'Thank you, sergeant,' said Pluke, not acquainting the detective with the fact that he had also called at the bus station. He wanted to discover whether this team had elicited any information which he had not discovered. 'What did you learn?'

Eiffel efficiently presented the information that he and DC Jameson had gleaned, including the girl's reference to travelling down the A19 from Newcastle by hitch-hiking, and everything corresponded to that which Pluke had acquired – with one important addition.

'I rang the CID at Newcastle,' continued Eiffel, 'and I explained our interest in the movements and identification of the blonde female victim. I was told, sir, that it is not uncommon for Scandinavian girls to cross the North Sea by the ferries which sail into Tynemouth, some as students, others to seek work and others as tourists. There are several ports of embarkation – the Swedes come from Göteborg, which we call Göthenburg, and they come into Tynemouth, the Tyne port.'

'Swedes?' Pluke asked.

'Yes, sir. There are other ferries which serve the Tyne too, crossing the North Sea between Tynemouth and places like Bergen and Stavanger in Norway and Esbjerg in Denmark. Each of those Scandinavian ports might also be of interest if we are to make enquiries of the ferry lines.'

'An excellent suggestion, Detective Sergeant Tower. I have to say that I am particularly interested in the Swedish link. I would like you to address that one first and to treat those enquiries as a matter of some urgency. Have you commenced enquiries from any of the ferry lines?'

'Not at this stage, sir, that's why I thought I had better discuss this with you first.'

'Excellent. Yes, you did absolutely right. So, yes, begin enquiries immediately, starting with the Swedish ferries; make sure you have a good description and photographs of the girl and a set of her fingerprints if you feel they are necessary. You will not ignore the other lines, though, in case our victim has come from either Norway or Denmark. You know I have established links with Interpol in an attempt to get her identified?'

'Yes, sir, I saw that in the file.'

'Then perhaps you could contact the officer to whom I addressed my original enquiry? He was called Inspector Binn. He should remember my call, it was only yesterday. Liaise with him about this development but I want you to pursue your own enquiries through the ferry lines.'

'We can go immediately, sir.'

'Then do so. As an act of courtesy, ring Newcastle CID first, let them know you will be conducting investigations in their area. I have no objection to you and DC Jameson travelling to Newcastle to make direct enquiries; in fact, it would be far better than doing it over the telephone or involving Newcastle CID. You will have to establish whether or not enquiries from the Göthenburg offices can be conducted from Newcastle, or whether that requires the intervention of Interpol.'

'Thank you, sir.'

'You know the sort of information we require? It is at two levels, Detective Sergeant Tower. First is the identification of the girl, and the second is her reason for coming to England with any known destination she might have planned.'

'Yes, sir, I understand. I will also seek to establish whether she travelled alone or was known to be meeting anyone in this country.'

'Of course,' smiled Pluke. 'Well done, Detective Sergeant Tower, this is just the sort of positive lead we require!' and with that the detective left his office. It was another very encouraging development but it was the Swedish connection that was of most interest to Montague Pluke. Why should a Swedish maiden come to this country and to Harman's Quarry in particular? Or even to Harman's Farm? Had she come to call on Eric Burholme for any reason and, if so, why had he denied knowing her? Was it possible he had no idea who she was or what she was doing on his premises? And further to that, who, knowing she *was* Swedish, would take the trouble to bury her with a mirror, in accordance with an ancient Swedish custom?

With Burholme in mind, Pluke had to ask himself whether a murderer would have taken that kind of trouble with a victim – and that was one reason why he continued to nurse a lingering suspicion that this death was not murder. The fact that the mirror had been buried with the girl was a strong indication that the person who had buried her *did* know who she was, that he was aware of her nationality – and that she was a virgin. That suggested a close relationship. It seemed likely that the person who had buried her was also Swedish or someone with a deep knowledge of Swedish burial customs of the past, someone who was prepared to spend a little time in ensuring the girl was buried according to the old tradition, and that her grave was correctly orientated east-west. A murderer would hardly accord a victim that kind of sympathetic treatment.

It was while reflecting upon those matters that Pluke reconsidered the telephone call from C.1 Department of Scotland Yard. As Pluke had suspected, Burholme was a mystery; that phone call confirmed it. However, the words used by Bromley of the

111

Yard were not a command to end the investigation – the London Metropolitan Police could not issue such commands for they had no jurisdiction over investigations in the provinces. The command came as a matter of internal British security and it was to say that if the traditional finger of suspicion indicated Burholme was involved in the death of the girl, then the matter should be taken no further. If the evidence implicated some other person, then a prosecution could proceed. Pluke was not sure of the ethics of the kind of action Bromley was seeking. The death of the girl had entered the public arena because Pluke had informed the newspapers, television and radio networks, and his officers were making widespread enquiries. A cover-up was therefore impossible – not that Detective Inspector Montague Pluke would ever sanction a cover-up but if, as he suspected, the death was due to an accident, however bizarre, then there would no case of murder to answer. Burholme, with all the security protection in the world, would not be at risk of prosecution. And if the case was not one of murder, then, whatever the circumstances, Montague Pluke felt that the public had a right to know the truth and that he had a duty to establish that truth.

The telephone rang again.

'Pluke?' Montague recognised the voice. It was Detective Superintendent Jack Hart calling from Headquarters.

'Sir,' responded Montague.

'What the hell is going on in Crickledale? I've had the Chief Constable on to me now because he's had a call from the Commissioner of the London Metropolitan Police who maintains you've got a murder suspect who's got some kind of top-level security rating. There's talk of the Home Office being notified, and the Foreign Office and the Security Services and the Prime Minister getting involved ... Just what the hell have you been doing, Pluke?'

'I have been conducting perfectly routine enquiries into a suspicious death, sir, and I have no such suspect for murder, sir.' Montague decided to be firm in his dealings with this matter. 'At this stage of the enquiry, there is no chief suspect, and we have no one in custody, there is no one within our cells helping with enquiries or otherwise under arrest. I am merely making routine enquiries into the suspicious death of a young woman, nothing more than that.'

'Well, you seem to have caused a mighty fuss of some kind Pluke. You'd better level with me, tell me exactly what's going on.'

Pluke gave a precise account of the investigation to date but decided to omit his own theories about Eric Burholme at this stage; he needed further evidence before he could implement his means of determining his own very deeply held ideas. He brought his supervisory officer up to date with the likely Newcastle connection and stressed that his officers were, at the moment, concentrating upon getting the deceased girl identified and tracing her last movements within the Crickledale district.

Hart listened without interruption; when Pluke had concluded his account he asked, 'You seem to have done all the right things, Pluke, but you have not yet interviewed this man Burholme? Not even for elimination purposes?'

'Not yet, sir. I want to keep that interview in reserve until I have established a great deal more about the background to the case – in particular, I want to know the identity of the girl and her place or country of origin. I consider it vital we know more about her before I begin to question Mr Burholme because he has already denied any knowledge of her.'

'But if he has denied knowing her, then surely you have interviewed him?'

'Only as a witness, sir; we talked at the outset because the body was found on his land. That has been his only involvement to date.'

'Did I hear you right when you said he's eighty years old?'

'That is what he claimed to be, sir. He doesn't look it, I must admit.'

'Hardly the age of a chap who would kill a girl and bury her like that. But fair enough. If he's speaking the truth and we can prove he has no links with the girl, we have no further interest in him, and the Home office need not get itself into a tizzy about this investigation. I have no idea what's behind all this, Pluke, I

113

will be honest with you. All I know is that you set up an enquiry which has produced a man who is flagged as being of security interest.'

'It surprised me as well, sir. There are some further enquiries I would like to make, however. I do need to know more about Burholme, and, at this moment, I have not put a team on to that aspect of my enquiry. It means Burholme himself has no reason to think he is under suspicion or even under investigation – I have adopted that tactic quite deliberately, sir, in view of the unusual background to this case.'

'You think there is something odd behind all this, don't you, Pluke? Maybe I have not given you credit for your perception.'

'From what I have seen to date, there are certain factors which do not appear to be as they seem. I cannot be more specific just yet. All I wish to do is to establish the truth, sir; what happens when I do will depend upon the decision of someone far more eminent than me. I shall simply determine the facts and present them to you for further consideration.'

'Well, it looks as though you've done everything right so far, Pluke, because it was not Burholme himself who sought sanctuary from your enquiries.'

'He's been extremely co-operative so far,' Pluke said.

'Obviously, he does not think he is under suspicion or investigation, so congratulations upon maintaining that aura.'

'When I do begin my in-depth investigation of him, sir, I might want help from a higher authority, due to the security aspects.'

'What sort of help?'

'Well, if he has a very high security classification, it means I will never have access to any of his files, even if he is a murder suspect. I may need to know if something from his past has provided a motive for his actions, for example.'

'So you want me to find out something, Pluke, from my own sources?'

'If Burholme is of interest to national security, and if my request for any previous record has triggered off this reaction, then one would expect some kind of relevant information to be held on file, sir. Special Branch, perhaps, or MI5 or MI6 or elsewhere. I don't have access to those sources. I am sure you

114

can understand that it would help if I had a starting point for my own enquiries into his background. I have some suspicions at the moment, but they are somewhat vague, rather too vague to divulge, even to you.'

'You're a deep individual, Pluke. You hold your cards very close to your chest . . .'

'It's most unlucky to steal a pack of playing cards, sir . . .'

'Give over, Pluke. I am not interested in your superstitious beliefs. Just get this thing sorted out without too much official-dom. Have the press mentioned him yet?'

'No, sir, they have merely published the fact that the body was in Harman's Quarry.'

'But you've searched his premises for the murder weapon and will search them again, and for grave-digging tools, you told me. You'd expect word of your interest in his premises to have filtered down to the local people, and for the resultant gossip to reach the press – they'd regard that as an indication that the police suspect the owner of the premises as being the killer.'

'We have searched his premises, sir, but not his house. I may do that later, if the evidence justifies it. But his farm is very isolated, people can drive or walk past without being aware of our presence on the land, and he did allow us to search his buildings – that was after I had pointed out that his open doors were an invitation for someone to steal a spade or hide the murder weapon. I would add that he has been most co-operative, sir.'

'He would, wouldn't he, if he has something to hide? Right, I shall do a little digging myself, that's between you and me. No one else must know, Pluke. Keep your head down and don't go upsetting our political masters and keep the enquiry moving. To be honest, I'm as keen as you to find out what he's been up to. An eighty-year-old agricultural engineer, you say?'

'Yes, sir, that's all we know at this point.'

'But you must have something else I can work on, Pluke. You don't think he's a retired international criminal who's hiding here, do you?'

'No, I've no reason to believe that, sir, and besides, that would hardly rank as being of security interest, would it?'

'No. A spy, perhaps, Pluke? Is he a spy?'

'I think he is rather too old, sir, although he could be a retired agent, even one with a price on his head, one who's here for safe keeping.'

'So that's all you can offer me as a starting point?'

'Except that he might be a Swedish national, sir,' said Pluke.

'Good God, why do you think that?'

'He uses the colours of the Swedish flag for his publicity material, sir, and he has a gold-headed cockerel as a weather-vane. Golden-headed cockerels were sacred to the war gods of ancient Scandinavia, sir; the pagan Norsemen believed that a gold-crested cockerel would herald the day when all things would perish, they called it Ragnnarok ... It's long been a tradition to use gold-headed cocks as weather-vanes in the Northern Hemisphere and even when Christianity replaced paganism, sir, the cock was used as a symbol of the corn spirit, to ensure good harvests, and always with a golden head ...'

'All right, you've made your point. I'll do a bit of quiet hunting, Pluke.'

'I do appreciate your help and support, sir,' and Montague Pluke smiled into the telephone.

'Not a word to anyone else about this!'

And Hart rang off. Montague smiled at this unexpected bonus and wondered if Hart was trying to score points over someone in a high position of authority ... but if it helped Pluke, then it would help his investigation. Pleased at this surprisingly furtive offer of help, Pluke now realised that Hart was as keen to solve the mystery as he was – and he'd never mentioned money during that call. Pluke's smile remained on his face as he left his office to walk into the incident room where Horsley hailed him.

'Ah, just the fellow,' he said as he spotted Montague. 'I didn't want to interrupt when you were on the telephone. Two more developments, both positive, I feel. First, I've just had a call from DS Forster; he's found a motorist who saw the deceased girl walking towards Barughdale on Friday evening, around five o'clock. He's been shown the photo and the artist's impression of her with the haversack and white anorak, and he has no doubt. He says the girl was walking briskly out of town towards Barughdale and she was facing the oncoming traffic. He was driving into town and saw her on the crest of Mill Hill, he got a good look at her.'

'Alone, was she?'

'Yes, Montague, quite alone. But it's a good sighting and it puts her closer to Harman's Farm. Mill Hill is about two miles away from both Crickledale and Harman's Farm – we can now put her midway between the two places, alone but alive and very close to the quarry. The timing's right too.'

'And our witness can be eliminated, can he?'

'Yes, Montague, he has been carefully interviewed, he's a local vicar and had been to see a parishioner. His account can be verified.'

'Good. So we know she was walking towards Barughdale as she'd led Mrs Cholmondeley to believe was her intended direction. What we need now, Mr Horsley, is someone to say she was seen at the far side of Harman's Farm, still walking briskly towards Barughdale. If no one saw her on that stretch of road, we might assume she entered the farm premises or the quarry.'

'Right. As we've said in the past, she might have decided to sleep in one of the outbuildings, Montague, without Mr Burholme knowing of her presence.'

'Yes. Remember, we are still talking about Friday evening. We think she remained alive until Saturday evening. We still have some twenty-four hours to account for, Mr Horsley. Where was she during all that time? Any sign of Detective Sergeant Wain?'

'He's not back from Barughdale, sir. As a matter of interest, we've had no positive news from our officers in Barughdale . . .'

'And that means there is none!' sighed Pluke. 'They always call in with any positive leads. So, what is the second item?'

'Mr Burholme rang, sir, only five minutes ago. He's discovered a spade's missing from his garden shed. He said you had asked him to make a search of the premises to try and establish if anything had gone, anything that could have been used to dig the grave.'

'I did indeed, Mr Horsely. So when did this spade disappear?'

'He can't be sure. He knows it was there a week ago – last Tuesday – because he used it to dig up a dandelion in the border of his front garden.'

'Very handy for keeping evil away from you, provided you gather them on St John's Day,' said Pluke in all seriousness.

'What are?'

'Dandelions,' said Pluke. 'But go on, Mr Horsley.'

'Well, he used the spade around tea-time on Tuesday last, cleaned the blade with some grass, and replaced it in his garden shed. After you suggested he search around for missing tools, he realised it was missing. He just discovered its absence before calling us.'

'We have a description of the spade?' asked Pluke.

'It was an expensive one, Montague. Stainless steel with a modern plastic handle, dark green colour. Worthington make. Worth about a hundred and twenty pounds, he reckons. He has searched his entire premises for it, it's nowhere to be seen.'

'I understand, but he has not found the murder weapon during this search?'

'No, Montague, and neither did our teams. They have finished, by the way. I have now detailed them to visit all farms which are close to Harman's, just in case we find something in their outbuildings. It's a long shot, but we have to do it. We'll make a search of all the hedges and ditches along the roads away from the quarry too, just in case the spade was thrown from a departing vehicle. Now, I have made a note for our files about the missing spade and will issue a description of it in the hope we can trace it, but we'll need a statement from Burholme. As he's claiming it's been stolen, we'll need a crime report as well. I'll send a team along, I think we can spare one of the house-to-house teams.'

'No, Mr Horsley, I would like to have an excuse for another visit to Mr Burholme. In fact, I'll go now and will show him a photo of the deceased.'

'What about the four o'clock news conference?'

'I will return in time for that, Mr Horsley. Now, have we someone who can drive me to the farm? Detective Sergeant Wain

118

is otherwise engaged at Barughdale so I shall require a car and a driver.'

'It will have to be someone from the incident room, Montague; we can use a pool car.'

'Excellent. I suggest one of the statement readers should drive me. None has viewed the scene and I think it would be sensible for them to do so, it will help them in their understanding of the investigation.' And he took a photograph of the victim from a folder on his desk.

'Good idea. I'll detail Detective Constable Helston to drive you.'

Clutching the photograph, Montague saw that Detective Constable Helston was a pretty young woman of about twenty-six with dark curly hair, a slim figure and a ready smile with beautiful teeth. She was a recent transfer from the uniform branch to the CID and this was her first murder case. She was clearly delighted at the opportunity to leave the humdrum of her statement-reading duties, if only to drive Pluke to the scene.

Paula Helston drove carefully and when they crested Mill Hill he requested her to slow her pace a little, explaining that this was where the deceased victim had last been seen. The verges at this point were broad and not yet fully grown with the flush of late spring. The road was quite wide with a white line down the centre: it was not a narrow country lane. He wondered if the girl had been the victim of a hit-and-run driver with some kind of protruding implement or adornment on his vehicle. Against that, she had not borne any injuries which were consistent with being caused by a motor vehicle.

As they approached the farm entrance with its name prominent on the gate, Pluke suggested that Paula slow down to take the sharp left-hand turn into the premises. She obeyed; the gate was closed, so Pluke emerged from the car in his ancient finery, opened the gate and waved her through.

'Now, Detective Constable Helston, take the first track to the left,' he told her. 'That takes us to the quarry where I shall show you the scene.'

He told her to ease to a halt at the quarry entrance, close by

119

the length of plastic-covered bales, and as they left the car, they saw the quarry was now deserted. Only the oblong hole in the bare earth was a reminder of the drama which had unfolded here so very recently.

'That is the victim's grave,' he said slowly without approaching the grave. 'It is invisible from the road, as you can now understand, and hidden from the farmhouse to which we are heading.'

'The poor girl,' said Detective Constable Helston.

'Now, let us see what Mr Burholme can tell us about his missing spade,' said Pluke, returning to the car. Under Pluke's guidance, they drove slowly along the farm roads and this time turned left to gain access to the farm buildings. Upon arrival, they parked on the tidy gravelled area in front of the huge house and Burholme emerged from his kitchen door to greet them. Most affably, he welcomed them inside and Pluke asked Detective Constable Helston to join him for the interview.

He told her it would be good experience for her, apart from which (he told himself) a second opinion about Mr Burholme, with all the benefits of feminine intuition, might be useful. As usual, Montague declined a cup of tea and went straight into the business of the meeting.

'So, Mr Burholme,' smiled Pluke when they were settled, 'tell me about this missing spade.'

10

Walking easily without the aid of a stick, the lithe Mr Burholme led Detective Inspector Montague Pluke and Detective Constable Helston out of the front door and around the side of the house into the walled garden at the rear. Surrounded by a high brick wall as protection against the worst of the moorland weather, it was a spacious garden comprised chiefly of a substantial vegetable patch neatly kept and showing signs of recent attention;

there were also currant and gooseberry bushes, a small orchard of apple and pear trees, a large lawn with substantial borders and a lean-to greenhouse against a brick wall at the distant end. In the southern corner of the plot, discreetly positioned behind a pair of conifers and with its back to the wall, was a small wooden shed.

'My tool shed,' said Burholme as he pointed to it, then led the way along the gravel paths.

'Was it locked at the time of the theft?' asked Pluke, anticipating the answer.

'No,' said Burholme. 'The door was closed, but I never lock this shed, there's never been a need. It's well out of sight behind the house and away from the road. In all the years I have been here, nothing has been stolen. Until now, that is.'

The shed, made of creosoted wood and in good condition, was some twelve feet long by eight feet wide, a substantial building with a reinforced glass window at one side. It was standing on stone blocks, elevated from the ground to keep rising damp at bay.

When Burholme opened the door, it revealed an impressive array of meticulously tidy garden implements, all having obviously been cleaned and oiled before being stored here. They ranged from a metal wheelbarrow with a green frame to a selection of plastic and metal watering cans large and small, by way of a lawnmower, several spades, forks and rakes, hedge clippers, plant pots, seed boxes, hoses and more besides, including garden furniture which had been placed in store until the arrival of the summer weather.

'We have a description of your spade at the office,' Pluke said. 'Stainless steel with a green plastic shaft and T-handle, an expensive sort of plastic, I am told.'

'That's right, Mr Pluke. It's one of a set – the fork, rake and trowels are still there.'

Pluke saw them and nodded. 'So where was it taken from, Mr Burholme?'

'Just inside the door,' Burholme said, indicating a pair of nails which had been hammered into one of the struts. 'It hung from

121

those nails by the T-handle. I kept it near the doorway because it was often required, even in winter sometimes to dig snow if my shovel was not immediately available.'

'You've searched this shed and your other buildings for it? Indoors and out? I wonder if you could have misplaced it?'

'I have searched, Mr Pluke. Everywhere. Your officers have been searching for grave-digging tools too, and they didn't find it in any of my buildings. It's not been misplaced, I can assure you.'

'So what do you think has happened to it?' Pluke asked Burholme.

'Well, if it hadn't been for that grave in the quarry, I'd have thought I'd put it somewhere and forgotten about it, lost it in other words. I'd have hunted high and low, as I've done in fact, and I suppose I'd have concluded I'd misplaced it. I would hardly suspect anyone of stealing it from such a remote place. But with this grave so near to me, and bearing in mind what you said on your last visit, I think someone could have taken it to dig that unfortunate woman's grave, and then disposed of it.'

'That would tie in with the theory that someone entered the quarry with the woman, killed her there and buried her immediately,' said Pluke. 'If that scenario is correct, or even partially correct, then the killer would have required a spade and, clearly, your establishment is the only place nearby at which one might be found at such very short notice, probably at night under the cover of darkness.'

'My thoughts exactly, Mr Pluke.'

'Now,' and Pluke turned to his companion, 'Detective Constable Helston. Have you any questions or observations while we are here?'

'I wondered if anything else might have been used during the burial, Mr Burholme?'

'Really? Such as?' He raised his eyebrows.

'Well,' she said, looking at Pluke and wondering whether her question was a silly one, 'I am assuming the victim was not killed precisely where she was buried. I realise the place of her death has never been determined, but taking my basic argument as a starting point, she must have been carried to the grave, even if it was only for a few yards. Dead bodies are notoriously difficult for one person to carry or move around – some additional assistance, mechanical or human, is generally required. I wondered, therefore, if the killer had also taken your wheelbarrow to enable him to move the body to the graveside.'

'Well, I doubt it,' said Burholme. 'I have just the one barrow, and it is there, exactly where I always keep it. To my knowledge, it has not been used by anyone but myself.'

'It is a very good question,' Pluke complimented the girl. 'We have not yet established exactly where she died, nor do we know how she was transported to the grave. But if the killer did make use of your spade, Mr Burholme, it seems strange that they ignored the wheelbarrow, if indeed transportation of the corpse was required, even over a comparatively short distance.'

'It is something I cannot answer,' said Burholme smoothly. 'All I can say is that there is no sign of the barrow being used. It is not dirty, and it is in its precise position in the shed. If the killer did use it, surely it would have either been left at the graveside, or removed for disposal, as was the spade?'

'Who can understand the mind of a killer, Mr Burholme? What is logical to sensible, intelligent people like ourselves might not appear sensible to a killer in the frantic moments of trying to dispose of a corpse. A spade is easily portable, even by someone on foot or on a motor cycle or even a pedal cycle. If the girl met her death at the hands of a hiker or tourist or camper, he might have been prepared to take away the spade to conceal its use, but it would not have been so easy to do likewise with a wheelbarrow. Anyone seen walking down the road in the middle of the night with a wheelbarrow would be ripe for suspicion, I would suggest.'

'Well, I just do not know, Mr Pluke. I have no idea whether or not my barrow was used – all I can say is that a valuable spade is missing.'

'And that is why we are here. Now, Detective Constable Helston will take a statement from you, for our murder files, and in addition she will complete our crime report – we shall record this as burglary, Mr Burholme.'

'Burglary, Mr Pluke?'

'Yes, that is the crime. Breaking into your shed – and it was broken into even if the latch was lifted without any other force being used – followed by the theft of your garden spade. Those are the constituents of the crime. You may wish to claim from your insurance in which case a police record of the crime is essential.'

'Oh, well, I never thought of that.'

'And we shall have to take possession of the wheelbarrow, Mr Burholme,' said Pluke.

'The barrow? But why?' Pluke did not miss the expression of surprise on Burholme's face.

'For forensic examination, Mr Burholme. We have samples of earth from the grave so we can examine the wheel to see if it crossed that land. And we can examine all the surface areas of the barrow, including the edges of the container section, for fibres, Mr Burholme. If the woman was placed in this barrow, there is every possibility that a quantity of fibres from her clothing, or even other minuscule deposits, were left behind. A strand of her hair, for example, a drop of blood from her wound, some flakes of skin, things invisible to the naked eye. If any such deposit is there, we shall find it, and then we shall know whether or not your barrow was used to carry the body. And, of course, we shall keep in touch with you.'

'Oh, well, I suppose if they came for my spade, they could have taken the barrow as well.'

'Very likely indeed, Mr Burholme. Now, if you can spare five minutes to make the necessary written statement to Detective Constable Helston, we need not detain you much longer. But there is another small matter before we leave. Photographs. As promised, I have a photograph of the girl found in the quarry.'

With no more ado, Pluke took an envelope from his overcoat pocket, extracted a photograph and passed it to Burholme. The old man looked at Pluke, his features displaying what might be regarded as disbelief that the police would photograph a dead person and show the picture to members of the public. Burholme's jaw clenched and his eyes grew moist as he accepted the print.

'Tell me if you know the woman.' Pluke spoke with surprising softness as he studied the facial expressions of the old man.

But Burholme shook his head slowly, handing the photograph back to Pluke.

'Sorry, Mr Pluke, I don't know her. I've never seen her before; she's certainly not connected with any of my customers or personal contacts.'

'All right, thanks for checking. And now DC Helston will take that statement.'

As Paula Helston began, using a chair and table in the garden shed, Pluke manhandled the wheelbarrow into the rear of the car. He took care not to touch those places likely to have been held by the anonymous grave-digger. There might be fingerprints on the handles or even on the metal bodywork of the barrow. Having stowed the barrow securely, Pluke waited in the car until DC Helston had finished her work.

On the way back to the office a few minutes later, Pluke asked, 'Well, Detective Constable Helston, what did you make of that experience?'

'It was enjoyable, sir, and most useful. It will help enormously in my statement reading. I'll be able to picture the scene in my mind each time I read something.'

'That was my intention. Now, you did very well to consider the possible use of that wheelbarrow,' he complimented her. 'Any thoughts about it?'

'Well, sir, if the grave-digger did make use of the barrow, why would he return it to the garden shed? Why get rid of the spade and not the barrow?'

'An extremely good point, Detective Constable Helston. A very good point indeed. And there is an extension to that question, is there not?'

'Is there, sir?'

'If the barrow was used to convey the body, why return it precisely to the place from which it was taken? Especially in darkness as has been suggested – even to find it in darkness was a considerable achievement. From the tidy state of the garden shed, it is clear that Mr Burholme keeps things in a very ordered way, something reflected in the overall condition of his premises. So if the killer used the barrow, why not leave it elsewhere, even near the grave? Why return it precisely to its place in the shed – and Mr Burholme did tell us it was in its normal place?'

'So you are saying you don't think it was used, sir?'

'No, I am not saying that. Think, young lady. What is the other alternative?'

For a few moments, she pondered his question while driving back to the police station, and then asked, 'You mean that Burholme used it himself, sir?'

'If it was used to convey the corpse, Detective Constable Helston, then only Burholme would replace it in precisely the place from which it had been taken, wouldn't he? Everything has its place in that shed. If anyone else had used it, they would not replace it precisely where Burholme wanted it, would they? They'd dump it fairly quickly in the first suitable place in order to get clear of the scene before they were spotted.'

'It's funny you should say that, sir, because another thought occurred to me.'

'Go on,' he invited.'

'It's a thought that occurred to me while we were in the garden, sir. The garden is at the back of the house, walled in except for the entrance we used. You have to walk along the side of the house to gain access; the garden is out of sight from the front of the house, it can't be seen from the area in front of all those farm buildings, nor can it be seen from the road which leads across the fields and into the farm premises. Not even the high walls are visible from those points, especially at night, and I doubt if the garden would be illuminated. I saw no garden lights.'

'And you can't see the garden from the quarry either, can you?' he smiled at her.

'No, sir. I think that is significant. I checked deliberately during our journey here, to see exactly what might be visible from various points bearing in mind the sketches and plans we have in the incident room.'

'So what do you deduce from this?'

'It seems so unlikely that anyone who killed the girl in or near

126

the quarry would come all this way to the farm to search for a spade and a barrow to bury her – if they'd killed her in that quarry, they'd have got away from the place as fast as they could, even if it meant leaving her unburied.'

'And what is the logical conclusion to be derived from that scenario?'

'That she died somewhere on this farm, sir, in the buildings possibly or near one of the agricultural machines, even by accident, and that someone wanted to move her body away from the premises – so they put her in the barrow, took the spade along at the same time, probably under cover of darkness, and, possibly under the cover of a tent, buried her in the quarry.'

'My thoughts precisely,' beamed Pluke.

'So you think Mr Burholme killed her?' she put to him, wondering why he had never suggested this to the teams when briefing them.

'I would not go quite that far,' he said. 'But I do think he buried her. The snag is that Mr Burholme steadfastly denies knowing or seeing the girl – that is why I need more facts before I begin to interrogate him as a suspect rather than a witness.'

'You mean we are looking for a killer as well as an accomplice, sir? Two suspects?'

'Not necessarily,' he said. 'I have not yet ruled out accidental death. I do not want you to mention this to any other parties, but I do want you to bear the likelihood in mind while reading all those statements and abstracting the relevant information.'

'But with the idea that Mr Burholme buried her?'

'Yes. I want you to consider, among all the other possibilities that come your way, that the girl could have died accidentally, and that Burholme buried her in some kind of panic, or even very coolly in order to cover his tracks.'

'You mean Mr Burholme has something to hide, sir?'

'I am sure he has, Detective Constable Helston. My problem is, what on earth has he done which would compel him to bury a girl in such a manner? What on earth has he done which might provide a motive for murder – that's if he has murdered her – or what has he done which would cause him to dispose of the body of someone who died accidentally on his premises?'

127

'I have no idea of the answer to any of those things, sir, but it does seem a strange way to die, sir, that hole in her temple. I remember thinking that when you briefed us.'

'A very strange way to die indeed,' nodded Pluke as they turned into the police station complex. 'Most odd, in fact. Now, that was a most productive outing, Detective Constable Helston.'

'Most useful, sir.'

'I'd be obliged if you would keep most of what you have learned to yourself but bear it in mind as you study all those statements.'

'Yes, I will, sir,' she said. 'And I really did enjoy my outing.'

'Me too,' said Pluke, thinking this was a truly charming and intelligent young lady, ideal as a future member of his department. Next, though, he had to consider whom he might instruct to deal with the wheelbarrow. A moment's reflection told him that Horsley was just the fellow; he was just the type of man who would be accustomed to arranging the forensic inspection of wheelbarrows. And now it was time for the afternoon news conference.

Upon returning to his incident room office, Pluke summoned Inspector Paul Russell for a brief consultation prior to the arrival of the reporters and photographers for their news briefing.

'Two things must be highlighted at this news conference,' Pluke told him. 'One is the sighting of the deceased at five o'clock on Friday afternoon as she was walking on Mill Hill. That is midway between Crickledale and Barughdale, as you know, and she was heading towards Barughdale which she called Barrowdale. She was alone too. We need to find anyone else who saw her on that road, inspector. Lots of local cars do use that stretch of road, so let's concentrate on the local papers, radio and TV programmes. Following that appeal, it's important we discover whether she was seen anywhere in this district on Saturday – to date, no one has reported seeing her at all on Saturday. That is most peculiar. Saturday is a total blank in our investigation, so link those two appeals, will you? The second thing is the missing garden spade. There is a description in the file – you might even find an identical one in a local shop or catalogue. It might be useful to have a picture of it, in colour preferably. So can you persuade your journalistic friends to highlight those two stories?'

'No problem, sir. Now, one or two have asked if you could make yourself available for a picture or even an interview.'

'Yes, as the officer in charge of the investigation, that is my responsibility. Acquaint me with your requirements, inspector, and I shall do my best to accommodate you and your friends from the press.'

As Pluke was discussing the news conference, Wayne Wain returned from Barughdale and waited for the opportunity to discuss the results with him. Satisfied that Inspector Russell could cope with the press, Pluke dismissed him to go about those duties while he admitted Wain to his office.

'Ah, Wayne. You've completed your enquiries in Barughdale?'

'Yes, sir, thanks to the teams already there. I was able to confer with them which considerably shortened my visit. I did not want to go over the same ground as them, although I did visit a few houses and premises which they had not yet crossed off their lists. And I called at the few farms, garages, cottages and inns which can be found on the road between Harman's Farm and Barughdale.'

'And?'

'Nothing, sir. No one in Barughdale is expecting a visit from the deceased. It's a tiny place, as you know. There are only two bed-and-breakfast establishments and one pub with rooms to let, but none had a prior booking by a single girl nor a phone call on Friday to ask about vacancies. No one knew her, the description did not mean anything and, so far as we know, she has never been to Barughdale on a previous occasion. She was not expected there and did not arrive on Friday or Saturday.'

'And there are no further sightings of her walking towards Barughdale on Friday?'

'The teams are continuing to explore that angle, sir. Some of the people who drive that road from Crickledale to Barughdale around five o'clock are office and shop workers. The teams are waiting for them to come home tonight, when they'll be questioned. I was unable to talk to them this afternoon. People who did drive along the road earlier have been interviewed – shoppers, shift workers and so on – but we've got nothing from them. In my view, sir, it supports a belief that she never reached Barughdale.'

'And, Wayne, it might even suggest she never *intended* to reach Barughdale.'

'You are inclined to the notion that her intended destination was Harman's Farm, aren't you, sir?'

'I am, Wayne, I am indeed,' and he provided Wayne with a brief account of the outcome of his visit with Detective Constable Helston, after which he said, 'A very nice girl, Wayne, a very nice girl indeed, and very bright. She has the makings of a good detective.'

'I might try to get to know her better, sir,' offered Wayne. 'So you think the victim came to visit Mr Burholme at Harman's Farm and that he knows much more than he's revealing to us?'

'I'm convinced of it, Wayne, but I do not know why he is being so secretive, nor do I know why the girl wanted to visit him. That is a very important question and for an answer, we must await her identification. Someone who knew her might enlighten us. I am confident we shall get her identified, though. You are aware of the development at Newcastle?'

'Newcastle? No, sir!'

'Or my discussions with Headquarters about the security aspects of our Mr Burholme?'

'No, sir. Good heavens, you have been busy in my absence!' grinned Wayne Wain.

'Certain aspects of the enquiry are really moving at a rapid pace, Wayne,' agreed Pluke, 'but it has something of a circular aspect to it in that I am going around in rings and getting nowhere very fast. But I must admit I am increasingly concerned about the part played by our Mr Burholme and I shall pursue the matter until I learn the truth. I think he is a devious and very cunning person, Wayne, one we must not underestimate. Charming certainly, kindly without doubt, but very clever.'

'Are you saying it is time we had him in for interview, sir?'

'I don't think so, Wayne. Not yet. I do not want to interview him until I have more evidence, until I know more about the girl, or even until I have news about the wheelbarrow, Wayne.'

'The wheelbarrow, sir?'

'Oh, didn't I mention that?'

Pluke had omitted to refer to the wheelbarrow theory, so he then acquainted Wayne Wain with all that had transpired since Wayne had driven over to Barughdale. Wayne listened intently, showing a keen interest in Detective Constable Helston's wheelbarrow theory and the lack of any sightings of the victim since Friday tea-time.'

'I am positive she did not visit any house or establishment on Friday evening to seek accommodation, sir,' said Wayne. 'Either she slept out of doors—'

'In the quarry?' asked Pluke.

'Yes, she might have slept out of doors in the quarry on Friday night, sir – not Saturday, the day she died – or she might have obtained accommodation at the only available place along that stretch of road.'

'Which is Harman's Farm,' said Pluke.

'Yes, sir, which means she sheltered there either with or without the knowledge or consent of Mr Burholme – on Friday night.'

'She could have used one of his outbuildings to sleep in, that is what you are implying, Wayne?'

'Yes, or if she did go to the farm to ask for his permission to use an outbuilding, he might have taken pity on her and invited her in. Or he might have allowed her to camp in the quarry ... even providing her with a tent. She had no tent or sleeping bag of her own, we know that.'

'Or he might have allowed her to use one of his spare bedrooms?' said Pluke. 'He does have seven bedrooms, he told us that.'

'You don't think he tried to sleep with her, do you, sir?' asked Wayne. 'Murder and rape are often the consequences of a girl refusing to allow a man to have sex ...'

'He is eighty years old, Wayne! Besides, there is no evidence of a sexual attack and she was a virgin, remember. That's another odd aspect of this case.'

'Have we considered the possibility that she did not arrive at the farm by accident, sir? Is it feasible she might have been heading specifically for Harman's Farm? That she was in the area in order to visit Mr Burholme?'

'I am increasingly drawn to that argument, Wayne, but Burholme claims he does not know her and was not expecting such a visitor. He has seen a photograph too, and says he does not recognise her.'

'Which is exactly what he would say if he wished to disassociate himself from her.'

'I appreciate that, Wayne, but there is a chance that Burholme was speaking the truth. I did detect some emotion as he examined her photograph in death. Nonetheless, it is feasible that he did not know her and that he was not expecting her.'

'You mean she was coming anyway but intended to surprise him?'

'It is always a possibility. Let us consider that he has something to hide, Wayne. I am sure he has – and I am sure he has strong Swedish connections. I am now inclined to believe he is the Swedish link, not the girl. Let us consider that she might be a journalist or an investigator of some kind and that she uncovered a nasty truth about his past, then decided to pay him a visit to either question him or photograph him or merely to embarrass him ... without him knowing of her plans or her visit in advance.'

'Would he murder her if she had uncovered his secret? Is that what you are suggesting, sir?'

'It's possible if his secret was of such a serious nature,' said Pluke. 'And whether or not he killed her deliberately, it is possible he buried her to conceal his past. That is my theory.'

'And you have some grounds for that theory, sir?'

'I have indeed, Wayne,' smiled Detective Inspector Pluke. 'The evidence is all around for those with eyes to see!'

'So what is the basis of your theory, sir? Are you going to enlighten me?' asked Wayne Wain.

'Indeed I shall, Wayne. Now this is how I see things. I drew my well-considered conclusions from a wide range of clues but the first intimation I received was—'

But before he could complete that sentence, there was a knock on Pluke's office door. 'Come in,' he called.

Inspector Russell appeared in the doorway and said, 'Sir, the news conference is over but I have received several requests for you to appear before the cameras. Regional TV for starters, sir, and also newspapers. They want you to appear in person to highlight your search for that spade. I have obtained an identical spade, by the way, on loan from a shop in town; it's for you to show the viewers. The TV people need the pictures urgently, so they can be processed for this evening's regional news programmes.'

'Then I shall not keep them waiting, Inspector Russell. Where am I required to go?'

'Without exception, sir, they have requested a shot from the graveside, if that can be arranged. Grave and spade shots. They will carry a lot of impact, you see, the viewers and indeed the newspaper readers will relate to pictures of that kind . . .'

For just a second, Pluke wondered about the ill fortune that might befall him if he walked on the grave or even on the ground immediately surrounding the grave, but rapidly decided that the hole in the quarry floor was no longer a grave. It did not qualify because it did not contain the remains of a dead person and in any case, it was not an official grave. It had not been created in consecrated ground nor had it been dug in any other approved place. It was that thought which reminded him once again about the burial of Mrs Burholme – he could now dimly recall she had not been buried in a consecrated grave. That was something he must check.

From the point of view of encouraging bad luck, however, there seemed to be no problem. Smiling, he therefore agreed to the proposals.

'I shall drive you to the scene,' said Inspector Russell before Wayne Wain could offer his services. 'And will it be in order for the TV reporter to join us in the car? He can discuss his requirements with you during the journey, that will save both his time and yours.'

'By all means,' consented Detective Inspector Pluke.

And so, leaving Wayne Wain to ponder the nature of his boss's enlightenment and to log the outcome of his afternoon's visit to Barughdale, Pluke dressed himself in his voluminous old coat and panama hat with its blue band, checked that his four-leaved clover was still thriving in its pot on his desk, then joined Inspector Russell. With him was a tubby but youthful TV reporter called Jonathan Kipling. They strode towards Inspector Russell's car and within minutes were heading once again towards Harman's Farm with the TV crew vehicle immediately behind. As they progressed along the road towards Barughdale, Kipling was outlining his plans.

'I was thinking, Mr Pluke, that we might get a shot of Mill Hill as well, with you explaining how the girl was seen there on Friday. You could explain to camera that you want viewers to contact you with any other sightings of her, especially those which might have occurred later on Friday evening and all day Saturday. Those shots will take only a few minutes, once we get the equipment in position, and then we could visit the quarry and do a sequence with you at the graveside. I think the shot we need is one of you holding the look-alike spade and talking to camera, asking for the public to look out for similar spades which might have been thrown away or sold in car boot sales or whatever. I am really pleased you have agreed to this because our viewers do appreciate being able to examine the actual scene of a murder, Mr Pluke. It carries such great impact and our news editor does like to incorporate realism in our programmes.'

The outcome was that Montague Pluke, in his oddly distinctive overcoat, panama hat and spats, stood on the roadside at Mill Hill and made an appeal for viewers to report any further sightings of the deceased. When the item eventually appeared on the TV screens, it would be accompanied by an artist's impression of the girl, complete with white anorak and black haversack, a drawing based on official photographs and descriptions provided by witnesses.

Newspaper cameramen who had also wanted pictures of Pluke at Mill Hill and the graveside had followed the TV car and thus they achieved their objective too. The Pluke motorcade then headed for the quarry, with Inspector Russell depositing Pluke and Kipling while he went off to notify Eric Burholme of their presence. That was a small courtesy insisted upon by Pluke. Pluke was then asked by Jonathan Kipling to stand close to the hole in the ground with the spade in his hand. He explained that the camera would look across the open grave which, when on screen, would appear directly before Pluke. It would present a dark and empty oblong hole almost at his feet. A very emotive picture, they all felt, a telling illustration of the emptiness and futility of death, particularly when the grave had contained the mortal remains of one so young and beautiful.

After one or two spade-waving takes with Pluke explaining the urgent need to trace the identical spade which had dug this grave, the crew expressed their satisfaction with the TV recording session whereupon the newspaper journalists did likewise. In that modern manner, therefore, Detective Inspector Pluke managed to put across his vital messages. He felt sure lots of people would respond to his appeal and contact the incident room with sightings of the girl; likewise, he believed that lots of others might wonder where they had seen that spade. Perhaps they would wonder why the spade they had bought at that car boot sale had been such a bargain . . .

Everyone having expressed their satisfaction with the photographic sessions, the news men departed to process the results of their work. It was while Pluke and Russell were preparing for their return to the incident room that they noticed the tall, slim figure of Eric Burholme watching from a distance. He made no effort to approach Pluke or any of the camera teams, and when they all departed, Burholme quietly retreated towards his massive house.

Pluke watched him and said to Inspector Russell, 'That's Eric Burholme, inspector, the owner of this farm and the quarry. I mention that so that you are familiar with one of the leading players in our Crickledale drama.'

'Yes, Mr Pluke, I know. I'd never met him until a few minutes ago. I told him we were on his land, filming. He's a suspect, isn't he? We've got him in the frame, in the incident room, even though he's not been formally interviewed.'

'Really? In the frame? Then I must ask that his name be removed from the frame, inspector,' said Pluke without giving his reason. 'Suspect he might be; a candidate for our racecourse-type frame he most definitely is not.'

'But, Mr Pluke, it's part of our tradition, the tradition of all incident rooms which deal with murders. When I was in CID, it was a long-standing custom that the names of all murder suspects were placed in a frame—'

'Who said anything about Mr Burholme being a murder suspect, inspector?' asked Pluke. 'I have not confirmed the death as a murder; it has always been described as a suspicious death, no more than that, and I regard our investigation as a murder-*type* enquiry. I do realise that others persist in calling it a murder and am happy for that to continue in order to maintain its high profile. I trust Mr Burholme will, in due course, be eliminated from any suspicion of murder.'

'Oh, I see. I thought he was under intense investigation.'

'Investigation, yes, Inspector Russell. But investigation is not necessarily suspicion. So please do not consider him as being in the frame. And I trust you will ensure your newshound friends never refer to him as a suspect.'

'I'll see to that, of course. Will you remove the name from the frame?'

'I will indeed,' said Pluke as their car left the quarry and returned to Crickledale Police Station.

It was around this same time that detectives returned to the incident room for a brief break. They relaxed and refreshed themselves with a mug of tea and a biscuit or two before

136

continuing work until 9 p.m.; it was a useful break when experiences were discussed, yarns exchanged and a good deal of very pertinent information gained. Pluke enjoyed this rather informal system.

'I am going to join my officers over a welcome mug of tea,' he told Wayne Wain. 'I need to learn what they have discovered during the first part of their day's activities. Will you join us?'

'Yes, sir,' enthused Wayne Wain, still anxious to know what had caused Pluke to come to his secretive conclusions about Eric Burholme. But such delicate and confidential matters could not be discussed within ear-shot of a crowd of intelligence-gathering, ear-wigging detectives. In police stations across the country, walls have more ears than most normal walls, and secrets can easily be revealed, so Wayne Wain was prepared to wait. Pluke would explain in due course.

Not every operational detective returned to the incident room for this afternoon tea-break; a few were quite simply too far away at the time, or involved in such intense questioning that a break would interrupt their train of thought and not be conducive to good CID work. But where possible, the majority did try to reach base for a hectic half-hour or so of swapping yarns, drinking tea, munching biscuits and trying to persuade the female civilian staff to join them for drinks in the pub when the day's work ended. Wayne Wain was especially to the forefront in the latter schemes. Pluke took this same opportunity to meet and chat somewhat informally with his officers. It was a relaxed 'meet-the-staff' exercise, or a periodic general human resources co-ordinated consultation, as it might be termed in these enlightened times. Circulating with a mug and a biscuit in his hands, Pluke wandered among the detectives, chatting to them and listening to accounts of their activities.

During that half-hour, he learned that the house-to-house visits in Crickledale and district had not produced any positive sightings of the victim. Even those along the Crickledale to Barughdale road had not produced any further sightings of the walking girl although she had been spotted at a garage. On the edge of the town, just before ordered suburbia became dramatic countryside, there stood a petrol service station with a shop attached – it was one of those garages where it was difficult to obtain a sparking plug or distributor cap for the car but very easy to buy a bunch of flowers, tin of biscuits or bar of chocolate. Sometime around four thirty on Friday afternoon, the lady cashier, Mrs Rafferton, had noticed the arrival of the hiking blonde; she'd approached the garage forecourt where she had attracted the attention of Mrs Rafferton because she had no motor vehicle with her. Then she had entered the shop, bought a bar of chocolate and a carton of blackcurrant drink, paid cash and departed. She had been alone at the time and no one had waited outside for her. She had spoken nicely with no discernible accent. When shown the photographs of the deceased, Mrs Rafferton was able to confirm it was the same woman. Half an hour later, she'd been seen walking at Mill Hill – the timings supported the theory that she had walked all the way. But there was no other sighting of her at this stage, either in Crickledale or beyond.

The next negative return followed the scrupulous examination of dozens of differing types of farm machinery by the massed ranks of officers of the Task Force and some from Pluke's incident room. They had scrutinised a bewildering variety of agricultural machines throughout the district and their examination had included all those currently laid up, whether for servicing or use later in the year. Pluke discovered that every machine had been checked for signs of damage, blood or missing parts of the kind which would have caused the deceased's head injury but nothing suspicious had been found. Pluke did accept that it was virtually impossible to be one hundred per cent sure that no small part from any of these monsters had been involved in the death but he had to concede that it did begin to appear that the victim's head injuries had not come from a component part of any of Mr Burholme's machines nor indeed those belonging to any other person.

A similar exercise at the town's Camping and Outdoor Activities Shop had also produced a negative result. Detectives had been shown a bewildering array of tent pegs, tent poles and other curious camping, mountaineering or rock-climbing aids, all with pointed ends but made from metal, wood or plastic. Some nine-inch spiked tent pegs made from metal did appear to have similarities to the wound in the girl's head but when these were examined by Mr Meredith, the pathologist, the pegs were shown to be too large. Something slightly more slender had killed the girl.

A search of other likely objects in the shop failed to find anything which could have produced that particular wound. Pluke reminded them that craft shops should be examined, along with those premises occupied by sculptors, farriers, blacksmiths, stone masons, wood workers, tool makers and repairers, garden centres and any other place which might sell or make use of sharp pointed objects of the requisite dimensions. It was indicated to Pluke, however, by one of the detectives, that if a foreign visitor to this country had used such an implement on the girl, then it might not boast the same measurements as something of British manufacture. A peg or pole for use with a foreign tent might be of a completely different size. Pluke said he would bear that possibility in mind, and it then occurred to him that a person who carved the words on ornamental gravestones and memorials of various kinds might have the sort of tool that would cause such an injury. And such a person, if he was employed in the burial business, might have grave-digging expertise too, or even a spade. He suggested a detective visited Crumble and Smirch, Undertakers, Embalmers, Funeral Carriage Masters and Ornamental Stone Masons of Crickledale, to see whether anyone had removed such a tool from the premises, or whether anyone had encountered the blonde victim. They might even enquire whether any member of staff had dug the woman's grave or had loaned or hired a spade in recent days.

More specifically, the absentee blonde Dutch au pair Marijka de Jong, had been traced to a new employer in Norwich where she was alive and well; similarly, the current blonde girlfriend of Mr Hebden, the Romeo show-attender from Pasture House Farm, had been found alive and well, as were other women from his recent relationships. None of Mr Burholme's other customers appeared to have unsavoury romantic secrets and their blonde wives and girlfriends were all accounted for.

As Pluke gathered the available intelligence, it became very evident that it consisted entirely of negative news, other than the positive sighting in the garage shop. Even that welcome incident did little to further the investigation, other than to support the theory that the girl had walked from Crickledale towards Barughdale and Harman's Farm. In a sense, it confirmed the Mill Hill sighting by providing further evidence that the same girl had been spotted and that she was indeed the quarry victim.

From this, Pluke drew the conclusion that the girl had hitch-hiked alone from Newcastle-upon-Tyne via the A19 on Friday, arriving safely in Crickledale in mid-afternoon where she had spoken to Mrs Cholmondeley. She'd wanted to know the way to Barughdale, by service bus if possible, and upon leaving Mrs Cholmondeley's had gone to the bus station, on foot in all probability. There, she'd enquired about bus times to Barughdale, using an Ordnance Survey map to clarify her request because her pronunciation of Barughdale had confused local folk, and once she had learned there was no bus in the next couple of hours, she'd decided to walk. Before setting off, she had opted for a snack in the bus station cafeteria. Once on the road, she'd been seen at the garage shop, and later at Mill Hill – then nothing. She had not arrived in Barughdale, only two miles away from Mill Hill, and was not known there, nor was she expected there. It was quite likely that Barughdale had never been her intended destination.

And she had turned up a day and a half later, dead in a grave in a roadside quarry. There was a possibility she had travelled to this country by ferry from Sweden, for Pluke was convinced, because of the mirror in the grave, that either she was of Swedish nationality or the person who had buried her was Swedish.

Pluke knew that such an attractive girl could not disappear from the face of the earth without someone noticing her presence when alive – if she had been on that road after five o'clock on Friday, then someone must have seen her. If no one had seen her, then it suggested she had not walked much further. As he contemplated this scenario, he wondered whether, instead of walking to Harman's Farm through the main gate and via the road across the fields, she might have taken the footpath over the stile and through the field of red cows. That path did lead towards the quarry and onwards to Harman's Farm. Being a public footpath, it would be shown on an Ordnance Survey map from which she would have been able to see that it provided a modest short cut to the farm. Pluke now realised he had not, in his TV appearance or his radio and newspaper interviews, specifically asked ramblers, hikers and campers to report sightings of her. But surely they would contact the police if they had viewed his other appeals?

He could only wait until his general appeal was broadcast in tonight's television programmes and tomorrow's daily papers. But the more he analysed the situation, the more he concluded that the answer to all his riddles lay within Harman's Farm and possibly the quarry. His enquiries had placed the victim on the road which ran past the farm entrance – she'd not been seen alive anywhere else apart from those known locations in Crickledale.

Although he dearly wished to interview Eric Burholme, he had to steel himself to wait until the girl's name was known, along with her reason for coming to the Crickledale area or Harman's Farm in particular. If Burholme was taking active steps to conceal his past and perhaps some of his more recent behaviour, then Pluke needed as much information as possible before questioning him as a key suspect. He would not let Detective Superintendent Bromley of the Yard realise Burholme was being questioned as a suspect, of course; if challenged, Pluke would say the interrogation was that of a witness, not a suspect.

Pluke turned his attention to the map which adorned the wall of the incident room. It was an inch-to-the-mile Ordnance Survey map of the locality, one used extensively by the teams, and although Pluke had made use of the map during this investigation, he had never studied in detail the footpaths around the quarry. He now saw that if the girl had had this edition of the map – the most recently published – then she would indeed have noticed that the path across the red cow field would provide a short cut.

Pluke went closer to study the map. He found the Crickledale to Barughdale road and with his finger traced its direct route across the moors. He found Mill Hill, named after a derelict mill which had long since been demolished. And then he saw another

141

footpath; it left the road near Mill Hill and led towards the quarry. This was not the one he'd used yesterday. Pluke had not noticed any footpath signs along the road near Mill Hill but that did not detract from the fact that the path existed.

Even if the sign had fallen down or been vandalised, the path was clearly shown and it led diagonally from the road towards the woodland near Harman's Quarry. Not far from Harman's Quarry, it joined the major path which Pluke had used, and which Michael Wardle had been using before he'd found the body. By using that path from Mill Hill, the journey to the farm was reduced by at least a mile. So, Montague reasoned, if the girl had been heading for Harman's Farm on foot and making full use of the map in her possession, then she would surely have taken this route? And if she had taken that route soon after five o'clock, it would explain why no one had seen her on the road beyond that point. She'd have left the road by the time the office workers had travelled this way. He decided to wait until his appeals had been broadcast and the officers had completed today's enquiries before further considering the importance of this unsigned path – but its presence did mean that more hikers, ramblers and campers would have to be sought and interviewed.

At that point he remembered that a team had gone to interview Michael Wardle in depth. He remained a prime suspect because he had found the body and he had not yet been eliminated. Pluke went over to Inspector Horsley.

'Mr Horsley,' he said. 'The man who found the body, Wardle. Have we had any report from the team who were sent to interview him?'

'Just a preliminary report, sir, to say that when they arrived at his house this morning, just before noon that was, he was not at home. The teams asked my authority to await his return rather than make a second journey all the way to Portrack-on-Tees. Enquiries from the neighbours did not reveal his whereabouts.'

'He had no idea our officers were *en route*?'

'Oh, no, they wanted to surprise him. He has no job, so he's probably out walking. Or shopping.'

'It was a genuine address then?' Pluke asked with just a hint of apprehension.

'Oh, yes, he gave us his correct name and address when we interviewed him at the scene.'

'So we await the outcome of their enquiries?'

'We do, Montague. Why, he's not really a suspect, is he?'

Pluke then explained his discovery of the unsigned footpath and suggested that any ramblers, hikers and campers using the path on Friday might have seen the girl. He did not lose sight of the fact, however, that few could be expected on that path during a weekday out of the holiday season. Weekends were the busy time for such routes – Wardle had been hiking on a Sunday. But if the girl had been observed on that path, then it was surely an indication she had been making specifically for Harman's Farm rather than the village of Barughdale.

Having listened to his detectives, Pluke now returned to his own office as the men began to drift outside, refreshed and keen to get on with the remainder of their enquiries. Before settling down, however, he pressed the intercom and asked Horsley to come in and see him.

'Ah, Mr Horsley,' he said when the detective inspector came into his office. 'Out there we have Eric Burholme high in the frame, as a suspect, that is.'

'That's right, Montague. It's logical, the body was found on his land.'

'I have to ask you to remove his name, at least for the time being,' said Montague. 'Please don't ask me why – I am not allowed to say, except I will tell you that the order has come from somewhere on high. Very high, in fact.'

'But you will be interviewing him, surely?'

'I will, Mr Horsley, you can be sure about that. But if anyone asks – anyone on high, that is – then you may tell them I am treating him as a witness, not a suspect.'

'But I don't understand, Montague, neither will our teams. In fact, I'll tell you this. They've put money on him, he's five-to-one at the moment. Favourite in fact, with Wardle at ten-to-one and all others at a hundred.'

'Favourite for what, Mr Horsley?'

'Being arrested for murder, Montague.'

'You must be aware that I have doubts whether or not this is murder, Mr Horsley, consequently I am describing it merely as a suspicious death which is being investigated in a murder-type manner. I do not categorise it as murder.'

'Well, you know what detectives are. They think they know best. But I will remove Burholme's name from the frame. I think I will allow the bets to stand.'

'Yes, that will be acceptable. I should hate the Chief Constable or Detective Superintendent Hart from headquarters to come in and see Burholme's name so prominently featured in our frame.'

'Right, leave it with me. Now, while you were out, Inspector Binn from the Yard rang, from the Interpol office. It's not urgent, he said he'd ring back.'

'There was no message?'

'No, none. Nothing important.'

'I shall ring him,' said Montague.

'No, there's no point, he said he had to pop out and would call back.'

'Then I shall await his pleasure,' smiled Montague.

Horsley left to go about the business of running the incident room and, as he left, Wayne Wain entered.

'Caught you on your own at last, sir,' he beamed, closing the door and easing a chair forward. 'So what's all this about Burholme, sir? You have a theory?'

'Well, Wayne, it is somewhat complicated, but this is how I see the situation—'

And then the telephone rang.

'It's Binn from the Yard,' said the voice when Montague responded.

12

'Detective Inspector Pluke, Crickledale CID,' Montague announced into the mouthpiece.

'It's Binn from the Yard, Mr Pluke,' repeated the friendly voice

144

from the Interpol office. 'I have an update for you, although I'm sorry it's negative. We've contacted the Swedish Embassy here in London as well as the police authorities in Sweden, and to their knowledge there are no missing Swedish women who fit the description of your dead woman. Rather like the British police, they don't maintain records of all women who have left home; they list only those for whom there is special concern, or perhaps a criminal association. They don't list those who have run away with another's husband, for example. We have received copies of the photographs of your victim, and her fingerprints, thank you – E-mail is a wonderful device, is it not? – and we have sent copies to the Swedish authorities. But at the moment the simple message is that no girl of that description has been reported missing in Sweden. That's all I can say.'

'Would your office have lists of Swedish women who might have travelled to this country in recent weeks?'

'If one fled the country while being sought for a serious crime – murder, robbery, drugs or whatever – then yes, we might be informed, otherwise, no. To trace the movements of a woman *not* suspected of involvement in any criminal activity, you'd have to contact the respective immigration and emigration offices.'

'I realise that. Now, since my initial call to you, Inspector Binn, I have some reason to believe our victim came into this country by ferry from Göthenburg, arriving in Newcastle-upon-Tyne as recently as Friday. She appears to have hitch-hiked from there to Crickledale and it seems she was alone.'

'Yes, your officers have been in touch with me, but if your woman arrived on Friday, presumably on a routine visit of some kind or a holiday, then she will hardly be considered missing at this early stage. Certainly, she would not feature upon our lists – unless, as I said, there was a criminal link of some kind.'

'Thank you for your help, Inspector Binn. Am I to understand that you will register my continuing interest?'

'Your enquiry will be logged and marked for regular updating, Mr Pluke, and if our computers later generate a response which is of interest to you, then of course I shall be in touch. I would also ask you to let me know her identity if and when it is established, Mr Pluke. We can then compare the name with our records – who knows what we might turn up?'

'Yes indeed,' responded Pluke, wondering if Interpol knew anything about the past life of Eric Burholme. 'Thank you for your help.'

After replacing his telephone, Pluke looked at Wayne Wain and said, 'Well, Wayne, no luck with Interpol,' and then explained the situation. 'So it looks as if all depends upon our men in Newcastle.'

'If you have grave suspicions about Eric Burholme, sir, surely it would be wise to bring him in for interview now?'

'No, Wayne, not yet. That is my decision.'

'I was thinking it needn't be a very formal interview, sir, not the sort of grilling you'd give to a real suspect. We could get him to detail his movements on Friday and Saturday without delving too deeply into his background and I think we should search the farmhouse as well, for her fingerprints or any belongings.'

'If what I suspect about Eric Burholme is correct, Wayne, there will be no evidence of that girl in his house. No fingerprints, no belongings, not a scrap of evidence of her presence. And he will have convincing answers designed to persuade us that he was not known to her, and that she did not come to his house. Remember, we do have his wheelbarrow, though.'

'You've obviously got strong reasons for coming to your conclusion – you were about to explain your theories, sir, before we were interrupted.'

'I was indeed, Wayne, for I think you should know my reasoning, you being my deputy. Now, this is what I have concluded. I would ask you not to discuss this with anyone else, not at this stage. When the first important piece of evidence—'

And then the telephone rang. Wayne sighed as Pluke picked up the receiver and said, 'Detective Inspector Pluke, Crickledale CID.'

'Front office, sir,' said the voice. 'I'm holding a call from a man who thinks he might have seen that girl, sir. I can't put him through to the incident room, the line's engaged. I wondered if you would speak to the man?'

'Yes of course, put him through.'

Pluke listened as the telephone made noises which indicated a connection was being made, and then a voice said, 'Hello.'

'This is Detective Inspector Pluke of Crickledale CID. To whom am I speaking?'

'The name's Stanton, Mr Pluke. Jim Stanton from Quenby.'

'And how can I help you, Mr Stanton?'

'That lass that's been found at Harman's Quarry. Me and the missus might have seen her.'

'Really?' Pluke's eyebrows registered his excitement and interest as he asked the question he felt most important at this stage. 'When do you think you saw her?'

'Saturday morning.'

'Saturday?' Pluke's eyebrows rose even higher. 'What time – roughly, if you can't be precise?'

'Half-ten or thereabouts, I'd say. Me and the missus were going to the supermarket in Crickledale – we thought we'd get there in good time. So we took the car and drove from our house, through Barughdale and past Harman's Farm, then into Crickledale. She was standing on the gate, Mr Pluke, like a kid would do. You know, standing on the second or third bar and looking over the top.'

'The farm gate, you mean?'

'Aye, the big five bar gate.'

'Was she alone?'

'Aye, she was. Nobody with her. We thought it funny because we know Eric Barholme and reckoned she wasn't anything to do with him. We thought she might be camping in that quarry of his – lots do, Mr Pluke.'

'If I despatch one of my officers to talk to you immediately, Mr Stanton, with a photograph of the girl along with her description, perhaps you and your wife could tell us if this is indeed the same person?'

'Aye, glad to help. We'll be in for the rest of the evening. We heard about it on the radio just now, BBC Radio Cleveland. On the five o'clock news.'

Pluke then appreciated the speed at which journalists could operate – this item had probably been telephoned into the news room immediately after the conference, to catch the first available slot.

'I am delighted you heard the item, Mr Stanton. And your address?'

'Beckside Cottage, it's right opposite Quenby War Memorial, Mr Pluke. You can't miss it. We're five miles from Crickledale, by the way.'

'I know your village quite well, Mr Stanton, you have a very fine horse trough near the War Memorial, dating to the seventeenth century. A very fine specimen indeed, made of Pennine granite and bearing the arms of the Quenbys.'

'We're right proud of that trough. You obviously get around, Mr Pluke. Right, well, I'll expect your chap when he gets here.'

'It will be Detective Sergeant Wain,' Pluke advised him before replacing the handset.

'A witness, sir?' Wain had heard only one side of that conversation and so Pluke acquainted him with the necessary facts, adding, 'This suggests she was seen alive on Saturday, Wayne, by two witnesses. And on Burholme's land.'

'She could have slept in his outbuildings that night, or the quarry, without him knowing.'

'She could indeed, but it does put her on his land on *Saturday*, Wain. It is our first confirmation she was alive on Saturday morning – and on Harman's Farm.'

'You want me to go immediately?'

'I do, Wayne. So we'll talk later. Isn't this good news?'

'This could be just the breakthrough we've been looking for,' and Wayne Wain prepared to leave for Quenby. Minutes later he was *en route*.

In an attempt to maintain the impetus in the Plukedom, Montague left his office and went through to the now quiet room and told the resident staff the good news; it meant the time chart, now prominently displayed on the wall, could be updated to show that the victim had been alive on Saturday. When the operational detectives rang in or called in for consultations, they could be notified of this development. This was the first positive evidence of the power of local radio. Pluke was justifiably pleased.

But another call rather jolted him. It came minutes after Wain had left for Quenby. His telephone rang and when he responded, there was a young, tearful woman at the other end. She spoke with a distinctive Tyneside accent.

'Is that Crickledale CID?' she sobbed. 'Is that the people investigating the murder of the young woman in the quarry?'

'Aye, pet,' said Pluke, slipping easily into the accent. 'That's us.' He felt it might make the caller feel more comfortable if he lapsed into the local idiom; she was clearly a young woman from Tyneside – someone who had made contact with the Swedish girl perhaps? He added, 'So how can we help?'

'Well, I hope I'm not being silly, mind, but well, when I heard about the girl on radio, in the quarry that is, well, she's just like a nun from the convent.'

'Nun?' questioned Pluke, thinking of the virginity of the victim.

'Aye, man, a nun.' The caller's voice had ended its sobbing sounds and was getting more confident by this stage. 'From the convent in the hills near Ponteland, you know, Sister Bega.'

'I see. So why do you think the girl in the quarry grave might be Sister Bega?'

'Whey, man, it sounds just like her, you know. Thirties, blonde bobbed hair, blue blouse, jeans, not much with her except a shoulder bag . . . I met her on a retreat I went on, she was lovely, chatty, friendly like and she said she was ganning down to Crickledale this week,' and at this stage, the girl resumed her loud sobbing.

'And who are you?' Pluke spoke very gently.

'Me? Why do you want to know my name?'

'One of our officers will have to come and talk to you—'

'Oh, no, I couldn't do that, man, no, never, not the polis. . .' and the line went dead.

Responding immediately, Pluke pressed 1471 to be informed of the number from which that call came; he was given the number, checked it and discovered it was a telephone kiosk in the suburbs of Newcastle-upon-Tyne. But at least he had a lead – a nun called Bega from a convent near Ponteland. A nun who had talked about a visit to Crickledale. But he did not have a name for the convent nor its precise address. In an attempt to determine that, he could ring either Northumbria police or British Telecom's Talking Pages.

He selected the latter at this juncture and after checking the list of religious organisations in the area, was informed of the existence of the Convent of Our Lady of the Hill, with an address near Ponteland. It was the only one in that area, and he was provided with its telephone number. Now, he was faced with two choices – either he could drive up to Northumberland, a journey of about two hours from Crickledale, and then knock on the door, an action that would surely alarm the sisters in residence, or he could ring and make initial enquiries, even if the call did similarly alarm and upset the residents of the convent. Bearing in mind the shortage of official funds, he opted for the latter.

'Our Lady of the Hill Convent,' said a gentle voice when his call was connected.

'My name is Detective Inspector Montague Pluke,' he began in a formal and informative manner. 'I am the officer in charge of the Criminal Investigation Department at Crickledale in North Yorkshire.'

'Oh dear,' said the voice. 'Is something wrong, officer?'

'That is something I cannot be sure about until I have had words with someone in authority,' he continued in a stern, formal voice.

'I am the duty sister for this evening.' The voice had now hardened slightly. 'I deal with everything in the absence of Reverend Mother, she is in London at the moment, at a conference.'

'Ah, well, thank you. I think I understand, sister. And your name is . . .?'

'Sister Agnes,' she said, now with a somewhat curt tone to her voice.

'Thank you. Well, Sister Agnes, I am ringing to ask if you have a nun within your establishment who is known as Sister Bega.'

'Yes, we do,' and there was a starchiness to her voice by this time.

'Is she with you at this moment?' asked Pluke.

'No, she is not. Might I ask why you are asking all these

questions, Mr Pluke? It will soon be time for us to gather in chapel, you see, before our supper, before we go to bed . . .'

'Do you know where she is?' persisted Pluke.

'She was given leave, Mr Pluke. She is enjoying a short break from the convent, a few days, no more than a week. It is not unusual.'

'And where has she gone? Is that something you can tell me?'

'We do not pry into our sisters' private lives, Mr Pluke, we accord them our confidence in the belief they will not abuse the permitted relaxations.'

'So you don't ask where they are going or why?'

'Not any longer, Mr Pluke. In the past we exercised extremely strict control over our young nuns, but not any more. In these enlightened times, discipline is much more relaxed, discipline comes from within, not without. It is a personal matter now. Our nuns are permitted a break from here, two weeks each year, and we do not impose conditions, we do not ask them to specify their destinations for example, although I must say that most like to spend time with their families.'

'And money, sister? How do they travel without money?'

'We give them pocket money. Families help as a rule, with things like bus and train fares. Mr Pluke, might I ask why you are asking me all these things?'

'Sister, before I answer that, can you tell me if your nuns have shorn heads or any other distinguishing features?'

'No, Mr Pluke. Our regime is much more relaxed than it was in, say, the sixties and seventies. We allow our nuns to keep their hair and even to wear light make-up or modest items of jewellery. A relaxed appearance helps in our work with young girls. But, Mr Pluke, why are you asking all these questions? Is Bega in trouble?'

He took a deep breath and said, 'Sister Agnes, yesterday – Monday – the body of a young woman was found in a shallow grave near Crickledale. She was suffering from an injury to her head.'

'Oh, Mr Pluke, oh, no, surely not . . .'

'The victim is about thirty years of age with short bobbed hair, blonde, and she was dressed in a light blue blouse, jeans and trainer shoes. There was no means of identification with her and, apart from a handkerchief, she had no possessions.'

'Oh, Mr Pluke, oh, this is dreadful . . . it does sound like Bega, yes indeed.'

'I have photographs,' he said, 'of the body. And if it is her, we should require someone to come to Crickledale to make the formal identification.'

'I do not know what to say, Mr Pluke, really I don't. Do you really think it is Bega?'

'We received a telephone call, not many minutes ago, from a young woman who said she'd met Bega on a retreat, and the description tallied. Unfortunately, the caller rang off without leaving a name.'

'That's understandable, we do a lot of work for orphans and the under-privileged as well as helping girls who have been forced into drugs and prostitution. I can understand that caller not wishing to get involved with the police.'

'If I drive to your convent, Sister Agnes, I can be there within a couple of hours, with a photograph of our victim and a description of her clothes. Could you make time to meet me?'

'In the circumstances, yes, of course, Mr Pluke. Of course.'

'Then I shall leave immediately,' he told her and, after obtaining directions to the convent, he replaced the telephone.

Pluke then realised he had no driver. Wayne Wain was at Quenby interviewing vital witnesses so Pluke approached Horsley and asked if he could spare Detective Constable Paula Helston once more. As soon as Horsley realised the importance of this lead, he readily consented.

Pluke asked Horsley to ring Northumbria police to acquaint them with the fact that he was soon to enter their area to undertake these enquiries. Within minutes, Pluke was sitting beside the young detective as she guided a white, unmarked Astra from the police station yard.

'This enquiry might necessitate a little overtime by you,' Pluke told her after giving her directions to the convent. 'But I think, in view of our destination, it is wise to have a female presence. I am not quite sure how to deal with nuns, Detective Constable Helston.'

'They are no different from other women, sir!' She smiled at his discomfort.

'I am not really very good at dealing with women at all,' he said in all seriousness. 'Now, tell me about yourself, tell me about your aims and aspirations as a detective.'

While Pluke and his driver headed north along the A19 to Tyneside, Wayne Wain was sitting in front of the fire at Beckside Cottage, Quenby, with a file of paper and statement forms on the floor, while enjoying a large slice of fruit cake and a mug of hot tea. This was the homely abode of Mr and Mrs Jim Stanton. Jim and Judith, as they had introduced themselves, were both in their fifties; Jim worked for the Forestry Commission and Judith had a part-time job in a stationery shop in Crickledale. Having established the background of the couple, Wayne began to question them, his charm and good looks winning over Mrs Stanton within minutes; she thought he looked like Pete Sampras, the tennis player.

'So,' he began, 'when you rang our office, you told us you had seen the girl on Saturday morning, at the gate which leads into Eric Burholme's farm. You got a good look at her?'

'Judith better than me,' Stanton said. 'I was driving, heading for Crickledale. I noticed the lass standing on the gate, looking over it, and pointed her out to Judith.'

'And she was alone? You are sure of that?'

'She was, there's no doubt about it.'

Wayne eased a photograph from his file and passed it to Judith. 'I'm afraid that's all we have,' he apologised. 'We haven't issued this to the press yet, but can you say whether that is the girl you saw?'

'Oh yes,' she said without hesitation. 'That's her. Pale blue blouse, jeans ... that blonde hair bobbed like it is ... oh, yes, sergeant, that's the girl.'

'And you don't know her?'

'No,' said Mrs Stanton. 'I've never seen her before. I've no idea who she is but, as Jim said, we thought it was one of Eric's girls.'

'Eric's girls?' puzzled Wayne Wain. 'You mean he has daughters?'

'Oh, no, he didn't have a family,' Judith said. 'His wife was handicapped, physically, I mean. She broke her back in a horse-riding accident, years ago, sergeant, not long after he came to live here. He got domestic assistance for the house while he looked after his wife – he did everything for her. Fed her, washed her, dressed her, real devoted he was. But he employed girls to clean and cook, that sort of thing.'

'Devoted to his wife, he was. He's a real nice chap, sergeant,' Jim Stanton confirmed. 'He was devastated when she died.'

'And when was that?'

'Oh, a long while back. Fifteen years mebbe. Then he never bothered with domestics after that, he did it all himself. The housework, I mean. He couldn't bear to sit around doing nothing after he'd worked night and day to look after his wife, so he extended the hire business as well. Keeps the place immaculate, he does. He never stops work, sergeant, and makes good money but gives most of it away. A very decent bloke all round. Very set ideas on some things, though!'

'Set ideas?' asked Wayne. 'Such as?'

'Well, he's not a Christian, he doesn't believe in God. He reckons nature rules the world and everything in it. Keeps things very tidy and straight, always cleans up after himself. I once went to a demonstration with him, at the North Yorkshire Show. We had wine and a buffet, and when he'd finished he started to clean up the table we'd been using, instead of leaving it. He laughed and said he always did that, cleaned up after himself so you'd never know he'd been there. He's very strict with himself, you know. Never lets himself go . . .'

'Well, he is entitled to his own opinions and lifestyle,' said Wain. 'So if he has not employed domestics recently, it is unlikely this girl worked for him?'

'Yes, you're right, but that was my first reaction,' said Jim. 'He usually managed to pick pretty blondes! Us local chaps always said he had an eye for a good-looking woman!'

'Had he a reputation then, for womanising?'

'No, not at all. Too devoted to his wife, he was. But he liked having pretty women around him. His wife was pretty as well, a blonde.'

'If this girl had nothing to do with him, we wondered if she had been camping in the quarry or sleeping in his buildings,' Wayne told them. 'There is a possibility she went there to shelter from the thunderstorms.'

'Not on Friday night or Saturday morning, sergeant,' said Jim. 'The radio said you'd seen her in Crickledale on Friday, but the thunder didn't come until Saturday evening, around tea-time. And there was none on Friday. We saw her on Saturday morning, long before it thundered.'

'Yes, that's right, she was seen in Crickledale on Friday,' Wayne reminded them. 'We have a positive identification. You work in Crickledale, Mrs Stanton. Did you see her at all, in town or walking this way around five?'

'Sorry, no, sergeant. I finish at one o'clock on Fridays and get a lift home with a friend. So I'd not have been on the road at the time she was.'

'OK, thanks. Now we know she was seen walking towards Harman's Farm, she was spotted at Mill Hill around five or five thirty. On Friday afternoon, that was. And she was not seen again on Friday or Saturday. Yours is the only Saturday sighting.'

'Well, if Eric didn't take her in, I suppose she could have camped out in the quarry on Friday night,' admitted Jim. 'She had no camping gear when we saw her, she carried nothing in fact. Not even a handbag, that's why we thought she might have been at his house, going out for a morning walk after a late breakfast. But we'd never know if she was camping in the quarry, sergeant, it's impossible to see into it from the road. She could have gone into Eric's buildings, I suppose, if she wanted somewhere dry to sleep, mebbe without him realising. She must have been somewhere around that area on Friday night, mustn't she? On his land or in one of his buildings? Have you asked Eric?'

'We have,' said Wayne. 'And we've shown him that photo-graph. He says he's never seen her and doesn't know her.'

'Well, he's not the sort of chap to tell a lie, sergeant, a very straight man, is Eric Burholme, always has been. Honest and trustworthy, something that's too rare among businessmen.'

'Well, thanks for your help,' said Wayne Wain, rising to leave and gathering up his papers. 'You have been extremely helpful.'

'You don't think Eric murdered her, do you?' suggested Judith Stanton as the couple followed him to the door.

'My chief thinks not,' said Wayne Wain. 'He tends to think she met someone in the quarry, probably not by design.'

'Well, yes, that does make sense. You never know who's wandering about these days. Eric would never do a thing like that, would he, Jim?'

'He wouldn't hurt a fly, he's much too decent. But if he had killed her, I reckon he'd make a good job of cleaning up after himself!' laughed Jim Stanton as Wayne reached his car. 'There wouldn't be much left for you blokes to find.'

Thinking about this character assessment, Wayne was soon heading back to Crickledale and the Plukedom. Pluke would be delighted at this news – but he'd be puzzled too.

And hadn't Eric Burholme said something about being away in Harrogate on Saturday? Bearing in mind the girl was at his gate at ten thirty that morning, Wayne wondered what time Burholme had left the house.

13

Pluke was unable to hear an account of Wayne Wain's interview because he was heading for the wilds of Northumberland. Later, a combination of Montague Pluke's map reading and Paula Helston's driving brought them safely to the front door of the hilltop convent a few miles north of Ponteland, pronounced Ponteeland. It was a massive place, a former fortified farmhouse, and it was surrounded by neat gardens and well-kept lawns with some conifers in the northern corner. A gravelled drive led towards the front door where Paula saw a sign which said 'Parking for Visitors'.

'You had better accompany me into this essentially female establishment.' Clutching his briefcase somewhat nervously, Pluke studied the imposing front door, a massive structure of wood and iron fittings. Above it was a wall-mounted platform supporting a colourful statue of the Virgin Mary. Followed by his driver, he climbed out of the car and approached the building. To the right of the front door was a brass bell-pull, highly polished. He pulled it. Deep inside, they heard the sound of a mighty clanging and, after what seemed a considerable wait, the sounds of approaching footsteps echoing on the marble floor within. There was a clanking of bolts being withdrawn and the huge door yawned to reveal a tiny nun in a dark blue calf-length dress-style habit with white epaulettes and cuffs. She wore no hat, and her dark hair was held back from her face by a white ribbon. There was no sign of grey in her hair, her face was unlined and Pluke reckoned she would be in her early fifties – a capable woman no doubt, and not one to tolerate any nonsense. He could almost visualise her as a matron in a private hospital.

Standing in the doorway, she looked in undisguised amazement at the peculiarly clad gentleman with the briefcase. Sporting dark-rimmed spectacles, he now stood before her with his vintage overcoat of tatty colours, his panama hat with its blue band, his spats and his blue bow tie. The young lady who accompanied him was more soberly dressed in a smart green jacket and skirt, offset nicely with a white blouse and brown shoes.

'Oh,' she said, as an apology for so readily opening the door to strangers, 'I was expecting the police . . .'

'We are the police,' beamed Montague, producing his warrant card and showing it to the nun.

'Oh,' she said in a small voice, doubtless thinking that Northumbrian detective inspectors did not look like this.

'We are Detective Inspector Pluke and Detective Constable Helston from Crickledale CID. I spoke to Sister Agnes earlier. We are expected.'

157

'I am Sister Agnes. Well, you must come in, detective inspector. We do get quite a lot of visits from the local police, as I am sure you can understand. It is due to the nature of our work with girls in trouble. Now, follow me.'

She led them from the marble-floored hall with its pillars and curved staircase into an ante-room to the right of the main door. Splendid though the surroundings were, this room was sparsely furnished with a solid oak table in the centre surrounded by half a dozen chairs. Colourful paintings of religious and biblical scenes adorned the pale blue emulsioned walls and a crucifix hung above the fireplace. The mantelpiece contained photographs of some nuns from a bygone age, sepia-tinted copies portraying fierce-looking women carrying rosaries, and there was a vase of flowers on the window ledge. His belief that Sister Agnes was efficient was proved by the presence of a brown folder on the table.

'Please sit down, both of you. May I offer you a drink? You have come a long way.'

Normally Pluke would have refused but on this occasion, bearing in mind their lengthy journey and sensing that a community of nuns was not likely to bribe a British police officer, he accepted. Tea was offered, with biscuits, and Sister Agnes pressed a bell-push on the wall; seconds later, another nun appeared at the door from whom tea and biscuits were ordered and the interview began with them sitting at the solid table. Pluke outlined the case in considerably more detail than he had during his telephone call, saying that Detective Constable Helston would take notes of the meeting. Having prepared the way, Pluke took a photograph from his briefcase and passed it to the nun.

'I know this is harrowing, Sister Agnes, but can you tell me whether this is Sister Bega?'

Although she was well prepared for this, tears misted the eyes of the little woman as she nodded and then made the sign of the cross on her head, breast and shoulders.

'Yes, Mr Pluke, yes, that is Bega. God rest her soul. We shall pray for her.'

'Then I am afraid I need to ask you lots more questions about her, sister, and I shall also require someone – a member of the family preferably – to visit Crickledale and make the formal identification . . .'

'She has no family, Mr Pluke; we are her family.'

'I see. Well, perhaps, with your help, I can establish a few facts before we consider the identification processes. I know this has been a shock but our investigation does carry a certain urgency and I would appreciate your co-operation.'

'I shall do everything I can to help, Mr Pluke, and please do not worry about the time. I am at your disposal.'

At that point, tea and biscuits arrived; it helped break the gloomy atmosphere and Pluke felt the interruption was very timely. The new nun, an elderly soul who was not introduced, laid out the plates, cups and saucers, poured the tea and quietly departed. After that pause, Pluke resumed.

'Sister Agnes,' he said, 'in cases of this kind, we can become extremely intrusive and I therefore beg your forgiveness before we start. I need to know everything about Sister Bega, her background and her recent movements. I also need to know why she decided to visit Crickledale and who she was going to see there – and why?'

'There is no guarantee I can answer all your questions, Mr Pluke, but I will do my best.'

'First then, her background. Is Bega her real name, for example?'

With an effort of will-power, Sister Agnes relegated the shock of her friend's death to the back of her mind, and opened the file which lay before her. It was Bega's personal file.

As she spread the papers before her, Agnes said, 'Before you arrived, Mr Pluke, I managed to contact the Reverend Mother and she has authorised me to give whatever co-operation is necessary. As I said earlier, we do work closely with the local police, and therefore we understand your requirements. Your visit is not all that unusual, therefore. Now, to begin, her real name is Miriam Ripley, and she was born on 14 July 1968.'

'And this is her home address?'

159

'It is. She has no other home.'

'And where did she come from, before she entered the convent?'

'She has always been here, Mr Pluke. She was placed in our care when she was a baby. She was reared in the convent, went to our school and later decided to join the Order.'

'She was an orphan, then?'

'No, but she was born out of wedlock, Mr Pluke. Her mother, Josephine, came from a strict Catholic family and when she got pregnant, Josephine's parents sent her here to have the child, out of the sight of family and friends. After giving birth, she returned to her parents in Newcastle, and the baby remained with us. Such secrecy was a feature of some staunch Catholic families, Mr Pluke, but it is not our practice to condemn. Our Order cares for such girls, and so we cared for the baby Miriam.'

'So she has always lived here, and became a nun. When?'

'She became a novice when she was eighteen and professed when she was twenty-four. I might add she has always been a valued member of our Order, a hard-working, intelligent young woman. She will be missed, Mr Pluke . . .' and the nun pulled a handkerchief from her robes, wiping her eyes and blowing her nose. It looked just like the handkerchief found on the body of Sister Bega – standard issue.

'And her parents? Where are they now?'

'The name of her father was never known, Mr Pluke, it is not even given on her birth certificate which simply says "Father Unknown".' Sister Agnes produced it from the file, passing the document to Pluke as if to support her claim. 'But you will see that her mother was called Josephine Ripley and that her profession is shown as domestic assistant.'

'A local woman?'

'Yes, Mr Pluke.'

'So where is she now? She will have to be informed of her daughter's death before we announce the name to the media, sister.'

'She died, Mr Pluke, only a matter of two months ago. And her own parents – Bega's grandparents, that is – are also dead. There are no other members of the family, Mr Pluke. Upon her

160

mother's death, Bega was utterly alone – apart from us, of course. As I said, we are – were – her family.'

'And did Bega's mother – Josephine – keep in touch with her?'

'Yes, she did. You see, we did not adopt Miriam, we merely cared for her along with other girls in a similar situation. Josephine's parents would never allow her illegitimate child in their home – a sad reflection on people who claim to be Christians, Mr Pluke. But Josephine always refused to give up her daughter completely; she would not have her adopted and always remained her mother in legal and practical terms. She loved Miriam, you see, Mr Pluke, and often came to visit her daughter here. Josephine never married. She always lived with her parents, Mr Pluke, she could never afford to buy a place of her own; she had no skills or professional qualifications and could never have survived without parental help. Following the death of her parents, Josephine inherited their home, a modest terrace house in Jesmond. They died about ten years ago, within months of one another. She continued to live there. It gave her some independence at last – she had no rent or mortgage to earn and she took various rather mundane jobs to support herself. She managed very well, better than anyone thought. She was only sixty when she died, a heart attack, we understand.'

'A sad story, Sister Agnes. So the house would be inherited by Bega?'

'Yes. Her mother did not leave much – the house came to Bega, and most of the furniture, fairly cheap stuff really, was sold by auction.'

'So, although she inherited a house, Bega did not want to leave the convent?'

'No, Mr Pluke. By that time, she had professed so she donated the house to us, to the Order. This is her home, you see, and we are in the throes of selling the house now, to help with our finances.'

'You rely on such help?'

'Entirely, Mr Pluke. We do have benefactors, of course, people to provide us with an income through donations, and we do ask parents to help with funding their children here. Various social agencies help too, with government grants and so forth.'

161

'So you survive?'

'Yes, but only just.'

'So Bega never went to live with her mother?'

'No, but she did spend some time with her. She had a holiday with her last year, for a long weekend. Even if Bega had not joined us, I don't think she would have gone to live with her mother. They were very different people, Mr Pluke.'

'Thank you for all this. Now, her holiday, this holiday in Crickledale. It has resulted in such sadness, sister. Did she say why she wanted to visit Crickledale?'

'I talked to her shortly before she left, Mr Pluke, and she seemed very excited. She did not explain the reason for her excitement, though, almost as if she was doing something secretive. She did tell me she was going to the Crickledale area and had managed to get a map of the district. She said she was going on a journey of exploration, Mr Pluke. That was the word she used. Exploration.'

'Exploration? That suggests she had never been there before. She never mentioned Crickledale at any earlier time, then?'

'No, never. It was only after her mother died that I heard her mention the place – perhaps her mother, or her mother's family, had some links with the area, Mr Pluke?'

'Did she mention any particular place or person? What we need to establish is who she was going to see, or where she was intending to stay.'

'No. Other than this rather mysterious exploration idea, she did not give us any idea of her intended destination.'

'And you never asked?'

'No, but if one of our nuns is staying with her family, we expect her to leave an address or telephone number. In Bega's case, she said she would obtain bed-and-breakfast and ring us if she found a more settled place.'

'And did she ring?'

'No, Mr Pluke.'

'And, I suppose, that would add to the mystery of her whereabouts?'

'It did, rather. I must say she did appear somewhat excited,

Mr Pluke. I got the impression something had resulted from her mother's death.'

'And again, you have no idea what that might be?'

'Sorry, no. She never told me. We are – were – good friends, Mr Pluke, I've known her since she professed. After her mother's house had been cleared, she brought a suitcase full of things here, her mother's private papers and so on. There wasn't much but, as next-of-kin, she had a few legal matters to deal with.'

'And where are those things now, sister? The suitcase, I mean, and its contents.'

'I expect they will be in her room, Mr Pluke. She did keep the case there, while she sorted the contents.'

'We shall have to examine it, sister.'

'Must you, Mr Pluke? I'd have thought such things were very private.'

'It is the examination of the very private matters of victims and murderers that enables us to detect crime, Sister Agnes.'

'So when do you want to see her room, detective inspector?'

'In a very few moments – with you present, if you would not mind.'

'Of course, I have authority to provide you with every possible assistance.'

'Now, before we examine her room, when did she leave for Crickledale?'

'Around mid-morning, Mr Pluke, on Friday. She received her holiday money – fifty pounds – and a packed lunch, then set off. Our own transport took her to Newcastle city centre and we thought she would be catching a train to Thirsk or York perhaps. She was given a week's holiday, we expected her to return the following Friday – the coming Friday, in fact.'

'We have reason to believe she hitch-hiked, sister. She told a lady in Crickledale she had hitch-hiked from Newcastle to Thirsk on a lorry, and then got a lift in a private car. With no trouble, I might add.'

'To save money, no doubt, in spite of the dangers.'

'She was seen in Crickledale on Friday afternoon – we have a confirmed sighting – and later the same day she was seen walking towards a village called Barughdale. We have reason to believe she got no further than Harman's Quarry – that's where her body was found, sister. It is part of a complex called Harman's Farm which is on the road between Crickledale and Barughdale.'

'Harman's Farm, Mr Pluke? Is that connected in any way to Harman's Agricultural?'

'Yes, Harman's Agricultural is a farm machinery hire business which is based at Harman's Farm. Why do you ask? Does the name mean something?'

'Harman's Agricultural is one of our long-term benefactors, Mr Pluke. In fact, that's where Bega's mother used to work as a domestic help. Is it near Crickledale? I do not know the geography of that area.'

'You say her mother worked there?'

'A long time ago, Mr Pluke, thirty years ago or thereabouts.'

'Now I do find that most interesting. And to answer your question, Crickledale is about four miles from Harman's Farm. Tell me about the support given by Harman's Agricultural.'

'They have been supporting us for many years. I recall the name – one of my duties is to administer the income from our benefactors, you see, and to compile our annual statement of income and expenditure for audit. All our benefactors receive a copy.'

'Really? So Mr Burholme is a benefactor of this convent? He is the man who runs Harman's Agricultural, sister.'

'So far as I can recall, we have never known the name of the man behind the business. Several companies do provide us with support, Mr Pluke, invariably done year by year by banker's order. We do not know who is behind the business – that does not mean it is secret or secretive, it's just the way business operates. We have several supporters within the business community of the north of England.'

'So if Sister Bega went to see Mr Burholme, or paid a visit to his business premises, why do you think she would do so?'

'I have no firm idea, Mr Pluke. She has helped with the accounts from time to time, and with other administrative matters, so she might have recognised the name – Harman, that

164

is – while passing by. She might have popped in to say thank you, or merely to see where her mother used to work. Perhaps her mother mentioned this to her? It's the sort of spontaneous reaction one could expect from Bega.'

'Right, well, can we now have a look at her room? Remember, this is a murder investigation, sister, otherwise I should not have embarrassed you with this. Detective Constable Helston, come with us, please. I'd like you to carry out the more intimate of inspections which may be necessary.'

By that, Pluke meant the searching of the nun's clothing in her wardrobe and dressing table. They were taken upstairs to a long corridor whose floor was covered with brown highly polished linoleum. Sister Agnes led them to room number 8, tapped on the door as a matter of habit, smiled apologetically, and then led them inside. It was a small, plain room with a linoleum floor containing a single bed, a bedside cabinet with a bedside light, a wardrobe and a dressing table containing six drawers. There was also a small desk and chair facing one wall, above which was a crucifix. The room and its contents were immaculately tidy and clean.

'Perhaps the dressing table to begin with?' Pluke suggested to Paula Helston.

'What am I looking for, sir?' she asked,

'We shall not know until we find it,' was his rather evasive answer. 'But I need to know, if possible, why she went to Crickledale and whether she went to Harman's Farm in particular; if so, when. Also we need to know whether there are any people in her life that might be of interest to us. An address book, perhaps? Diary . . . seek and ye shall find, constable.'

While the keen young detective began her task, Pluke concentrated on the wardrobe. Other than a few items of clothing there was very little – then he saw the small brown suitcase lying in the bottom of the wardrobe, almost hidden by a long coat. He eased it out.

'Her mother's?' he asked Sister Agnes, who was clearly embarrassed that this man should be hunting through a nun's private belongings.

'Yes, that came from her mother,' whispered the nun as Pluke

165

opened the case. Inside there seemed to be family photographs, a few items of feminine jewellery, some glass ornaments, a crucifix and rosary, a Catholic missal and some fairly recent birthday cards signed 'Miriam'.

'Which of these ladies is her mother?' asked Pluke, passing some photographs to Sister Agnes.

She flicked through them until she came to one of a good-looking blonde woman standing near a sundial in what looked like a walled garden.

'This is Josephine,' affirmed the nun, handing the photos back to Pluke. 'It's the best likeness – she's about forty-five in that picture.'

Pluke accepted it from her and passed it to Paula Helston for her to examine, saying, 'I would like to keep this for a while, to show potential witnesses.'

'I understand, Mr Pluke.'

'Now, you said Josephine died two months ago,' he continued. 'Where was she buried, sister?'

'Buried? She was a Catholic, Mr Pluke, the funeral was at her local church, the one at Westwood, Newcastle.'

'A small funeral, I would imagine?'

'Yes, there was a small congregation, a few friends and neighbours, former work-mates, several of us from here and Bega, of course. Josephine had no brothers or sisters. She was very much on her own.'

'No tall, distinguished gentlemen attended the funeral then?' Pluke had to ask.

'No, definitely not. I'd have noticed.'

'A sad story,' Pluke almost muttered to himself. 'So very, very sad.'

Their hunt through the meagre personal belongings of Sister Bega revealed nothing which would provide Pluke with a reason to explain why Sister Bega had travelled to Harman's Farm. He realised, of course, that if this suitcase had contained anything relevant, such as a photograph or letter, then Bega would probably have taken it with her. So where was it now? And if she had been heading for Harman's Farm in particular, it would surely have been for some very personal reason.

166

The search thoroughly conducted by Pluke and Paula Helston produced nothing of value to their enquiry, save a small pile of handkerchiefs in one drawer, all identical to the one found with the body. When they had finished, everything was replaced in exactly the same position, a point Pluke made to Sister Agnes. It was impossible to see that a search had been made.

'Thank you, sister,' he said. 'We had to undertake that, but it has not provided us with much information, except this photograph which may or may not bear fruit. But there is one thing – would Sister Bega have carried a small mirror with her?'

'A hand mirror?'

'Yes, one with a handle, a pink plastic frame and a round glass.'

'Yes, we all have them for our travels. Our make-up needs are modest, Mr Pluke. A mirror and a comb are usually all we need.'

'Handbag?' asked Paula Helston.

'No, we have no need for handbags, we do not carry make-up or credit cards or lots of money . . .'

'When Bega was seen in Crickledale, she had a black hold-all,' Pluke told the sister.

'Yes, we all use those when we are travelling, Mr Pluke, they hold all our requirements from spare clothes to money to food.'

'Well,' said Pluke, 'I think we can leave this sad little room. Please convey my deepest sympathy to all the sisters. But there is one final thing before we go. Could I see your record of payments from Harman's Agricultural?'

'Well, I am not sure, Mr Pluke, I would have thought such records were highly confidential!'

'Sadly, nothing is confidential in a murder investigation, sister, and we could always apply for a warrant to conduct a very thorough search for any material evidence . . .'

'Follow me to the office, then.' She looked flushed now.

The office was very orderly too, and within seconds she drew a ledger from a shelf; it contained an alphabetical list of benefactors with the amounts they paid and how they made the payments.

Not computerised, it had been completed by hand and provided rapid access.

'I am not concerned with your other benefactors, merely Harman's Agricultural.' Pluke tried to assuage some of the nun's anguish at having to show this to someone from outside the convent.

'They have been making a monthly payment to us since October 1968.' She indicated the appropriate entry. 'At first, as you can see, Mr Pluke, the amount was modest – £60 a month – but it has risen due to inflation. We now receive £600 a month from Harman's Agricultural.'

'A steady record over thirty years, sister! Has Mr Burholme ever been to visit the convent during that time?' asked Pluke.

'Not while I have been here, Mr Pluke, not during the past thirty years or so, not since the commencement of those payments, in fact. I have been here all that time. I remember the payments starting but I do not know whether he and his wife did visit the convent prior to that. I have never seen him, Mr Pluke. His wife is dead, you know, she was an invalid. When she died, we had to amend our records, that's how I know about Harman's . . .'

'And he does not maintain contact?'

'No, other than continuing with the banker's order. I once located the original banker's order, Mr Pluke, which is buried deep in our filing system now, and both Mr and Mrs Burholme had signed the authorisation. They were joint directors of the business. I found it while checking back before I amended our records. I remember thinking it was an unusual job for a woman, directing an agricultural machinery hire business, but it was nice to get her support for our causes.'

'So both provided that support?' He frowned at this news.

'Yes.'

'And has Mrs Burholme any earlier links with the convent? As a schoolgirl perhaps? She was an invalid, and I wondered if she had ever come here . . .'

'No, Mr Pluke. She had no links with us, she did not attend our school – in fact, they were not Catholics. Neither of them. They were not even Christians, which made their work for us that much more rewarding. They lived very good lives though, charitable and helpful to others.'

'It would be interesting to know why they chose your charity,' said Pluke. 'Mr Burholme does appear to have kept his distance from you. He seems to be a person who did not get close to anyone.'

'Well, Mr Pluke, for us it was a business arrangement, nothing more.'

'Can I ask something?' Paula Helston asked.

'Certainly,' agreed Pluke.

'Did Mr Burholme send Christmas cards to the convent, or to anyone in it?'

'No, not to my knowledge,' replied the nun. 'He does not know anyone here, does he? Except those who run the establishment.'

Pluke smiled and said, 'Well, we must leave you now, sister, with grateful thanks for all you've done. I now feel I know a lot more about this case.'

'You do?' The nun frowned. 'I felt I had not been very helpful.'

'You have been most helpful, but there is one further matter, I am afraid. I refer to the formal identification of the deceased. In the absence of any relations, someone from the convent will have to visit Crickledale to view the body. A distasteful task, but very necessary. It cannot be tonight because the mortuary will be closed.'

'I will come,' said Sister Agnes. 'Just let me know.'

'My office will arrange a suitable time and will contact you,' promised Pluke.

Minutes later, they were driving away from the peaceful place, with Pluke sitting in the passenger seat in his heavy overcoat and Paula Helston beside him at the wheel.

'Well, Detective Constable Helston.' He regarded her with a thin smile. 'What did you make of all that?'

14

'I wondered if that nun was trying to hide something,' was Detective Constable Helston's first comment as they drove from the grounds.

'I didn't think so,' countered Pluke. 'By that statement, I mean I don't think she was trying to conceal anything criminal, she was not trying to frustrate our enquiry. I think her reticence was chiefly due to her role as temporary custodian of the convent. After all, it's not very pleasant, when you are in temporary charge of an establishment, to have the police appear with a demand to inspect your sources of income, and the room of a recently departed friend, and to ask probing questions about her family. I think, under the circumstances, Sister Agnes was behaving with considerable restraint.'

'They don't own much, do they? Those nuns. Personal things, I mean, sir, the sort of things a woman would normally have. My dressing table's like a chemist's shop with make-up, face creams, hair spray . . .'

'To us, their life does seem sparse, and yet they do not have to earn a wage, buy a house, clothe themselves, make their own meals or support a family. Everything is provided, including the roof over their heads. And even their handkerchiefs. Did you notice that the clean handkerchiefs in Bega's dressing table were identical to the one we found on her body? Standard issue, I believe. A job lot. But by having very little, they do have quite a lot, Detective Constable Helston.'

'You asked me what I made of our visit, sir. I don't quite understand your question.'

'Well,' he smiled, 'would you say our investigation has progressed?'

'Yes, we have an identification for our victim, sir. That is very important.'

'Vital to any such enquiry indeed. But what else have we learned?'

'Not a great deal more, sir, except that there is a definite link between this convent and Harman's Agricultural.'

'Precisely,' he nodded. 'But it's more than that, is it not? We have now established a link between the dead girl and Harman's Agricultural. We are now firmly of the opinion that Sister Bega knew of the existence of Harman's and that she also knew her mother had actually worked there. From that, we might even assume that Bega knew of the man who runs it. Eric Burholme, in other words.'

'Knew of him, sir?'

'You are alert. Yes, I did not say "knew him". Perhaps she did not know him personally, but I am sure she knew of him, knew something about him, was aware of his existence. Enough to persuade her to visit him, perhaps?'

'I can understand that, sir. If she'd worked in the office of the convent from time to time, looking after the accounts perhaps, she would probably know about Mr Burholme and Harman's Agricultural. If she had known her mother used to work there, then the name would become more important to her. Not everyone knows where their mothers worked in their youth, of course – I haven't a clue where my mother worked before I was born. But these facts are too closely linked to be ignored and I now believe she was making for Harman's Farm. You don't think she did just happen to be passing last weekend, recognised the name on the gate and, on the spur of the moment, popped in to express her appreciation for years of support?'

'Is that what you think?' he returned the question to her.

'Well, no . . .'

'And neither do I! I think it was quite a deliberate act on her part, a journey of exploration as she told her friend. I wonder what she expected to find there?'

'Did she go to meet a person, perhaps? You asked that nun about tall, distinguished gentlemen at Josephine's funeral. Were you thinking of one such man, Mr Burholme, sir?'

'Yes, I was.'

'But why did you think he might have gone to the funeral of a woman like that, sir, a domestic? It was years since she'd worked for him. He'd never have known she'd died, she lived nearly ninety miles away.'

'He didn't go to the funeral, that's the point. I agree he was hardly likely to know she had died. Who'd tell anyone that a domestic servant who'd worked for them thirty years earlier had died? It's not impossible, I agree, but it is unlikely and suppose Josephine worked for him a little more than thirty years ago?'

'Oh . . . sir . . . good heavens . . . yes, I think I see what you are saying. You are saying that he might have had an affair with Josephine while she was working in his house, and that Sister Bega – Miriam – was the result? That means she could be his daughter!'

'I thought that was what you were suggesting when you asked about Christmas cards?' Pluke smiled.

'Well, sir, I did wonder if he knew anyone here, a friend perhaps, or relation. I thought it odd that he supported the convent for no apparent reason.'

'Well, perhaps there is a very good reason, Detective Constable Helston. If Bega was his daughter, then his wife would have been alive at the time which would mean he could not marry Josephine to formalise the birth. Besides, her parents, who were very strict, so it appears, took her away from the farm and from the influence of Eric Burholme. She was made to give birth in secret.'

'Josephine did enter the convent to have her child, sir, we know that.'

'Yes, we do, and that child was Miriam. There is no doubt about that. Consequently Burholme, said to be a nice, generous gentleman, decided he should pay for the girl's upkeep – and he did so with his wife's knowledge and consent. He set up that system of long-term donations to the convent.'

'Which he continues to pay to this day, sir.'

'Indeed he does. Another fine example of his munificence.'

'In that case, you'd think he would have shown some interest in the child he was supporting, sir, especially as she matured into such a very sincere young woman.'

'Yes, that's what I would have thought but it seems there was no contact between Burholme and Miriam for thirty years. Is that the reason she turned up on his doorstep, probably unannounced? To confront him about the discovery she'd made in her mother's papers? I have a feeling she might not have known the identity of her father until she examined the contents of the little suitcase left by her mother. And then she set out to meet him. That was her journey of exploration.'

'But surely, sir, if that is the case, he would not have killed her, his own daughter, not after all the support he'd given. He'd never have resorted to murder to conceal that kind of secret . . .'

'It is that very thought which makes me feel sure he did not kill her. Right from the outset, I have not been convinced we are dealing with murder. But whatever the cause of her death and in whatever circumstances it happened, I am sure that he buried her.'

'But why, sir? Why try to conceal the fact she had died, especially if it was through a tragic accident? There is no shame in that.'

'That is what is puzzling me. That is what we must establish, Detective Constable Helston. That is why I am delaying an interview of Mr Burholme. I am waiting until I have amassed as much information as possible about this strange affair, facts which I can put before him and which he cannot deny.'

'She has a look of him, hasn't she? The dead girl, I mean. There is a resemblance to Burholme.'

'Tall, blonde . . . yes, and a similar helpful outlook. Everyone says Burholme is helpful and kind and thoughtful . . . and that is how I assessed Miriam's character. A chip off the old block, as they say. So, Detective Constable Helston, whereas my investigation was going around in circles, it now seems to have taken the shape of a triangle.'

'A triangle, sir?' she frowned.

'A three-cornered square, Miss Helston. A triangle with Burholme at one point, the deceased Miriam at another and the third point carrying the mystery which links them both and which Burholme apparently wishes to conceal. But the fact that she was found buried at Harman's Farm does prove she *did* arrive there.'

'It doesn't prove she met him, though, does it? Or is there some other mystery, sir? Something in addition to her probably being his daughter?'

'Let us not be too hasty in assuming that she is his daughter. We have been speculating, Detective Constable Helston, no more than that. We have no proof of his paternity. But if this young woman died accidentally on his farm, why would Eric Burholme take such drastic steps to conceal her presence? That is the question we must answer.'

'It's more than not wishing to admit to that paternity, sir?'

'It's much more complicated than that, Detective Constable Helston. There is an argument that he has already admitted paternity by giving money to the convent who raised Miriam, alias Bega. He did so throughout her life, and yet there is no sign of his love for her. I find that odd.'

'Then blackmail, sir? Did Bega discover his true role and decide to leave the convent for a new life, raising money by blackmail? Recognising that business and farm as her rightful inheritance perhaps? Even exploring the possibility of going to live there with her real father?'

'They're feasible theories, but I did not get the impression that Bega was unsettled, or unhappy in the convent, or that she was the sort of woman who would resort to blackmail. I very much doubt if she would have abandoned her chosen life to live with a man she did not know, whatever the relationship. No, I think she turned up unexpectedly on his doorstep and died soon afterwards in some kind of freak accident, whereupon he decided to bury her in the odd way she was found. But I cannot be sure why he would want to do that – and, remember, at this point we do not know whether he realised she might be his daughter. It's feasible he might have had no idea of the relationship, if indeed there is one.'

'But you have some idea, sir? About his other secret?'

'I have a very vague notion which I shall not reveal just yet – simply because I might be totally wrong. But time will tell.'

'Then you'll have to ask him, sir?'

'Yes, I will, won't I?' and he settled down in his seat to enjoy the rest of the drive back to Crickledale as darkness enveloped

174

the landscape. Suddenly, however, after some fifteen minutes, he jerked into action and sat bolt upright in his seat, clutching at the dashboard of the speeding police car.

'Oh dear,' he gasped. 'I have done a dreadful thing!'

'What is it, sir?' The shock had caused Paula to wobble the steering wheel, an unintentional act which created a small weaving motion of the vehicle, and which resulted in someone blasting a car horn behind. But Pluke never noticed the near mishap as Paula asked, 'It's obviously very important.'

'Very!' he said. 'I forgot to warn Millicent that I would be late home this evening. She will have prepared my dinner, it will be as dry as a horse trough in a drought.'

'Oh, I thought your reaction was connected to our enquiry!'

He looked at his watch. 'I think, under the circumstances, I should return home directly, without going into the incident room – it will be closed anyway. And you may do likewise. We shall meet tomorrow morning when I shall deliver my summary and my thoughts to the conference of detectives.'

'Yes, sir,' sighed Detective Constable Helston, wondering what sort of an ogre lurked within Mrs Pluke.

During Montague's absence that day, Millicent had shown photographs of the deceased girl to her friends and social acquaintances, but none had recognised her. At the mention of Eric Burholme, however, Mrs Plunket-Greystone did relate a curious incident. Mr Burholme had kindly given her a lift home to Greystone Manor following a demonstration of a new piece of machinery in the Yorkshire Dales. As they drove down the dale in his BMW, an oncoming car had caused Mr Burholme to take evasive action and he'd finished his journey in the ditch.

The offending car had departed. Burholme had managed to reverse his own vehicle from the ditch where it had not suffered any damage, other than acquiring an adornment of pieces of hedgerow and clumps of grass. Before leaving the scene, Burholme had meticulously removed every piece of grass and twig from the bodywork of his car, and had then raked over the tyre marks in the verge with a piece of wood. By the time he departed from the scene, there was not a trace of the accident. Upon leaving, he'd said to his passenger, 'No one will ever know I was there, Mrs Plunket-Greystone.' And he had driven home without further explanation. Millicent felt she ought to tell Montague about that. Montague would know he'd been there, she smiled to herself.

The following morning, Wednesday, after checking with Sergeant Cockfield pronounced Cofield in the control room, opening his post and providing Mrs Plumpton with sufficient work to keep her busy, Pluke went into the incident room. Already, his detectives were gathering but it was Wayne Wain who first hailed him.

'Sir,' he said as he followed Pluke into his office, 'I came here last night and waited and waited and waited . . .'

'I had to travel to Newcastle, Wayne, on a matter of great importance.'

'Yes, sir, Mr Horsley told me. I tried to contact you by radio but you were out of range. I had some important information for you, vital in fact, and apart from that, you promised to explain things to me, your beliefs, your suspicions.'

'There is no time now, Wayne. I shall present my views to the conference and you can listen in. Now, I had a very fruitful visit to Newcastle yesterday evening.'

'To the ferry company, you mean?'

'No, to a convent . . .'

Wayne wondered if horse troughs were the reason for such a visit to a convent, and decided he must immediately acquaint Pluke with the result of his enquiries. 'Sir, I must tell you this. I had a very successful visit to Quenby and established that our victim was seen – positively seen – on Saturday morning at Harman's Farm! That's our first sighting on the Saturday, sir, and I have two witnesses. It means she must have been there overnight on Friday, and even staying there on Saturday.'

'That is excellent news, Wayne, brilliant news in fact . . .'

'And I discovered Burholme had a penchant for good-looking blondes, sir, although he appears not to have been a womaniser.

He had women working for him, sir, according to my witness, when his wife was incapacitated. Domestics, sir, doing the cooking, washing and cleaning while he cared for his wife. I bet they had to be first class, he seems to have been a purist, never liking to leave things lying about,' and he told Pluke of Burholme's clearing of the table at the agricultural show.

'Excellent news, Wayne, absolutely wonderful! Mrs Pluke told me a similar tale about him clearing up after a near-miss with a motor car. Now, I need to know where the late Mrs Burholme is buried, and I would also like to know whether any of our emergency services were called to Harman's Farm on Saturday. Can you do those tasks for me, before I convene the detectives' conference?'

'Well, yes, sir. But what happened in Newcastle? Did you find a rare horse trough? You seem buoyed up, sir, if you don't mind me saying so.'

'I completely forgot to examine the grounds of that convent for horse troughs, Wayne, but I have learned that our deceased is not a Swedish girl who came here by ferry. Her name is Miriam Ripley and she is a nun from a hilltop convent near Newcastle. Her religious name is Sister Bega. We shall soon have a positive identification – and, Wayne, we have established a very positive link between her, the convent, Harman's Farm and our man Burholme.'

'That's great, sir! But a nun? She wasn't dressed like one, although I suppose that explains the virginity. But why on earth would a nun visit an agricultural machinery hire business?'

'That is the question we have yet to resolve, Wayne. Now, if you could see to those two small enquiries, I shall prepare for my conference of detectives, and for the subsequent news conference.'

'Very good, sir. By the way, how did you get to Newcastle?'

'I was driven, Wayne, in an official car, by Detective Constable Helston. Now there's an intelligent young woman, Wayne. As I said earlier, I must consider her as a potential member of my team . . .'

'Really, sir? Does that mean I have competition as your deputy? I think I'd better get those enquiries sorted, then.'

'I think you had, Wayne,' smiled Pluke.

Seated before his desk in the full realisation that he had not attended the closing conference following yesterday's enquiries, Pluke was pleased to see that Detective Inspector Horsley had provided him with a brief summary of the outcome of Tuesday's investigations. The main result was that enquiries from the Swedish ferry lines sailing in and out of Newcastle had produced a blank.

In the light of the identification of the nun, of course, that was to be expected – certainly, six girls broadly matching Bega's appearance had arrived from Sweden but all could be accounted for; the enquiry had thus produced a nil return. Now, of course, Pluke welcomed that!

Another result concerned the wheelbarrow recovered from Burholme's garden shed – fibres had been found on the rim of the barrow. These had been compared with fibres taken from the victim's blouse and jeans, and a match had been made. Furthermore, particles of soil in the tread of the wheel of the wheelbarrow proved it had recently been pushed over soil which surrounded the grave – samples taken at the time of the discovery of the body proved that. So Pluke knew the barrow had been used to convey the body – but who had used it? No discernible fingerprints had been found on the rubber handles or any other part of the barrow; certainly, there were none which might be compared with those of Eric Burholme.

All undertakers, grave-diggers and graveyard attendants within a five-mile radius of Crickledale had been interviewed but none could help. None had lost any of their grave-digging tools and none of the stone masons visited reported the loss of any of their tools. All could be eliminated from the enquiry.

The remains of all the camp fires in the quarry had been sifted by the Scenes of Crime officers and analysed in the hope they would reveal traces of some of the victim's belongings, such as a burnt haversack, anorak, sleeping bag, map, spare clothing, or comb. A burnt passport could no longer be considered because the girl had not travelled from overseas. So far as other evidence was concerned, none of her belongings had turned up anywhere else and neither had the spade which was reported missing from

Burholme's garden shed. The search for those items would be continued today with Task Force officers checking every inch of the hedgerows and fields in both directions from Harman's Farm entrance.

Continuing checks on the owners of crossbows had not revealed any in the Crickledale district and the local sports shops claimed that no one in recent years had ordered replacement bolts or spare parts from them. Pluke therefore felt that a locally owned crossbow could be eliminated as the cause of Bega's death, and the pathologist had already ruled out a humane killer.

Michael Wardle, the man who had found Bega's body, had been interviewed following a long wait at his house by detectives. He had not been avoiding them, his absence being due to nothing more than a visit to his married sister who lived in Redcar. He had been quizzed in depth about his background and particularly about his movements on Friday, but there was nothing which could link him to the body, other than his misfortune in discovering it. The detectives who interviewed him thanked him for his patience, saying that his ordeal was an unfortunate part of every murder investigation. He said he hoped he found no more human bodies during his excursions. If he did, he would think carefully before reporting it. Perhaps an anonymous telephone call via the 999 system?

Among the other enquiries which had been completed, a study of the types of motor vehicle seen at night on the Barughdale to Crickledale road revealed nothing of consequence. Checks had been made between midnight and six the following morning. One vehicle, a Volkswagen car, had been logged by police night patrols on Friday/Saturday at 3 a.m. Saturday – its owner had been traced and eliminated. It was a vet returning from treating a sick cow. Similarly, Saturday/Sunday night's check revealed a few more vehicles – five in total, and all moving around 1 a.m. and 2 a.m. – but all could be eliminated. Each belonged to a young man seeking solitude with a girlfriend aboard.

Photographs of the pink-framed mirror had been displayed around shops and hairdressers in the town in the hope someone might remember selling such an item, but none did. It was a cheap mirror, they felt, more like a tourist's souvenir or child's plaything than a mirror bought by a discerning young woman. In fact, Pluke now knew it belonged to the victim.

It was while Pluke was studying all these notes that Wayne Wain entered his office having completed his brief enquiries by telephone.

'First,' he said, 'the emergency services. I've checked them all, sir. None of the local hospitals or the ambulance service received a call to a casualty at Harman's Farm or the quarry on Saturday evening or night, or in the early hours of Sunday. Or at all, in fact. I asked for those times in particular, but they checked on a wider scale. I've done a telephone call of doctors' receptionists too, sir. There are only two surgeries, but I got the same answer. No call out.'

'If the girl did have an accident, then, it seems she was dead when she was found, would you think, Wayne? Beyond human help, in other words.'

'That's feasible, sir, yes. Now, the burial of his wife. I rang the vicar, sir; the Crickledale parish does include Barughdale and here's an odd thing. She died in hospital, sir, Crickledale General to be precise, from a heart attack. She'd been ill a long time and died the day after being admitted. There is no suggestion of foul play, sir, none at all. Anyway, she was buried at Harman's Farm, sir, in a private plot.'

'That's it . . . I remember the fuss now! And where is this plot, do we know?'

'The vicar did not know, sir, because he took no part in the burial service. Apparently, Burholme is not a Christian, sir. Years ago, he got planning permission to bury his wife among some trees on the edge of the moor, on his own land. He will be buried there too, when the time comes.'

'So who actually carried out the burial, do we know that, Wayne?'

'Yes, sir, Crumble and Smirch the Crickledale Undertakers, Embalmers, Funeral Carriage Masters and Ornamental Stone Masons. I had words with Mr Smirch, sir, he remembers the funeral. There were no mourners, he told me, other than Eric Burholme. The body was lowered into the grave, in a cardboard coffin, and Burholme read some words over the body as it was

180

committed to the ground. Mr Smirch couldn't understand what he was saying, sir, he thought it might be Latin.'

'Swedish, I would guess, Wayne. Now, was anything buried with the corpse? Did you think to ask that?'

'Swedish, sir? But there was nothing, sir, except her wedding ring, although the lady's hair was braided, sir, so Mr Smirch said.'

'That's an old Swedish custom for married women, Wayne. There is a lot of Swedish influence on that farm. Well, thank you for that. Now, is there anything else before I call the teams together for the conference?'

'There is a note asking you to ring Detective Superintendent Hart, sir. Control passed it to me just now. He rang last night, apparently, when you were out.'

'Then I shall do so immediately. Sit down, Wayne, you need to be fully informed of events, and Mr Hart might have some news for us.'

Pluke rang his boss's number at Headquarters and when a deep voice said, 'Hart, Headquarters,' Pluke responded with 'Pluke, Crickledale, sir.'

'Ah, Pluke. Good of you to ring back. How's it going?'

Montague updated his boss on the more important aspects of the enquiry, particularly the identification of the girl, albeit yet to be confirmed by an inspection of the body by one of the nuns, and Hart expressed his pleasure.

'Now, Pluke, as I said, I have been doing a little digging into the background of your Eric Burholme. I have not bottomed this enquiry, though, not by a long way, because your man is the subject of some highly secret files which are not kept at our Headquarters and not even in Scotland Yard. They're held by the Security Services and not even I have been allowed access to them. But one thing is certain – his former name is Erik Bjurholm, he is Swedish, he is eighty as he states. He came to this country, as an alien, in 1947 and later applied for naturalisation. He Anglicised his name at that stage. He was not married, by the way, and lived where he is now, at Harman's Farm; he worked as a conventional farmer with grain and livestock, but later developed his machinery business. His application for naturalisation was approved and later he married an Englishwoman called Elsie Butcher. He has no criminal record and to all accounts is a citizen of exemplary conduct.'

'But I must not accuse him of murder?'

'If your enquiries suggest he is guilty, contact me in confidence, Pluke. But the mystery remains ... I cannot delve any further without someone in high places getting worried about my motives. Sorry and all that. But don't rock the boat, Pluke. Softly, softly is the word on this one.'

'And if I prove he did not commit murder?'

'Then no more need be said, need it?'

And Hart replaced the phone.

Pluke did likewise, sighed and said to Wain, 'Right, Wayne. Get the teams assembled for our conference, and afterwards I shall embark upon my interrogation of Eric Burholme.'

15

While the detectives were assembling in the Plukedom for their Wednesday morning conference, Pluke asked Horsley to contact the convent in Northumberland and Meredith, the pathologist, to arrange for a nun, Sister Agnes preferably, to come to Crickledale to make the formal indentification of the dead girl. A police vehicle would convey her to the mortuary if necessary; the sooner she arrived the better, Pluke exhorted Horsley. Pluke also briefed Inspector Russell, the press officer, about the theme of this morning's news conference – once more it would concentrate upon trying to secure sightings of the victim in and around Crickledale, although the name, occupation and home address of the dead girl could not yet be released because she had not been formally identified. There should also be a renewed appeal to trace the missing spade and personal belongings of the dead girl.

As Pluke waited for the signal that everyone was ready, he hurried outside, found a pair of fresh four-leaved clovers and returned to his office to replace the one on his desk which was wilting. He slipped the other into the buttonhole of his jacket, a sure method of ensuring good fortune during the coming day.

Then Wayne Wain tapped on his door and came in.

'Everyone's here, sir,' he announced.

Pluke felt rather as an actor must feel before going on stage to produce a stunning performance because this conference was going to be rather different from normal. Instead of giving them their tasks for the day, he was going to present his arguments and ask his officers to challenge his theories by producing conflicting evidence; he needed this kind of reaction before interviewing Eric Burholme because he wanted all the counter-arguments tested.

'Be sure to tape record this conference, Wayne,' he instructed his sergeant. 'I may need to remind myself of portions at a later date.'

'No problem, sir.'

'Thanks. Now, let's get it over, Wayne.' Pluke spoke softly as he touched the four-leaved clover. His confidence thus reinforced, he led the way from his office.

'Good morning, all.' He mounted the small dais someone had thoughtfully positioned on the floor so that he stood head and shoulders above his audience, a distinctive figure in his old yellowish-brown jacket, blue dicky bow, spats and half-mast drainpipe narrow trousers.

'Good morning, sir,' was the chorus of response.

'This morning,' he began, 'I am going to acquaint you with my suspicions and beliefs about this very odd case. I want you to consider them carefully and if you have any evidence or theories which would counter my suppositions, then you must tell me now. Each of you will be aware that one suspect, Eric Burholme, has not yet been interviewed – I have had my reasons for that, and I can now say it is my intention to interview him once I have assembled and analysed every piece of available evidence. And that moment, I think, has almost arrived.'

He paused for them to absorb his words, then continued with a résumé of the case, highlighting the manner in which the body had been discovered, the place where it had been found, its condition when examined by both the police and the pathologist, the mirror in the shallow grave which had been created so close to a public footpath, and the curious head injury and other wounds sustained by the dead girl. He reminded them of the positive sightings of the victim in Crickledale, along the road to Harman's Farm and at Harman's Farm itself, and of the fact that, at no stage, had the victim been seen in the company of anyone else, male or female.

He followed with an account of his visit to the convent, and told them that they had a provisional identification for the victim, and that she was a nun. He stressed that this information was currently highly confidential and was on no account to be released to the public or to the media. That would be done when the identification had been formalised by Sister Agnes. Pluke then turned to Horsley.

'Mr Horsley, as I proceed, there will be scope for new actions, chiefly aimed at confirming what will emerge during these discussions. Perhaps you could make a note of them and allocate them when I have completed my synopsis?'

'Sure, Montague,' nodded Horsley.

'Right,' said Pluke. 'These are my primary thoughts. It has been my belief throughout this enquiry, a belief which has been strengthened as time progressed, that the girl died as the result of a tragic and highly unusual accident and that she was unlawfully buried. I do not think she was murdered. Those core beliefs have coloured my approach to this investigation although I have maintained an open mind. So why do I subscribe to the accident theory? The answer lies in the grave. The dead girl was not hastily buried in a makeshift grave, which is what most murderers would have done. She was buried with considerable care. She might even have been buried with love but I would prefer the word *care*. The grave, which was carefully and cleanly dug with a spade, was orientated east to west, an indication of care, attention and a desire to do things correctly. She was lying with her head to the west, a further indication of care and attention. That is not the sort of care or attention one would expect from a murderer. If the person who dug the grave did make a mistake, it was the fact that the ground immediately

184

below the grave was solid rock – it meant he could only bury the girl in a very shallow grave. While that might have been an error, on the other hand it might not. Placing the grave there might have been a very deliberate act. As the grave was close to a public footpath which is popular with ramblers and hikers, it is not surprising that a rambler's dog unearthed the body. In view of the care taken to bury the body, for however temporary a period, I think the person who carried out the burial *wanted* the body to be found, and found very quickly. That, in itself, is puzzling. Why bury a body in the hope it will be quickly discovered? Thus, in my opinion, the shallowness of the grave, and its proximity to a footpath, might have been very deliberate indeed. The ground in that quarry was obviously shallow with a rock base because it housed heavy machinery – quarries are like that, ladies and gentlemen, even disused ones. Many have very solid floors. A quarry user would know that.'

'But a shallow burial, sir, unauthorised like this in a deserted place, of a victim with a head wound caused by a weapon that has been hidden – surely that suggests murder . . .' The speaker was Detective Sergeant Warriner. 'Everything points to murder.'

'Precisely, Detective Sergeant Warriner. That is exactly what was intended but I think the care shown in the burial rules out murder. Nonetheless, I believe that the person who buried her wanted it to look like a case of murder. I know that sounds a most unlikely theory but it will be explained as I proceed.'

'It's usually the other way round, sir! Most murderers try to make their crimes look like accidents!'

'They do indeed but not this man. That is why this is such an interesting case. Bear that in mind, all of you, as you continue your enquiries.'

'But why would anyone want to make an accident look like murder? That's crazy, sir . . .'

'Not entirely.' Pluke remained calm. 'We are dealing with a very clever and skilled deceiver, a practised operator, I believe. Now, to continue. As you all know, a small but inexpensive hand mirror was buried with the body. I believe that was no accident. For one thing, I now know the mirror did belong to the dead woman and, even though her other belongings have not

185

been traced, this particular item was buried with her. That is very significant. It used to be the custom in Sweden to bury a mirror with a maiden; married women were buried with their hair braided. At first, because of that, I thought the victim was Swedish – her appearance added to that supposition – and I also thought that the person who buried her knew of her nationality. I was wrong, she is English – the person who buried her was Swedish. Eric Burholme, the owner of Harman's Farm and of the quarry, is a naturalised Swede, ladies and gentlemen. He is also old enough to have remembered superstitions and customs still in use in the early years of this century. I mention that because I believe he buried the girl – but I do not believe he killed her. Oddly, he does deny knowing her. Allow me to continue.'

He paused again for them to absorb his unusual theories.

'Think about that mirror.' He spoke softly now, knowing that by lowering his voice, they would strive to listen more carefully. 'A mirror was customarily buried with maidens in Sweden – and that tells me that the person who buried the girl *knew* she was a maiden, even if she was a good-looking woman of thirty. And if he knew she was a maiden, an old word for a virgin, then he knew who she was; she might have been merely unmarried, but I think he knew she was a nun. And, of course, the fact that he knew about that old superstition suggests that the person who buried her is a person of considerable age. I doubt if the modern generation of Swedes follow those practices. And Burholme is eighty, remember, he has been away from Sweden since the end of the Second World War. Burholme has constantly denied knowing her – the mirror in the grave suggests otherwise. That means Burholme is lying, but if the girl died in an accident, why would he lie like this? And why go to such extremes to deal with her body when a call to the emergency services would have sufficed? That is my next question.'

Pausing again he took a deep breath and said, 'Now, a little more about the grave. Its location. As you know, it was in a quarry, the only access *by road* being through the Harman's Farm gate and across Burholme's land. Access by foot from the Crickledale to Barughdale road is possible via public footpaths and a stile, then over a field for a distance of about a third of a mile or thereabouts. Our own investigation showed no motor vehicle had entered the quarry – tracks would have been easily identified in the ground which had been softened by Saturday's rain. Checks on the fence between the quarry and the road revealed no fibres from the clothing of the deceased. In other words, she was not brought to the quarry by any of those routes when she was dead. It would be impossible for one person to manhandle and carry a dead body all that way, over fences and a stile, through a field and along a public footpath . . . And we are positive she did not die in the quarry. So how did the body get there? Where did it come from? Where did she die?'

As they pondered the significance of those words, Pluke said, 'I think she died out of doors at Harman's Farm, during the thunderstorm and rain on Saturday evening. It would explain the dampness of her clothing. And I think Burholme came home from his meeting, found her dead and conveyed her body to the quarry in his wheelbarrow – forensic evidence now supports that theory. Here he made a mistake – being a meticulously tidy person, he replaced the barrow in precisely the same place as he took it from. Had it been placed anywhere else, or left in the quarry, we might have been tempted to believe someone else had borrowed it.'

'So, sir . . .' A detective raised his hand. 'If Burholme claims his spade has been stolen – clearly because he has got rid of it – why did he not do the same with the barrow?'

'He used them both, I am sure, but I planted in his head the idea of his spade being used by a murderer, Detective Constable Crowther. I suggested to him that someone might have used his tools or one of his spades to dig the grave . . . his buildings are never locked and so access was quite feasible. But I did not refer to the barrow. So he went along with that and sought to strengthen my belief by disposing of the spade. And I did tell him that I suspected murder – which is what he wanted me to believe – murder not by him, but by some other person. He has not framed anyone – he has just made the girl appear to be a murder victim. Furthermore, he is of the age where the miracles of modern forensic science are unknown to him. I do not think for a moment that he realised we could link the body so positively to his wheelbarrow – he doesn't know that we have done so, of course, not yet. But even so, he could claim another person had used it to convey the body – except that it was replaced so precisely, as I have already mentioned. So the evidence is beginning to point to Eric Burholme . . .'

'You crafty old devil – sir!' smiled one of the senior sergeants.

'Perhaps I have been dangling poor Mr Burholme at the end of a long fishing line,' smiled Pluke. 'I have been letting him think we suspected death by agricultural machine, for example . . .'

'You've ruled that out, have you, Montague?' asked Horsley. 'I thought we might spend days looking for a damaged machine or a component part with blood on it.'

'Yes, I know what caused her death, and how it came to cause her death; it is there for all to see, quite boldly displayed – but I will come to that in due course. Now to the deceased herself. I shall not trouble you with a repeat of her physical description but we do know this – Miriam Ripley, whose father has never been named, was brought up in a convent having been born illegitimately to a woman called Josephine Ripley. She used to work as a domestic for Burholme. That was thirty years ago – the deceased is thirty years old or thereabouts. Burholme, through his agricultural business, has been supporting that same convent for the past thirty years, paying substantial amounts but never once entering the place. He maintained a discreet distance between himself and the convent which was in fact the girl's home – it is where she was brought up, where she was schooled and where she subsequently entered as a nun. It is a relaxed regime by some standards, the sisters being allowed to wear long hair and modern clothing. Miriam – by this stage known as Sister Bega – was happy in the convent, we are told. Then a couple of months ago, her mother died. She was buried in Newcastle. Burholme did not attend the funeral, but we believe Josephine left some personal papers in a suitcase which came into Miriam's possession. As a consequence, it appears Miriam asked to leave the convent for a short holiday, to undertake what she called a journey of exploration. I think she had recently discovered her mother had worked for Harman's Agricultural, that the owner of the business was Eric Burholme and that the

188

business in question was a long-standing and generous benefactor to the convent in which she had spent her entire life. In
the belief that this man was her natural father, Sister Bega –
Miriam – made her journey of exploration to Harman's Farm.
Naïvely, she hitch-hiked from Newcastle last Friday with her
sparse belongings, including a pink-framed mirror, and found
her way to Crickledale. Unfamiliar with the area, she asked
directions for the road to Barrowdale, which is pronounced
Barfdale but spelt Barughdale, and then found herself at Harman's Farm. That is precisely where she was heading. I think she
carried the personal papers inherited from her mother, and I
think she was anxious to meet the man she believed was her
natural father. I'm sure she met Burholme at the farm. Although
she arrived unannounced on Friday evening, I think Burholme
admitted her to his home where she stayed overnight although I
am sure he would have had doubts about her motives and
indeed her genuine identity. But he had an important appoint-
ment the following day in Harrogate. He left home around ten
thirty on Saturday morning. A customer who'd been to his farm
earlier that morning did not see the girl – quite understandable.
Mr Horsley, I don't think we have confirmed that visit to
Harrogate? A good action for someone while I am interviewing
Mr Burholme? Like any daughter would do, when Burholme left
the house Bega went with him to the gate, opened it and waved
him off. Two witnesses saw her there. She would have awaited
his return and might even have prepared a meal for him – just
as her mother had done. But he did not return until Saturday
night – meanwhile, there had been a thunderstorm . . .

'Bega died out of doors in that storm and, upon his return, he
found her lying dead on his premises. So what could he do? If
she was dead, there was no point calling the emergency services
. . . and what story had she told him? Who did he think she was?
Why had she come to find him? We don't know – but we do
know he buried her. Or to be honest, *I* know he buried her.'

'Sir,' called a voice from the floor. 'This is all speculation on
your part, is it not?'

'Not speculation, Detective Sergeant Harlow. Reasoned deduction based on the available evidence.'

'But if she was his natural daughter, why not deal with her death in a more rational manner? I mean, sir, for God's sake, why bury her secretly in a bloody quarry, as if she was a dead cat or something?'

'His wife is buried in a wood behind the farm, quite legitimately,' said Pluke. 'He is not a Christian, he follows nature. Once a thing is dead, it has no further use, there is no need for emotion . . .'

'I can't believe he would do that with the body of the woman he thought was his daughter, whatever his beliefs! If this girl died in some freak agricultural accident, the authorities should have been informed and there should have been an investigation followed by an inquest. That's the way things are done. He would surely know all about the formalities, being in the business of hiring agricultural machines. Then the burial could have been formalised, even if it was intended to be a pagan burial in a wood behind the house. Unless he is mad, of course.'

'That is what a reasonable person would do,' smiled Pluke. 'But he did none of those things. There has to be a reason for his odd behaviour.'

'Perhaps he never admitted being her father, sir?' suggested Harlow. 'I think he couldn't face up to it, so he concealed things by faking her murder, to take the pressure off him. He engineered things so that someone else would find her and have to bury her properly and he could disassociate himself from her. In other words, he wanted nothing to do with her, just as he has neglected her throughout her life.'

'It's an interesting notion,' said Pluke. 'I want to hear his story – and I want to hear him tell me what killed her before I reveal my ideas to you – but if it was an accident, then there is no murder and we are left with a minor offence of failing to register a death and perhaps a breach of the coroner's rules.'

'No undetected murder to darken our statistics, sir?'

'Absolutely,' smiled Pluke. 'Now, any questions?'

Surprisingly, there were none and so he dismissed the teams. Horsley said he had identified several actions, chiefly rechecking previously made statements from witnesses in the light of

Pluke's theories. One team would collect Sister Agnes and take her to the mortuary, another would visit the undertaker for a statement about the pagan burial of Burholme's wife, and yet another would be despatched to Harrogate to check Burholme's story about attending the showground for a demonstration. But the only person who could fully provide Pluke with the information he desired was Eric Burholme himself, a man who liked to cover his tracks . . . Now it was time to interview him.

16

'I shall be pleased if you will drive me to the farm, Wayne, and I think you had better accompany me during the interview,' and so the detective sergeant drove Detective Inspector Pluke to Harman's Farm.

It was eleven o'clock when they arrived, a fine day with a thin covering of cloud and the faintest hint of a westerly breeze. Sitting in the passenger seat, Pluke was dressed in his familiar old coat, panama and spats. As they drove along the road towards the farm, he said, 'He will be expecting us, Wayne, to discuss his wheelbarrow. Either he'll acquaint us immediately with his role in this affair, or we will have to present him with the facts, one by one, and gently ease the story from him. If the fellow has buried a woman who claimed to be his daughter, for whatever reason, there is bound to be a little emotion within him, in spite of his mysterious past. I shall be interested to learn whether he will reveal a little of that past to us, Wayne.'

'He's a cold fish, sir, he's not shown much love for that young woman.'

'You're suggesting he has not shown the kind of compassion a man would show his daughter, whatever the circumstances of her birth?'

'Well, for one thing, he never went to visit her, and yet he paid for her upkeep all those years . . .'

'He did not actually pay for her upkeep, Wayne. He made a contribution to the convent, or rather, his business made a contribution to the convent.'

'Well, in my view it amounts to the same thing, sir, he's been supporting that girl all these years with never a visit or a show of parental love.'

'There might be a very good reason for that, Wayne.'

'Well, if there is, I can't see it.'

'Then suppose she is not his daughter, Wayne? Burholme has said he has no children, he quoted an old war injury.'

Wayne paused, then asked, 'So if she is not his daughter, then who is she? What is her connection with him? And why would she come to see him?'

'They're exactly the sort of things we must establish, Wayne.'

'If she's not a relation, he wouldn't have made all those contributions, would he? It must have cost him a fortune, over the years.'

'He might have paid for the same reason he buried the girl in his quarry, Wayne, to maintain some deep secret. To prevent his past being exposed.'

'You seriously think that, don't you, sir? Are you suggesting blackmail?'

'Not necessarily. But, on the surface, his behaviour over the years does not make complete sense. It doesn't make sense to secretly bury an accident victim on your own land, does it? That is really asking for trouble, Wayne. The body is bound to be discovered and identified sooner or later with the resultant investigation. Yet he must have had what he thought was a good reason for doing so. It suggests he is under extreme pressure of some kind and I hope he will enlighten us.'

'He seems unusually tidy, sir, obsessive almost.'

'It seems he has a compulsion, an instinctive reaction, to cover his tracks, to remove evidence, especially if he thinks he is at risk in some way. That could be a relic of his wartime experiences,' mused Pluke.

'Even to the extent of creating a mystery by needlessly hiding this body, sir?'

192

'Yes, Wayne, precisely that. I think that is exactly what he would do.'

'You're way ahead of me with that kind of thinking, sir!'

And Pluke produced one of his enigmatic smiles.

When they arrived at the farm gate it was closed and Pluke saw that it bore a large blue sign with yellow lettering saying 'Harman's Farm' above smaller wording which read 'Harman's Agricultural'. When Wayne halted the car, Pluke climbed out, opened the gate and held it wide as Wayne drove through. Then Pluke closed it but, before returning to the waiting car, he climbed on to the lower bars and peered over the gate, looking up and down the road beyond as he thought Sister Bega might have done.

'A long straight road, Wayne,' he said. 'When she stood on the rails of this gate on Saturday morning, I think she was waving goodbye to him. Such an action would surely suggest friendship, would it not? Not blackmail?'

As they drove into the extensive yard which occupied the space between the front of the farmhouse and its range of outbuildings, Pluke observed the continuing cleanliness and tidiness of the premises. As they cruised slowly across the yard towards the front door, the wheels of the car crunching the gravel, he noticed that the morning sun was glinting from the weather-vane, the golden head of the cockerel reflecting its rays as the dull black vane moved easily in the gentle breeze.

'This farm is beautifully maintained,' Pluke said to Wayne Wain. 'I think she fell on this gravel which is spread before the house. And see, not a thing out of place and everything fully operational. Even the tiniest of breezes is making that weather-cock move . . . the bearings must be very well greased.'

'From my experience, weather-vanes usually squeak, sir, when they turn in the wind. They get on your nerves at times.'

'And some have been neglected to the extent that it takes a gale force wind to turn them, Wayne; in fact, some don't turn at all, so blocked up with dirt are they. The bearings get clogged with debris, you know. Like everything else that is exposed to the weather, vanes need to be regularly maintained and their bearings greased. And I would think that one, with its golden head, will need regular coats of new paint. As you will see, Wayne, that vane is in unusually good condition, and it is of a rather unusual design too.'

'Yes, sir, you mentioned that earlier. About the cock being an emblem of war and that the Norsemen believed the end of the world would be heralded by a cock with a golden head.'

'My interest is in the arrow, Wayne. Some vanes comprise merely a well-fletched arrow with a barbed tip which turns above the compass points, and others will have just the cockerel or other emblem which turns above the compass points. But this vane has two wind-operated devices, Wayne, the cock and the long, slender pointed arrow which lacks the barb. It is fletched in metal for this purpose, and I think perhaps the cock was added later, by Mr Burholme.'

By this time, Wayne was drawing the car to a halt outside the front door, but on this occasion, Burholme did not emerge to greet them.

'You seem to be paying a lot of attention to the weather-vane, sir. I thought horse troughs were your speciality.'

'I believe there is a weather-vane in Northamptonshire which sports a horse trough as its emblem, Wayne, and another in Durham with a horse drinking from a trough, although I must admit I have never seen them. But, yes, this vane does interest me. I would say it has been removed recently and that it has been serviced.'

'I cannot see why we should be interested in that, sir, at this rather delicate moment during our enquiry.'

'Suppose it had fallen down, Wayne . . . suppose, for example, it had been struck by lightning and sent hurtling to the ground, and suppose, just suppose, by a terrible misfortune that it struck someone walking beneath . . .'

'Oh, God, sir, yes! I see what you're getting at. A thing like that falling from the roof would kill anyone, especially if a chunk of masonry was attached . . .'

'Particularly if the arrow became embedded in the victim's head. Now, if that did happen, then the compass points, because

194

they protrude on long stems, would cause other wounds to the body . . .'

'I see what you mean, sir! She did have other minor wounds – so you think they will correspond with the weather-vane? And that arrow, sir, is a length of pointed steel with arrow fletches at one end . . .'

'And it is painted, Wayne. Freshly painted in this case, I would say. Come, let us find Mr Burholme.'

Parking the car, they knocked on the door but there was no response and so they entered the buildings and explored each of the huge hangar-like barns, eventually hearing the sound of tools being used upon metal. Guided by this, they found their way to a small workshop situated at the end of one barn. Pluke shouted in advance and Burholme heard their approach, halting his work.

'I'm making a flower container,' he explained. 'From iron bars. It'll be like a cradle and when it's bolted to an outside wall, I will fill the base with moss and then plant flowers in it. Like a hanging basket idea.' He smiled and said, 'But you have not come to admire my metal-work, Mr Pluke. You have come about the wheelbarrow perhaps? I cannot say your visit is unexpected. You and I need to talk. You'd better come over to the house, both of you. I'll put the kettle on,' and Burholme led the way to the kitchen.

Pluke, on yet another occasion in his long career, did not refuse the proffered coffee, this man not being considered by him to be a murder suspect. They sat at the kitchen table with the Aga fussing away behind them, and Burholme produced three coffees, indicating that they should help themselves to milk and sugar from the containers he provided.

Then he settled down opposite Pluke, smiled ruefully and said, 'Well, Mr Pluke? My wheelbarrow. Did it tell you anything?'

'It confirmed what I believed, Mr Burholme,' said Pluke.

'Go on, inspector.' It was not so much a challenge, more an acute interest to find out just how much this funny little detective had discovered.

'Where shall I begin, Mr Burholme? Perhaps I should begin

with Erik Bjurholm, a Swedish national who came to this country after World War II, and who was naturalised. A man whose country was neutral during the war, but in spite of that, a man who fought—'

'You know that?'

'You told me you had no children because of a war injury, Mr Burholme – something which has a bearing, I believe, on the woman found in your quarry.'

'I did not kill her, Mr Pluke. Earlier, you spoke of murder – well, it was not me.'

'I know you did not kill her, Mr Burholme. But you did bury her and I think you hoped that if the body was found, it would look like murder, murder committed by someone else. You had no wish to throw the blame on to any particular person – this was not an attempt to frame anyone – but you created a "murder" by person or persons unknown simply to divert attention from yourself.'

'Her death was an accident, Mr Pluke . . . a terrible freak of an accident . . .'

'The weather-vane?' asked Pluke. 'Knocked from your roof by a lightning strike, falling so that the metal arrow embedded itself in her head . . .'

'Yes, I found her like that, Mr Pluke, late on Saturday night, when I got home from Harrogate. She was dead, she had been dead a while, there was nothing I could do, nothing would have helped her. She was beyond the help of a doctor or ambulance so I did not call anyone. I don't know what caused the weather-vane to fall from the roof, but the stone base had been dislodged and the entire thing had come down. It is very heavy, Mr Pluke, and yes, you're right, the arrow had entered her head . . . poor woman. She didn't deserve that.'

Burholme spoke with a cool rationality with no sign of outward emotion.

'I am sorry . . .' Pluke paused a moment, then said, 'So this girl, young woman – whose name is Miriam Ripley, otherwise known as Sister Bega of the Convent of Our Lady of the Hill – arrived here on Friday, unannounced and unexpected?'

'Yes. I had never seen her before, I had never met her.'

196

'But she thought she was your daughter?'

'She told me she was, but she is not, Mr Pluke. I am unable to father children, as I told you previously. That was a slip on my part . . . I am getting careless . . .'

'Did you enlighten her?'

'No. At the time, I wanted to find out more about her, who she was, why she had suddenly turned up. Due to my past, I was highly suspicious of her and her motives. I wanted to be completely sure who I was talking to. For the time being, therefore, and so that I could assess the truthfulness of her reason for calling on me, I was content to let her continue with the idea she was mine . . . I might have told her the truth, had she lived . . . I had to be very careful . . . but she died before I could make my decision. She never knew I was not her father. She died thinking she had found her natural father . . . and that made her very happy.'

'Tell me about her arrival, Mr Burholme, on Friday.'

Burholme, wrapping his hands around his mug of coffee, told Pluke how, at tea-time on Friday, the girl had arrived at his farm. He admitted her and gave her a meal, during which she said her mother had died and she'd found a scrap of paper bearing Burholme's name and address, with other notes suggesting he was her father. She'd brought those papers with her and said she knew about his donations to the convent; to her mind, the evidence suggested he was her natural father. As it was late by the time they had finished talking – he had told Miriam that her mother had worked on the farm – Burholme offered her a room for the night, a father offering succour to his daughter. She accepted. As he had an important business engagement in Harrogate on the Saturday, he invited her to remain over the weekend and even into the following week when they could become better acquainted; he had hoped to use that time to know her better. In fact, she was accommodated in the same room her mother had used, the one all his domestic staff had been given. His absence meant she would be alone on the complex for most of Saturday. She did not mind, she was so happy to be there, especially as he'd promised to devote the following days entirely to her.

'Before we proceed ...' Pluke halted the man in his story-telling. 'If she was not your daughter, why did you support her school and the convent as you did?'

'How much do you know about me, Mr Pluke?' was his response.

'Considering we have been acquainted for many years due to your generous gift of the shoggling sticks, I know surprisingly little about you, Mr Burholme. But I suspect a good deal ...'

'Go on, tell me what you suspect.'

'Sweden was neutral during World War II,' said Pluke, 'and yet you suffered a war wound. This suggests you were involved in the war effort – but that is not very surprising. For personal reasons, many Swedes did fight in the war. But your arrival in this country after the war, your eventual naturalisation and your links with our security services all combine to suggest that your wartime role was something out of the ordinary. When I began to investigate your background, as we do with all murder suspects, I was told, in no uncertain terms, of your links with our security services. From that, I suspect, Mr Burholme, that you were deeply involved in some wartime work which remains highly sensitive to this day. I believe you proved yourself of inestimable value to Great Britain and the Allies.'

'You, Mr Pluke, and Sergeant Wain, are both subject to the provisions of the Official Secrets Act, are you not?'

'Of course,' confirmed Pluke.

'You are not wired, are you? Either of you?'

'No, you may search us if you wish,' was Pluke's surprising response and, even more surprisingly, Burholme quickly frisked both detectives.

Satisfied, he said, 'Good. What I am about to say to you now is off the record. Nothing must be in writing, and when I have finished, I shall deny everything.'

'I understand,' said Pluke while Wayne Wain continued to look somewhat baffled.

'Your reasoning is well based, Mr Pluke, and without revealing precisely what I did during the war, I can confirm that I worked for a branch of military intelligence. I was working deep within the German military high command. I was posing as a German officer and became very close to Hitler. He trusted me, I was privy to many secrets and in fact used a German alias. But I was a British spy, Mr Pluke, passing my information to the British through a network of trusted people. Happily my dual role was never discovered by the Nazis. After the war, though, my name appeared on lists of Nazis being hunted as war criminals. I was hunted under my German alias, Mr Pluke, a name which still appears on the dwindling list of wanted war criminals. But I was not a German and not a war criminal; I was an agent for the Allies, Mr Pluke, and that is why I was given shelter in England. And Bjurholm is not my real Swedish name either, I have had to make use of several false indentities in order to maintain my secret. But a lot of Germans, French, Danes and, yes, Swedes did help me and this means I cannot allow my past to be known. Too many people and their families are still open to reprisal, after all this time ... so I am Eric Burholme now, a successful English businessman.'

'I will not attempt to investigate your claims,' Pluke assured him. 'It would get me nowhere. So, in a more normal world, what is the story of your donations to the convent?'

'Josephine Ripley was a very attractive young woman when she worked for me, Mr Pluke, but I was not tempted by her many charms. With my background, I could not afford any kind of adverse publicity or a scandal; most certainly, I could not risk any kind of investigation into my past. I had to be extremely careful in everything I did, I had to cover my tracks throughout my life. Then one evening, I went into one of my outbuildings and caught Josephine in the sex act with a man, one of my customers at that period.'

'Go on, Mr Burholme.'

'I dismissed her on the spot and sent her home.'

'And later she found she was pregnant?'

'Yes, and to cover the disgrace and circumstances of her dismissal, she told her parents I was the father and that I had sacked her because she was pregnant and I was a happily married man. Her parents believed her and put the baby into the

199

care of nuns, Mr Pluke. They did not want it in the house, but approached me for maintenance. I protested to Josephine's mother that I was not responsible.'

'You could have proved it!' said Wayne Wain. 'Your war injury.'

'That is precisely why I could *not* prove my story, Mr Wain. They knew I was of Swedish birth – that was no secret locally – so how would a neutral Swede get a war injury? I could have claimed my injury was from another source but could not risk any kind of examination or investigation. You see the caution I had to exercise? I promised money to the convent school, but never admitted being the father – and for that reason I maintained my distance throughout her life. But I did get reports about Miriam from the Reverend Mother and realised the little girl I was supporting was worthy of my continuing support. So I maintained the payments – my late wife was in full knowledge of those contributions by the way, and the reason for them.'

'And Miriam's real father?'

'He was killed in a traffic accident, Mr Pluke, about eighteen months after I had caught him with Josephine. It meant the girl, Miriam, had no father – another reason for maintaining my support. Because I admire the work done by that convent, in caring for girls in trouble, I have continued my donations and will do so until I die.'

'I know you support many other charities too, Mr Burholme,' said Pluke.

'It is my way of thanking this country for allowing me to live here.'

'So far as Miriam was concerned, then, you were her father, if not by nature?'

'I suppose so. Now you will see my dilemma when she came to visit me. She caught me by surprise, Mr Pluke. At first, I was deeply suspicious, as you can understand. I wondered just how much she really knew about me. I wanted time to make an assessment of her, to determine whether she was genuine or whether she was working for the investigative press or some foreign agency. On the other hand, if she was genuine, then I wanted to spend time with her, to get to know her. I must admit

200

I liked her, Mr Pluke, and I said she could stay as long as she wanted. That would enable me to have enquiries made into her background, just to be absolutely sure she was not hunting me for wartime reasons. You know as well as I that people are still hunting down Nazi war criminals.'

'Even though you are innocent of such evils, you have done well to remain free all these years,' said Pluke. 'So she stayed on Friday night and then, on Saturday, you went to a meeting in Harrogate?'

'Yes, it was important, a business commitment. I did not wish to cancel it. I explained the situation and gave her the run of the house and farm. She came to the gate with me, to see me off, like a little girl would have done for her daddy. She waved, I watched her through my rear view mirror as I left her . . . I must admit I shed a tear, Mr Pluke. You see, I was thinking – hoping is perhaps a better word – that, at last, I did have a family, that there was someone else in my rather lonely life . . .'

'And you returned at what time?'

'Later than I expected, half-past nine or so. I thought I'd get home about six or thereabouts, and that I could share my evening with Miriam. She called herself Miriam when she introduced herself, she didn't use her religious name, possibly because I am not a Christian . . . but when I drove into the yard, she was lying there with her head under that weather-vane. She was dead, Mr Pluke. I've seen dead people, lots of them. She'd been dead for a few hours, I think. The vane and part of the coping stone had somehow been knocked off the roof. There was a storm, you see, earlier that evening . . .'

'A lightning strike, I believe, Mr Burholme. An act of God.'

'If there is a God, he would never be so cruel, not to one of his own, Mr Pluke!'

'A debatable point. Now, what was the condition of her clothing?'

'Wet, Mr Pluke, from the rain. Her whole body was wet . . . I broke down, Mr Pluke, I don't mind admitting that. I thought I was hard. I used to be hard. I had to be to survive as I did in the war, but after such a promising meeting, she was gone. Taken from me in a moment, and when I was not there to help. I sat and wept over her body, my tears adding to the dampness of her clothes ... but I recalled my operational orders, Mr Pluke; they remain valid until I die. I had not to court trouble, I had not to do anything which would result in deep investigations into my life by the police, the press or any other agency. I had to cover my tracks, I had to conceal anything that might incriminate me or reveal my past ... apart from my Nazi reputation, there are honest people still in Germany and other parts of Europe who helped me, and whose families helped me in my espionage work, you see. They must be protected. If I had called in the authorities, there would have been an enquiry, her past would have emerged and I would have found myself having to answer all manner of questions with undoubted interest from the press. I could not risk that. So I did what I have been trained to do. I established a diversion. To do so, I made use of the existing facts and evidence. This was my military training resurrecting itself. During the war, you see, if a German soldier died, even in something like a domestic fight or drunken brawl, where possible we made it look as if the British had killed him. We doctored the truth for propaganda purposes or political reasons. Faced with what was for me a dilemma of major proportions, I decided to make it appear as if the girl had been murdered and buried in haste by a passer-by, a travelling camper perhaps ... Secretly, though, I wanted her body to be found, which is why I chose the shallow earth near the footpath. And I wanted her to have a proper funeral in due course.'

'I knew you had buried her with care, Mr Burholme. Love almost.'

'Did I reveal that? You are very astute, Mr Pluke.'

'The grave was correctly orientated east to west, Mr Burholme, and dug neatly to the correct size. A grave prepared with care and thought. And yet you contradicted that by burying her in shallow soil near a public footpath, a combination of circumstances which almost guaranteed a swift discovery. One deed contradicted the other. That puzzled me and made me suspicious. I realised you would know the quarry had a base of rock – that's why you kept your heavy machinery there – and so I knew you would be wise enough never to dig a deep grave there

'. . . even at that early stage, I scented an inner conflict, Mr Burholme.'

'I did want her to be quickly found, yes. I wanted her to have a decent burial.'

'And her belongings? You disposed of them?'

'In the Aga, Mr Pluke, her family papers too. It consumes almost anything. And I have disposed of the spade, but not in the Aga. You will never find it.'

'We found gravel in some wounds in her hands, and in her jeans – from the yard outside, I suspect, where she fell. That would indicate her presence here.'

'It's the same gravel that covers hundreds of farmyards and car-parks in this area, Mr Pluke. It could never be traced solely to this place.'

'And the weather-vane. You replaced the weather-vane, after taking the opportunity to straighten any bent pieces, repaint the cockerel and arrows, and grease the bearings?'

'Yes. I have mechanical training and I do have skills in metal-work, Mr Pluke. I did that on Sunday, along with the coping stone. She was found on Monday.'

'You carried her body to the grave in your wheelbarrow, Mr Burholme. One mistake was to replace it exactly as it had been before making that use of it.'

'I realise that now. Clearly, I made mistakes which you noticed. Perhaps others less astute than you or your officers would not have noticed them. Maybe this will be my last military operation, Mr Pluke. I am getting too old for this sort of thing. I have not made such errors in the past nor have I encountered a man like yourself. In addition, I am not up-to-date with modern scientific methods, Mr Pluke. To locate those fibres on the barrow was remarkable.'

'It's routine these days, Mr Burholme, not remarkable.'

'You said using the barrow was one mistake, Mr Pluke. What was the other?'

'Putting her mirror in the grave, Mr Burholme. I knew a Swede had done that – it was you, I felt. Your Swedish links are evident around the farm, in the cock on the weather-vane and in the colours of your advertising banners. Then I suspected your background when you told me of your war wound, knowing Sweden was neutral...'

'I congratulate you on that. But so far as the mirror is concerned, it was an automatic action. When I was young, it was always done in our village, Mr Pluke, for maidens. One tends to forget that other cultures differ from one's own.'

'That small act told me you *knew* she was a maiden – so when you denied knowing the victim or even seeing her, I knew you were lying. I think you tried a further red herring by telling me about the car you heard on Saturday night, to add credence to the idea that someone else had killed and buried her. Now we have talked, your account confirms all that I suspected, Mr Burholme.'

'I congratulate you; you have shown some remarkable powers of deduction, Mr Pluke. So what happens now?'

'There is no crime of murder, Mr Burholme. We shall need to remove your weather-vane to compare the arrow with the wound in her skull, to confirm your account of her death, and then there is the question of minor offences relating to the registration of deaths, the infringement of the coroner's rules and wasting police time.'

'Mr Pluke, think carefully. For me, nothing has changed. There can be no prosecutions, even for minor offences. The security of those with whom I was associated during the war remains of the highest priority. I cannot be compromised in any way whatever. In accordance with my standing orders, valid even to this day, I have informed the Security Services of this incident, and they will be contacting your Superintendent Hart.'

'With what purpose, Mr Burholme?'

'To ensure that I cannot be connected in any way to this incident. It happened on my land – that is all. That can happen to any owner of land. I have told you the truth. But the official version will be along the lines that the girl was paying me a chance visit because of my long association with her convent. It will be stated that she was missing when I returned from Harrogate. My movements in Harrogate can be checked and her time of death can be established with some accuracy. I remember her clothing was wet because of the storm, Mr Pluke, and I saw the rain had washed a little blood down the side of her face. I know enough about your forensic pathologists to realise they can pinpoint the time of her death to the time of the rainstorm. That means she died when I was thirty miles away at Harrogate; it also means I have an unshakeable alibi, Mr Pluke. I know that and you know that. That is my strength, my salvation, Mr Pluke. It means I cannot be a murder suspect and thus I need not be investigated. So, it is now necessary to produce a cover story which will fit the available facts. There are several possibilities. Might we say she interrupted a burglary at my home, for example, and died as a consequence? Perhaps not. Someone from Security will contact you for a digest of all the known evidence so that a suitable story can be produced. Once the official version has been agreed, it will appear that the girl was murdered, possibly for her money which has never been traced or possibly for sexual reasons, and probably by a travelling person from overseas who was carrying a tent. The story will say that I did not miss the girl on Saturday night because I returned home fairly late and thought she was in bed; clearly, I had no wish to disturb a nun in her bed! On Sunday morning I noticed she was missing and it was while looking for her that I found the wheelbarrow abandoned in one of my fields. Thinking it was the work of a joker, I replaced it in my shed, not realising what it had been used for. I did not, of course, visit the quarry. Your enquiries will suggest that her killer used the barrow to convey the body to the grave and the fact that my spade is missing will confirm that someone killed the girl – although exactly where has never been determined – and conveyed her body to the quarry for burial. The report will assume that my spade was used to dig the grave but that will never be proved. The murder weapon will never be found either. Should anyone try to match the arrow on that weather-vane with the wound in her head, they will find that the arrow up there is far wider than her wound, Mr Pluke. And of course, the paint it bears will not match the paint particles which adhered to her wound – I saw them, remember, Mr Pluke. They were black; that arrow is now dark blue even if it looks black from this distance. But that is speculation, Mr Pluke, because I am sure the "murder" weapon will never be identified. You were most astute to find the cause of her injury. When the authorities contact you, you may find that the press would be interested to know that a European youth on a camping tour of this country is suspected. I believe you have already instituted enquiries through Interpol and with ferry operators? The mirror will have little relevance to other investigators, Mr Pluke; it belonged to her in any case and must surely have fallen from her clothing into the grave, don't you think? If the evidence cannot support the theory that she was attacked by a burglar, might it be better to concentrate on the hitch-hiker idea? Let's say it was someone who met Miriam while she was hitch-hiking. She was rather naïve, being a nun, and so when he invited her into his tent in my quarry for a lager or two on Saturday evening, she agreed. After all, she was alone in that huge house, and on holiday. A nice friendly man would be a wonderful diversion. But he expected more; she refused him sex and, in his anger, he killed her. That might be the better story. To support it, there are tent peg holes in the quarry, Mr Pluke, and camp fires to prove someone has used the site. That person either killed her or caused her to die from a wound, the source of which will never be determined. The killer has gone back to his own country and will never be found; your suspect will never be identified. There are several alternative stories from which can be produced a set of circumstances which will fit the available evidence. Already you have kindly eliminated any suspicion from my many agricultural machines. Maybe, to add support to the official version, my controller will arrange for an anonymous letter to come to your office from overseas – anywhere but Sweden, in fact – which you can show your coroner? It could be a letter admitting everything suggested by the evidence, albeit with regret? You could then close your books, Mr Pluke, and keep your crime detection record intact. I think it was your William Shakespeare who said that, to do a great right, one had to do a little wrong. Remember, I am still not entirely sure why that young lady wanted to visit me – I did not have the opportunity to fully question her. I hope she was genuine but I may never know. There is more work for me to do in that respect, work I need not worry you about, but I fear you will have a murder investigation on your files.'

'We can't have this, sir!' cried Wayne Wain. 'It is not right, not justice—'

'Sergeant,' said Eric Burholme, 'I am afraid that is what will happen. You are now privy to what might be termed state security, rather than rural policing. There is much at stake, even half a century after the end of the war, and those politics must take priority. My own superiors will contact you, Mr Pluke, perhaps personally or perhaps through your Chief Constable, to debate the available evidence. You are a member of a disciplined organisation, Mr Pluke, which means you must obey orders.'

'That is true, Mr Burholme.'

'Then I see no future problem.'

'But, Mr Burholme, if you had reported the accident for what it was, it would have been dealt with very speedily ... after all, it was an accident, nothing more. There was nothing to fear. You would not have been at risk in any shape or form.'

'I would have been at risk, Mr Pluke, which means others would also have been put at risk. For such an unlikely accident and the peculiar set of accompanying circumstances, the press might have begun to delve, my past might have been investigated. It is easy to find out I am a naturalised Swede. That would be sufficient for some to dig deeper. They have many sources; I could not risk any publicity. After all, the evidence shows I am a Nazi war criminal who is still being hunted! Furthermore, I would be associated with enquiries into Miriam's background and certain things would be revealed such as her mother's insistence that I was her father ... For all kinds of reasons, including those basic ones, I could not risk the tiniest part of my background being discovered and investigated, Mr Pluke. So, very hastily and knowing I had an unshakeable alibi for the "crime", I had to produce something at which I used to be very good – a cover-up.'

'I have no power to sanction this, Mr Burholme.'

'I am aware of that, Mr Pluke. That will be dealt with by your superiors, and the convent will be consulted about their part in all this. Now, as a final gesture, I want you to ensure Miriam has a proper burial. With a full Catholic service.'

'I will ensure that,' Pluke assured him.

'Let me know when and where it will be, and I will send a maiden's garland.'

'What's a maiden's garland?' asked Wayne Wain.

'It is a tribute to an unmarried woman of unblemished reputation, Wayne,' Pluke told him. 'A white garland of flowers or even linen, sometimes with a white glove in the centre, and adorned with white ribbons and rosettes. It is carried before the coffin to indicate the status of the deceased, Wayne. Very fitting for Sister Bega.'

'But not for politics, sir?'

'No, Wayne. Not for politics.'